I0538574

Muffalettas and Murder

Jann Franklin

Copyright © 2023 by Jann Franklin

All rights reserved.

No portion of this book may be reproduced in any form without written permission from the publisher or author, except as permitted by U.S. copyright law.

Contents

Also By Me

<u>Small Town Girl Series</u>

Jen's life isn't perfect, but it's beautiful. A beautiful mess.

Jen was living her best big city life, until her husband Mike uproots them to small town Louisiana. Life throws you curveballs, but you've got to keep swinging.
This heartwarming series resonates with joyful, almost nostalgic feelings of encouragement. Readers living in big cities will feel the quaint, small-town Southern charm leaping off the pages, and experience a yearning to visit their very own Graisseville. And readers from small towns will see versions of themselves and their own community in these characters, nodding and laughing along with Jen and her family. There is something for everyone to relate to and thoughtfully consider.
Trading Bright Lights for Lightning Bugs
Shining Stars and Mason Jars
Cheese Grits and Hissy Fits

<u>Small Town Girl Mystery Series</u>

Why is murder so much fun?

Evangeline Delafose found Graisseville, Louisiana just as she remembered—boring and uneventful. Until she solved a murder. Now she's hooked.

Follow Ev as she takes on each mystery, with her frustrating but loveable private investigator by her side. And, of course, a bit of insider info from the quirky residents of her small town.

You'll laugh, cry and roll your eyes at the antics of this charming small-town Southern sleuth and her exasperating private investigator.

Muffalettas and Murder

Boudin and Bloodshed

Fruitcake and Fraud

Mardi Gras and Mayhem

Sweet Tea and Suspects

FROM THE VICTIM'S EYES

What if I could run away, to somewhere no one knows me? Alaska maybe? I've always wanted to visit.

Michael slowed his steps up the sidewalk. Was Stella home yet? She said she'd catch a ride, but sometimes she'd call, with a lengthy excuse of why her ride fell through. Her job was only ten minutes down the road by car, so it wasn't difficult to pick her up. Just inconvenient. But then, everything about Stella was inconvenient—even as kids.

Michael opened the door slowly, so it wouldn't creak. Stella's key chain hung on the peg just inside. Stella's house key dangled from the pink glittery "S" key chain he'd bought her for Christmas. Good! Stella had found a ride home. *One less thing to do.*

Inching to the kitchen, Michael lifted his feet carefully, ever so slowly, so as not to make his arrival public.

I want to go through the mail before supper. Did Stella put out the chicken this morning to thaw?

Inspecting the sink, Michael confirmed his suspicions. His sister, once again, forgot her morning task.

Spaghetti for the win, I guess, his words angrily swirled in his head. *Do we even have pasta and a jar of marinara? Oh cool, we do! What is the weather like in Alaska right now?*

He grabbed the pot from beneath the cabinet and moved to the sink. As he filled it with tap water, he couldn't help his wandering thoughts.

I love music. I wonder what's popular in Alaska?

Noticing the overflowing pot, he shifted weight to his back foot and balanced it carefully as he turned again to the stove. Ten minutes later, a knock at the front door interrupted his thoughts.

Michael rushed to open it before Stella heard. No reason to give her a chance to come downstairs and start a useless conversation. He'd never get this unwelcome visitor out of his house with Stella involved.

Recognizing the figure on the front porch, Michael's eyes widened as his stomach tightened. *I thought...* His shoulders slumped, and he opened the door just a few inches. *Better not to start a fight. Just pretend everything is okay and I don't want to punch my fist through the door.*

"Oh, hi! I know this is confusing, because you didn't expect me. But if you let me inside, I can explain." Michael opened the door a few inches wider, narrowing his eyes in suspicion.

"My water's boiling, and I need to add the pasta. Let's go into the kitchen." He turned away from the door. "Why don't you go in first? You can fix yourself something to drink." *I don't trust you, not one bit.*

"Looks good, Michael! You really are a splendid cook."

Michael shrugged, his eyes focused on opening the box of pasta. They'd each spotted the lies lately, increasing the mutual distrust.

What was that? Michael's eyes tried to show fear, but his brain delayed the order. *Anger, Michael. You should be angry, not afraid.*

"What are you doing with that gun?" *Keep calm and think. What if...?* Before Michael's brain finished the thought, his arms flung the pot of boiling water towards the gun.

As the bullet tore through his torso, Michael heard a cry of pain. He slumped to the floor.

I'm not taking that trip to Alaska, am I?

Chapter 1

How did it happen? My adorable kids, all grown up, think they know everything. Last I'd heard, *I* was in charge of my life. Me, Dr. Evangeline Louise Bergeron Delafose, PhD. Yet, I didn't know a thing.

My youngest, the one who understood me best, announced one day that Nate was right—I needed to pack it all up and move closer to family. Not her, of course.

"Mom, that would be weird. My mother living in the same town as me? I'm a freshman in college! It's my time to spread my wings." Ellie was actually referring to my brother and my father, still in the town I'd fled thirty years ago.

Matty agreed, of course. "Mom, Ellie's right. You should live closer to Uncle Nate and Aunt Bonnie. Grandpa too. You need to make some changes."

Traitors. If Doug was here...but he wasn't. So, I packed up my stuff and moved. Not like I moved anywhere crazy. When Doug and I married, I'd made a vow to love, honor, cherish, and never move back to Graisseville (pronounced, *GRACE-vil*) in Louisiana. To quote a James Bond film, *Never Say Never*.

The parents of a Graisseville mayor built my home in 1928, giving it a wide front and side porch and majestic columns. The last owner painted the entire house white with slate blue shutters. Not only had someone raised a mayor in my home, but village gossip claimed that Bonnie and Clyde laid low in my adjoining carriage house for a few days. It sat in the center of the Pecan Street block, just outside the Historic District and snugly within the bounds of my brother's watchful eye. As a sheriff's deputy in East Baton Rouge Parish, Nate had sworn to protect and serve. Hovering was not part of his oath, though. I had checked, just to make sure.

Back in my hometown for three months, I was adjusting to the exciting population of 298 intriguing people. The casserole brigade descended upon me like vultures on roadkill. In my small-town experience, these senior ladies ambushed all men qualifying as available.

They sniffed out every single man over sixty within the parish, plying them with King Ranch casserole and enchilada pie. Why had they set their sights on me? Maybe I kept a stash of single men, ages sixty and up, in a storage facility somewhere? The brigade eventually discovered I had no stash, didn't know how to play bridge, preferred not to gossip, and led a completely boring life. The newness wore off, and they left me to my own devices.

Today was Thursday, my weekly supper with my brother. The day of the week I had to account for all my activities, as Nate frowned and shook his head. *Maybe I should have moved closer to Mad?* My younger sister's given name was Madeline, but she had a short fuse. Nate dubbed her Mad when he was about four, and we all agreed it fit. Her quick temper convinced me to move closer to Dad and Nate. Mad wouldn't critique my social life, though. Someone remind me again... *why* had I moved back to Graisseville?

"Ev, you've lost more weight. Did you eat the gumbo Bonnie sent over?" Nate's mouth curled up in a smile, but his eyes exposed the concern.

Why was everyone so worried about me? Was I that pathetic? "Yes, Nate, I ate Bonnie's gumbo. Yes, I read the book she gave me. Yes, I'm coming to Jack's football game and Syd's piano recital this weekend. Yes, I'll be at church on Sunday." My eyes jerked in my brother's direction and softened. He was trying to take care of me, like Doug did before he passed away. Only when Doug asked me if I'd eaten, his words weren't nails on a chalkboard.

My brother was relentless. "So, changing the subject, have you given any thought to starting another book? Writing, I mean—not reading. The guys down at the station still talk about your character, Lou Bergeron, and how authentic he is." Nate stopped, realizing he'd stepped in a big hot mess of...dog poop.

My series of books, featuring New Orleans police detective Lou Bergeron, had been reasonably successful. Lou was no Alex Cross, by any standard. But the royalties from my books supplemented my professor's salary. Along with Doug's detective pay, our life had been pretty darn good. Only...

"Gosh, I'm so sorry, Ev! Geez, what a moron I am!"

Only...Lou Bergeron *was* Doug. Which was why police officers were my biggest fans. He was authentic because Doug made him so. My husband was always the first to read my books, making my character an authentic police officer. With Doug gone, I had no desire to visit Lou down at the police station, to flesh out his cases and celebrate his successes.

"It's okay Nate, I know what you're saying. But Lou is Doug, and Doug is gone. I can't write about Lou anymore. I'm not sure I ever want to write again." There! I'd spoken the thoughts crouching under the rug. My words freed them, and they'd sprung into the middle of the room.

Nate nodded, his brown eyes revealing just a hint of tears. "No pressure! I just wanted to double-check, because the guys always ask me. But I understand, Ev, I truly do. On another note, I had an idea..."

Reaching into his briefcase, my brother pulled out a medium-sized manila folder and placed it gingerly on the cleared table. An East Baton Rouge Parish sheriff's department folder, from the looks of the official seal.

"This case is technically inactive. It's been eighteen months, and we're stuck." Nate's eyes took on the familiar sad puppy dog look, the one he'd always used to get what he wanted. Those eyes always worked on Mother, and usually me, too. Never Mad or my father.

"Ev, I can't let it go! This was a good kid. We like his sister for his murder, but we just don't have enough evidence to prove it. The D.A. won't touch it. So, I talked to the sheriff, and explained how you write, or used to write, detective novels for a living. Turns out he's a fan." Nate's eyes lit up with pride.

Who would've guessed that writing stories about my husband would score such a fan base?

"Okay, Nate. So, the sheriff is a fan. What do you want from me? Should I autograph the file?" Glancing at the manila folder before me, I couldn't help but flip it open. Doug had brought home many files, so these pages stared at me like familiar friends. Where do I put my autograph? Should I use my go-to pink glitter pen, or should it be black ink? My eyes shifted to Nate for confirmation.

"No, Ev, the sheriff doesn't want an autograph." My brother paused, then walked it back. "Well, he doesn't want an autograph on this file. It's a copy of the original. Your copy. He'd...well, we'd..."

Spit it out, Nate, because I'm not following you.

"We'd like you to look at the case through fresh eyes—hopefully find something we missed. Would you do that for us? For Michael Cook, the deceased?"

Hmmm...this was intriguing. Doug had often shared his cases with me after the kids went to bed. But I functioned as a sounding board, to nod or shake my head as he ran through his theories and clues. To play detective, limited as it would be, seemed...well, it seemed much more fun than playing bridge and definitely more interesting than joining the church decorating committee.

"I'll do it! *Umm*...I mean, if the sheriff's department would like my help, of course." C'mon Ev, rein in your enthusiasm. And yet...this could be so much fun!

Nate smiled in relief—did he actually think I'd say no? He didn't know me that well, I guess. Wait! Had the rock in my stomach shrunk several inches? Relief washed over my body, and I felt my shoulders relax. After three years of surviving without my husband, trying to get our daughter graduated from high school and our son through most of college, my reward had been banishment back to Graisseville. Ellie relinquished her need of a mother, and Matty had long since outgrown me. But the sheriff's department found me useful. Had I found a reason to stop surviving and start living?

October evenings in Louisiana summoned eighty-degree heat, but I still enjoyed a cup of hot tea and a light blanket. Gazing at the stars, I breathed in the small-town peace while my feet rocked back and forth. The realtor sold me on my house because of the front porch and its swing.

"You'll find peace in this porch swing, Ev. Come sit and you'll see." She'd plopped down on the creaky wooden swing, then patted the cushion beside her. Gingerly I joined her, and we rocked quietly. "You can see the stars from this porch swing in the evening. And enjoy a cup of coffee early in the morning. The neighborhood is quiet, with lots of friendly people. You're only two minutes away from Nate and Bonnie." The woman had me at the words, *porch swing*.

Before I opened the file on Michael Cook, I grabbed my trusty purple highlighter and pink Sharpie from the side table. Purple to note clues, and pink to mark potential lies or inconsistencies. My situation confused me at first, because normally I created the murderer, the victim, and the suspects. But this file contained all the characters already created. My job? To figure out who was who. *What have you gotten yourself into, girl? Maybe you should have put something stronger in the tea?*

Suddenly, peace filled my soul. Was it Doug, or more probably, my Heavenly Father? I'd take either or both, whichever one helped solve Michael Cook's murder. Let's begin, Ev. You can do this!

Perusing the file, I scribbled a slew of notes. The victim was Michael Cook, the bright star of a working-class family. Diligent in his job at the bank in Zachary. Parents died a few years ago, leaving their home to Michael and his older sister, Stella. Nate's notes mentioned Michael supported Stella, financially and otherwise. I hoped Nate didn't relate to Michael, younger brother supporting older sister? I'd never asked for a dime! Sigh...Focus, Ev! Move on.

My brother's meticulous notes continued: Stella Cook—recovering from substance abuse. Seriously, Nate? Not a crime, really. Could she kill her brother? I certainly couldn't kill mine! What would her motive be?

Nate outlined it all for me. Witnesses stated that Stella was jealous of her brother because he was on the right track, a young man with a career and a future. Then, of course, we had the standard statement: once an addict, always an addict. What the heck? That was not a motive to kill.

Angrily, I plowed through Nate's notes. Why was he focusing on the drug addicted sister? Ah, here was suspect number two.

Josh Fairchild, a person of interest. Prominent member in the community and owner of Best Dry Cleaners, where Stella worked. Witnesses stated he was a dear friend of the victim's parents, committed to looking after the children upon their death. Solid alibi and no motive, but Nate felt there was more to his story. He'd written the question, *Stella's drug supplier?* in the margin.

Another person of interest, or who I dubbed Suspect Number Three: Sam Hughes—Michael's co-worker at the bank in Zachary. Employees saw Sam and Michael arguing about a missed promotion. Missed promotion? That seemed pretty important. Men identify most strongly with their careers, while women count family as most important. A missed promotion might be a reason to kill. Why weren't there more notes?

Ooh! Suspect Number Four: Faith Dixon, Michael's ex-girlfriend. Checking the file several times, I came up short. Really, Nate? Mother's stories of my brother's exes rushed through my mind, the stalking and the phone calls at all hours. Women scorned can be crazy! Side note: Thank You Lord Jesus for Bonnie! She was a blessing to both Nate and our family. Otherwise, we'd have Crazy Anna, her nickname in the Louisiana State Penitentiary. Nate dodged a bullet. Turning back to the folder, I envisioned a similar tale. This girl needed to be investigated.

Rounding out the manila folder was Rob Dugas—Michael's best friend from high school. My eyes squinted as I read the small print. Ugh! Did I need a stronger prescription already? It had been a couple of years. Sigh...just another sign I was not getting any younger.

Turning back to the file, I noted the sheriff's office had arrested Rob multiple times for dealing drugs. Yikes! Doug would guess this kid needed money fast. My heart turned to my kids with good hearts. Matty and Ellie would give money to friends in need. Rob was Michael's friend in need. Did he finally say no?

Chapter 2

Refilling my cup gave me time to think. The coroner reported the cause of death as a gunshot wound to the torso. Ballistics confirmed Michael Cook Sr. owned the gun. The perpetrator wiped the weapon clean but left it in the kitchen. Detectives spoke with friends and neighbors. No one could confirm or deny who had the gun. No one had seen it recently, including Stella. Or so she said. Some people insisted that Michael Sr. got rid of the gun because he didn't want Stella to have access. Other people stood firm that Michael Jr. kept the gun as protection from Stella's questionable friends. So much for the weapon.

As I drifted to the porch, I remembered chasing after Nate when we were kids. He was ten years younger, and Mother tagged me as a babysitter more times than I could count. I spent my teenage years running after Nate, second-guessing his every move, and trying to predict his next steps. Pretty much what I was doing with his file. Nate had already interviewed, investigated, and concluded. His big sister was just coming along after him, trying to unravel the events. Hmmm...but what if?

Placing my cup on the side table, I focused my attention on maneuvering the blanket back into cocoon mode. What had I been thinking about? Oh yes! What if?

What if I could interview everyone myself? Ask my own questions and draw my own conclusions. If Nate didn't shut down my idea, the sheriff certainly would.

Unless they didn't know. Nate would kill me if he found out.

So, he couldn't find out. I recognized only twenty-five percent of the people interviewed. Being the new girl in town, why couldn't I ask questions? Just satisfying my curiosity, nothing more. It could work.

Tomorrow I could run to town, start at Maggie's Coffee Shop. Maggie knew practically everyone and probably knew a lot about them, too. The coffee shop was a good place to begin. Wait a minute! Shorty Cormier promised to come by tomorrow and fix my washing machine.

Shorty was Graisseville's resident handyman, a mechanical genius. If he couldn't fix it, then you might as well throw it away and buy a newer model. He'd come back from the Gulf War with a purple heart and a prosthetic leg. Working under machinery, the man hopped up and down off the ground like a pogo stick. Comical to watch, but he could make anything with a motor purr. Which meant Shorty was in great demand. Unfortunately, the best mechanic in the parish didn't have the strongest work ethic. Shorty only took on jobs if he needed money. If I rescheduled, who knew when he'd need money again? No, Maggie would have to wait, because I had a date with my handyman.

"Hey Shorty, it's Ev. How are you this morning?" Can't forget the traditional Southern small talk, before getting down to business.

"Oh, can't complain. How are you this mornin', Doc?

"Fine, thanks." Shorty had called me *Doc* ever since my graduation from LSU with a Ph.D. in English Literature. My parents bragged to everyone, including the entire village of Graisseville, that their daughter was a doctor! The word spread, a normal occurrence in small towns, and soon the story transformed. Skeeter and Muriel Bergeron's daughter, Evangeline, graduated from LSU medical school! Doug and I visited my parents after graduation and puzzled over people greeting me as *Doc*. My parents corrected no one, but eventually people figured it out. The first clue came when I returned for Christmas the next year, and Abe Taylor asked me to check on his pregnant wife to see how far she was dilated. We laughed over that for years. Shorty's family continued calling me *Doc* because they were incredibly proud of me. Why no one called my father, the veterinarian, *Doc* was still a mystery.

"Hey, how's your daddy doin'? I heard he was feelin' under the weather?"

Would this small talk never end? Sigh...hopefully I could steer this conversation back to my burning question: what time will my repairman arrive?

"Oh no, he's great. He's wondering when you're coming over this morning to fix my washing machine." Actually, Dad didn't know about my washing machine. Otherwise, my eighty-year-old father would be at my house on his knees trying to fix it himself.

"Doc, we've had this conversation before. First, I have my coffee and scrambled eggs, then I check my email and phone messages. Next, I feed the cows and the hogs. If I don't have any more farm chores, I pull out my list."

Oh yes, the magical list! Getting on Shorty's list was the simple part. It lived on the first seven pages, front and back, of a spiral-bound notebook. Getting to the top of the list was the trick. To achieve that feat, bribery came into play. Fortunately for me, Shorty loved my mom's cold oven pound cake.

"Okay, where am I on the list, Shorty?" Holding the phone with one hand, I rummaged through my pantry and refrigerator. Did I have the ingredients to make another pound cake? Shorty had already scored one baked good to put me in the top five. Another one might be in order to move me up the ranks.

"You're in luck! I don't have no more chores, and you are third on the list." He paused, waiting for my counteroffer.

"You know, I'm making a cold oven pound cake for Nate and his family this morning. I'd let you take it with you if you came to my house first. I can make another one for Nate this afternoon." Lies, all lies. Nate and Bonnie were on a low carb diet, and I knew better than to bring them a pound cake. Pulling out the recipe, I double checked the ingredients. Yes! Just enough eggs for one cake. Better start mixing up the ingredients.

"Yeah, that'd work. I'll be over in an hour." The man was shrewd. I'd give him that. Incredibly athletic too, since he regularly scored a pound cake a month from me with no extra weight to show for it. My baking wasn't his only bribe each month, either. Some families prepared entire meals to get Shorty on their doorstep, so I considered myself fortunate. Of course, Shorty's dad and my dad had been the best of friends. My dad, when he was the town veterinarian, spent many afternoons at the Cormier farm. My mother suspected most of those trips were to shoot the breeze, but it kept Dad and Mr. Cormier out of trouble. My widow status probably gave me an automatic jump up Shorty's list, too. He'd never say it to me, but Shorty had a soft spot for single moms and widows.

Shorty knocked on my front door, and I glanced at the timer. About thirty minutes left. The beauty of the cold oven pound cake was the baker didn't have to waste time preheating the oven. Thank goodness!

My handyman let himself in and set his toolbox on the kitchen island. "Mornin', Doc. Mmmm...that cake sure is smellin' good! How much longer?" The crows' feet around his brown eyes made him look wiser, not older. Why does age sit better on men?

Best to be the driver of this conversation.

"Thirty minutes. Just enough time to tell me what's wrong with my washing machine."

Shorty definitely wasn't my type, but I understood why single women within a thirty-mile radius brought him casseroles and desserts. And tickets for the Kenny Chesney concert in Baton Rouge. My handyman was the shortest male in his family, standing at six feet tall. His curiously sexy mop of dishwater blonde hair reached his shoulders, and it drove the women wild. Personally, I found long hair on a man, well, disheveled. But I was definitely in the minority. Women ages thirty to seventy swooned over the guy every time they spotted his beat-up Ford F150. At the coffee shop, I'd heard adjectives ranging from *rugged* and *outdoorsy* to *virile* and *charming* to just plain *yummy*. That last adjective came from my eighth-grade English teacher, Mrs. Collins, recently widowed.

Sean Connery as James Bond was my go-to for sexy, but many women thrilled at the wild mane of Travis Tritt or Trace Adkins. Besides, it was hard to resist a man who could fix practically anything. Despite all the female attention, Shorty remained determinedly single for his entire fifty-four years.

Oh geez, I hope he doesn't think I've fallen to his charms!

While pondering Shorty's attractiveness to women, I'd been gazing in his direction. Fortunately, he was texting on his phone, probably with one of his admirers. "Shorty, the laundry room's this way." Strolling past him towards the back of the house, I resolved to stop wondering about my handyman's animal magnetism.

Thirty minutes and a mountain of cuss words later, Shorty had coaxed my washing machine back to life. The man performed miracles. Emerging from my laundry room wiping his hands, he spied my pound cake cooling on the stovetop. Did he spot the to-go container perched strategically near the cake? My phone read 9:30 a.m., plenty of time to get Shorty out the door and head to Maggie's coffee shop for some sleuthing.

"Hey, Doc, that cake sure smells great! Think I could have a piece?"

Didn't he eat scrambled eggs a few hours ago?

"It will be perfect for eating when you get home." I spelled it out because subtlety didn't work on Shorty. Even then, he didn't always get my hints.

"Nah, I think it's perfect now. Mind if I have a slice?" He'd already reached into my cabinet for two dessert plates.

"Shorty, I really have a busy day today. I don't have time to eat cake at 9:30 in the morning." Too late. He'd already poured me a cup of coffee to go with my cake.

My friend handed me my cup while he balanced the plates. "Hey, let's go out on the front porch! It's gettin' cool in the mornings. Ya keep a blanket out there, don'tcha, Doc? Because it'll prob'ly be a little cold for ya." Hmmm...Shorty knew me better than I'd realized.

Following the leader on to the porch, I dutifully sat on the swing and snuggled under my blanket. Shorty placed my cake on the side table, then faced me in the wicker chair. Cake in hand, of course.

"We haven't chewed the fat in a while. How ya' doin'? How's everything goin'? How're ya' settlin' back in tuh Graisseville?" Shorty's eyes stared at me like interrogation lamps, attempting innocence but failing miserably.

Yeah, I smelled a rat. "Good, it's all good. Say, when's the last time you talked to Nate?" Shorty's gaze flicked from innocence to guilt. The man never could lie to me, even when we were kids.

"Okay, ya caught me, Doc. But Nate's jus' worried about ya, that's all. Me too. Yer practically skin and bones; ya won't even touch yore mama's cold oven pound cake. That's not normal." Shorty licked the crumbs from his lips and eyed my plate. I waved my hand towards my cake and Shorty eagerly pulled it towards him.

"Shorty, I'm fine. In three years, I've lost a spouse, my last kid left for college, and I've moved. Those are three major stressors that would cripple any normal person." To seal the deal, I locked eyes with him. Would he let it go?

The wicker chair creaked as Shorty relaxed his shoulders into its back. Good. For now, I'd satisfied my interrogator. Suddenly, he shifted and reached under his legs. Nate's file! Pulling out the now familiar manila folder, Shorty stared at it. The interrogation was back on.

"What's this? Why do ya have this file? Does Nate know about this?" Shorty's eyes darkened and he squinted at me accusingly.

"Yes, Shorty, Nate knows about the folder. In fact, he gave it to me. It's an inactive case he'd been working, and he thought I might have a fresh perspective."

Could someone's eyes actually light up like Christmas trees?

"Are ya dustin' off Detective Bergeron? Oh, Doc, tell me ya are! Ya know I'm not a reader, but I jus' love yore books!"

Oh, here we go! Shorty adored my Lou Bergeron books, and bragged to everyone that the author was his dear childhood friend. If someone hadn't heard of the book series (and many hadn't—I wasn't James Patterson by any means), Shorty sprang into action. He would pull out a dog-eared copy and demand the culprit take a picture, so they could purchase it later. Shorty had been one of my best marketing resources.

"No Shorty, I'm not. Nate's hoping the case will give me something to do all day. Since I've rejected his suggestions of knitting group, book club, and the decorations committee at church." I knew he did it for love. But the decorations committee, really? My idea of decorating was to hang some family photos and call it a day.

"Well, tell me about the file! Hey, did I tell ya I have my PI license?" The letters ADHD zipped into my brain. Shorty never stuck to one subject for long, and conversations with him became tiring after a while. Nope, not getting to Maggie's anytime soon.

"Let's start with your PI license. Tell me about that." This news could come in handy.

Shorty's eyes flew back to Christmas tree mode.

"Well, it's not as fancy as your *doctor-ite*, but it took a lot o' work."

Oh, please don't let my smile reach my mouth! Shorty always called my doctorate a *doctor-ite*, but his pride rang true. My mission failed, however, as my smile turned into a laugh. How could I turn this around?

"Oh, you've never been afraid of hard work, Shorty! Please tell me all about it!" Settle back into your swing, Ev, and finish that cup of coffee. Shorty's stories ran about twenty minutes or more.

Proudly, he reached into his wallet and handed me a card. Cormier Investigations, LLC. He eyed me carefully, making sure he had my full attention.

"Well, first thing, y'gotta' take a forty-hour course an' pass an exam. Let me tell ya, that course ain't no walk around Graisseville park! An' guess what, Doc? I passed it on the first go around." The warm glow of accomplishment filtered through his eyes.

His news didn't surprise me. Shorty had been a couple of grades ahead of me in school, but I'd heard the teachers talk about him. The guy had smarts but couldn't focus. We graduated before medications arrived on the scene to help kids with their classroom attention.

Shorty thrived in shop class, where he constantly moved around the room, working on different machines. Mother asked me several times to help Shorty with his schoolwork, even though I was two years behind. School came easily for me, so she thought I could help him. If I'd had more patience, I probably could have. Stuck inside helping a fidgety kid instead of hanging out with my friends? Mother and I fought over my lessons with Shorty for many days. That's why I had a soft spot for my friend—maybe if I'd had more maturity and patience and less silly teenager in me, he'd have done better in school.

"Doc? Did ya hear me? The first time! Howie says that don't happen often." Pausing so I could congratulate him, Shorty continued. "Howie's my PI sponsor. See, I had t'find a licensed PI t'sponsor me. This guy in Baton Rouge, Howie Robichaud, jumped on it. He helped me fill out all the forms, get fingerprinted, even took my pictures for the application." Shorty paused once again so I could congratulate him. The man wanted credit where credit was due, for sure.

"So you're a licensed private investigator in the state of Louisiana? You could help me with this case?" Perhaps divine intervention kept me from blundering into the coffee shop. Shorty could be a real asset.

"Yes, ma'am! Now I've also watched a lot of *The Rockford Files*, to get some first-hand experience. My fees are $200 a day, plus expenses. I normally just take cash, but since I know ya, a check is fine." He waited expectantly, his second piece of cake long gone. "Say, do ya mind if I get another piece o' cake? Oh, do ya want some more coffee?"

Shorty hobbled inside, my coffee cup and his plate in hand. The guy was unbelievable! *The Rockford Files* had been on NBC from 1974 to 1980. Starring James Garner, the show featured Jim Rockford and his career as a private investigator in Malibu, California. Obviously, Shorty didn't understand that watching a television show didn't qualify as a real-life experience. Jim Rockford charged $200 a day plus expenses, mentioning his fees in practically every episode. Come to think of it, we both used to watch *The Rockford Files* with our dads.

Shorty returned with his cake and my coffee and handed me the steaming cup. How should I burst my friend's bubble? With Shorty, the direct approach worked best.

"Shorty, I can't pay you $200 a day to work this case. I'm barely making it right now on Doug's pension. My retirement doesn't kick in until I turn sixty, which is eight years away. LSU offered me an adjunct position to teach Crime Fiction next spring, but that's a few months away."

My would-be PI gave me a hard look, squinting his mud-colored eyes. No wonder the guy had crows' feet.

"Who do those fancy pants LSU jerks think they are? Ya don't need a junk job! Yer a doctor for crumbs' sake!" Only, he didn't say crumbs. Shorty's mouth hung open and his voice trailed off. Eyes round as hubcaps, he began his apology. "Geez, Doc, I'm sorry about that. I know ya hate cursing, an' I try real hard not to do it in front of ya. I really do."

It was the same conversation every time. His spirit was sort of willing, but his flesh was extremely weak. As always, I tried to give him grace.

"It's okay, Shorty. Bad habits are hard to break. I'll make you a deal. If you work on cutting the cursing, I'll work on not being skin and bones. How's that?" He nodded in agreement, so I continued.

"For the record, it's not a junk job, it's an adjunct teaching position. There's a *t* on the end—*Ad Junk-t*. It means instead of teaching a full load of classes for a salary, I would just teach a couple of classes for a set amount per class. It would be lots of fun to teach a class on how to write a crime fiction book, but with LSU forty-five minutes away, I'm not sure a couple of classes are worth it." Was I ready to talk about Detective Lou Bergeron? From my conversation with Nate, I'd say not yet.

Shorty's head bobbed up and down, like the pedal on my grandmother's old Singer sewing machine. "Yep, yep. That's a mighty long way for a piddlin' amount of money. I'm not sure Nate and I want ya drivin' so far by yourself."

When did my handyman and my brother team up? To be honest, I'd rather have Shorty supervising me than Nate. Keeping tabs on me meant Shorty stayed out of trouble. Besides, Nate had his hands full with two kids and a career. Not to mention a wife that liked him home at night. But how to pay Shorty without breaking the bank?

"Didn't you used to gorge on my mother's muffaletta sandwiches?" Mother didn't serve sandwiches as a general rule. She believed any respectable Southern cook turned on the oven to make a meal. But she broke her cardinal rule on LSU game days.

A muffaletta (pronounced *MUFF-uh-LE-tuh*) is a classic Louisiana sandwich. New Orleans claims to serve the best, but my mother made them just as good or better. The bread is key—it's got to be wide and soft. Here in the pelican state, we have bread just for these sandwiches, called Muffaletta bread. If it wasn't available, my mother would wag her finger at the poor soul behind the bread counter and give a lecture that no decent store in Louisiana should be out of Muffaletta bread. Then she'd grab a loaf of French bread and storm off.

Mother also splurged for premium salami, prosciutto, mortadella (hot pork sausage), and provolone cheese. She made her marinated olive salad from scratch too. Even if LSU lost, her muffalettas made it a good day, anyway. Shorty and his brothers watched the games at our house. We had the bigger TV, and we had Mother's muffalettas.

Shorty's eyes took on a dreamy haze as he thought back to those Saturday afternoons. "Yeah, that was Heaven on earth—watchin' LSU in color and eatin' your mama's muffalettas. Why? Whatcha' got in mind?"

If only the electric company bartered like Shorty. "How about, instead of $200 a day plus expenses, I make you a muffaletta a day, plus expenses?" Shorty didn't need the money, anyway. The man led a simple life, funded by his Army pension. His lady friends took care of his extracurricular activities, and the family farm paid for his truck. Thank goodness the man loved to eat!

"Yeah, Doc, you've got yoreself a deal!" We shook hands and made it official. His right hand felt leathery and firm, reminding me of my dad's. A working man's hands.

"Okay, let's get started, Shorty. Tell me everything you've heard about this case." Did I actually think we'd get started immediately?

"Okay, but first I've gotta call my other customers an' tell 'em I'm not comin' around today. And ain't it time for lunch?" My new PI rubbed his stomach eagerly. "What're we havin'?"

Shorty broke the news to his customers, who didn't react well. He held the phone away from his ear, and I heard Bob Cahill yelling about calling the sheriff. Shorty just shrugged and stuck his phone in his pocket.

"What's ol' Bob gonna' do? He knows only me an' a guy in Baton Rouge can fix his hay baler. An' he's not gonna' haul it forty-five minutes down the road when I make house calls. Besides, he's not balin' hay til' Monday. Today's Friday—that's a whole four days away." Shorty was many things, including a procrastinator. Two bowls of tomato soup, and two turkey sandwiches later, my investigator was ready to work. "Okay, Doc, hand me the file and let me *puh rooze* it."

A snort escaped before I could contain it. "I think you mean *peruse*. And I'd rather you tell me what you know about this case, before Nate's investigation slants your opinions."

Shorty had found a bag of mixed nuts in my pantry and insisted on carrying them to the living room. The front porch had fallen to the heat, so we'd moved inside. He reached for a handful, then sat back to deliver his report.

"Well, Michael worked at the bank in Zachary, an' his sister, Stella, is a drug addict. Josh Fairchild felt sorry for Stella an' gave her a job at his cleaners in Zachary."

"Yes, Shorty, I know all that! Tell me about this Josh Fairchild. His family wasn't around when I grew up here." Shorty would be a great resource because he knew everyone. A great resource needing lots of food and focus.

"Yeah, he moved here after ya' left. He bought Best Cleaners—I think his daddy had money. Josh and Michael Cook Sr. were buddies from the Rotary Club, so Josh gave Stella that job. I heard after Michael Sr. an' his wife passed, Josh started comin' over tuh the house real regular. The story was they were working on the finances an' such, but it seems fishy to me, Doc—why wouldn't they do that at the cleaners? Some people think they're datin', but not me. My buddy knows 'im, an' he says Josh don't look at Stella like that. Y'know what I mean? He never saw no romantic-like looks from him."

A notebook! I needed somewhere to write other than the file. "Hold that thought, Shorty!" Like a jackrabbit, I leaped off the couch for my office. Before my PI could protest, I'd returned with a spiral notebook and a teal pen. Doug used to say I was having an affair with Office Depot, and he provided our credit card statements as evidence. A writer needs her pens and paper!

Scribbling furiously, I captured Shorty's clues. "Okay, I'm ready! Please continue." An impossible feat, because he had a mouthful of mixed nuts. Patiently, I waited, sipping my glass of iced tea.

"Mmmm hmm...those are some good mixed nuts, Doc! Make sure you stock up before I come back over."

Oh, good grief, was I now stocking the pantry for two?

"I think they got the right person, though." Shorty began, "My buddy in the sheriff's office said they found drugs an' needles an' stuff in the house. Michael Jr. told everybody Stella was clean, but sounds like she wasn't."

I still didn't like the argument once an addict, always an addict. Too convenient.

"Tell me about Michael's co-worker, Sam Hughes. What do you know about him?"

Shorty shifted gears. "My buddy Jake's the security guard at the bank where Michael worked, an' he told me Sam left at the same time as Michael the day o' the murder. Michael left first, an' Jake told him t'have a good evenin'. The guy waved back, but he looked like he had a whole plate full o' troubles on his table. Jake said Sam came out not ten seconds later, an' he waved to 'im too. But Sam was too busy chasin' after Michael. Jake said the whole building watched 'em yellin' at each other in the parkin' lot."

My original thoughts about Sam seemed on point. Maybe it was a stretch to kill over a promotion. But what if that was the last straw? Maybe there was a history of jealousy and competition? My notes about Sam grew longer.

"Hey, Doc! Ain't Rob Dugas a suspect too? That kid's had more run-ins with the law than my Aunt Mavis has bunions. My buddy at the sheriff's office said neighbors saw Rob's car in the neighborhood. He and Michael still hung out together, even though he deals drugs. My money's on that guy."

He reached forward for more nuts.

Several questions burned through my brain. Did Stella love drugs more than her brother? How deep did Sam's feud with Michael run? Was Josh as good-hearted as his reputation boasted? Would Shorty's offer of $200 a day be cheaper than the food he ate? Just how many bunions did Aunt Mavis have?

Chapter 3

My new PI insisted on driving me to the coffee shop. It turned out to be the better plan, because Shorty specialized in being nosey. People expected him to ask personal questions, and they felt comfortable sharing information. Shorty had his own dirty laundry that he easily aired, so no one felt ashamed to return the favor.

Shorty and I differed in that respect, for sure. Moving back to my hometown had been difficult. Personally, I preferred the anonymity of New Orleans, where I could run to the grocery store for milk without suffering an inquisition disguised as conversation. It sounds unfeeling, I'm sure. But sometimes I just want to go to the store with a baseball cap and no makeup, without whispers of "Have you seen Evangeline Delafose lately? Honey, that girl is worn slap out."

Maggie's Coffee Shop, a welcome addition to our community since I'd left, served two important functions. Most of the 298 residents purchased Maggie's coffee delights and scrumptious baked goods, marveling at how they'd survived before she opened. The coffee shop also gave the village a place to quietly eavesdrop on each other's lives. It became my saving grace, a place to dole out the bits and pieces of my life I didn't mind sharing, speaking just loudly enough that the entire shop could catch up. I always wore makeup, so I didn't look worn slap out.

The owner and namesake of my favorite coffee shop leaned against the counter, her smile widening in recognition. This woman was born to dispense coffee, from her hair the color of cold brew to eyes resembling her famous cinnamon dolce latte.

"Hey Ev, hey Shorty! What can I get ya'?" Maggie made everyone feel welcome, even if she didn't have a clue who they were. Most likely she knew a brother or a cousin, or a friend of her new patron. As she served each order, she took care to make the customer feel welcome. Her coffee shop reminded me of the 1980s sitcom *Cheers*, which would make her our Sam.

Maggie made hands-down the best chai tea latte, but her café americano was hard to beat. Most days I struggled with that life choice. Should I get the tried and true, or be adventurous? My brow furrowed like a rice farm before planting, when my partner eased my pain.

"Doc'll take a *chay tea lat-tay* an' I'll have my usual." He scanned the shop, spotting a couple of buddies.

Maggie chuckled at Shorty's pronunciation of my chai tea latte, but she covered well with a cough.

"Oh, hey Doc, this is part of my *plus expenses*—right? So you've got the bill." Not waiting for an answer, he moseyed toward his buddies. Sighing, I reached for my credit card.

"Since when do you and Shorty hang out together? I know your families have been friends for years, but...well..." Maggie's voice trailed off.

"Shorty fixed my washing machine, so I offered to buy him a cup of..." I paused. Obviously, I didn't know my friend as well as he knew me. "Hey Maggie, what exactly is his usual?" And how did he know mine?

Maggie laughed as if she'd heard a hilarious joke. "We call it, The Shorty—It's chicory coffee with cayenne pepper sprinkled on top, just like his mama Madie used to make. Except that he adds five shots of espresso."

"That explains a lot about Shorty! But how does he know my favorite drink?" This story had to be interesting.

"Oh, that's easy. He and your dad come in here a lot, and one time they got to arguing whether you preferred tea or coffee. They settled the bet by asking me which drink you order the most." Maggie's grin commandeered her face. "Shorty won, and your dad pouted for days."

Were all the men in my life hanging out together, conspiring to run it for me? Who was I kidding? They could do a better job than I had done lately. My dad and I would have to have a talk about his topics of conversations with his friends.

"Hey, Doc! When yer done jawin', come on over an' meet muh buddies!"

Jawin'? What exactly did Shorty think *he* was doing? That guy gossiped more than a ladies' weekly sewing circle.

Maggie flashed a knowing smile. "Don't worry, Ev. I'll have Avery bring out your drinks."

The table was full, but a twenty-something kid stood up and motioned that I take his seat. Courtesy from Gen Z didn't happen in New Orleans, and I thanked him for being raised right. The kid returned quickly with a chair from the back table.

"Fellas... I want ya t'meet Dr. Evangeline Bergeron Delafose." Shorty emphasized my title, pronouncing it *Dock Tuh*. "Ya'll know her daddy, Skeeter, an' her brother, Detective Nate Bergeron. She lives a coupla' blocks down from the post office, in the one story with the blue shutters an' the porch swing."

As the men nodded in acknowledgement, I had to chuckle. Small town introductions always involved both a genealogy and a geography lesson.

"Doc, this here's Bobby, Curt, an' Ken." He leaned in towards the center of the table and dropped his voice a few decibels. "Ken lives down the street from the Cook house."

Shorty turned to his friend and gave him the go ahead. The go ahead for what?

Ken cleared his throat. "Yeah, Shorty said you were asking about Michael Cook's murder, cuz your brother's workin' the case. Well, the cops came to my house about a year and a half ago to interview me. I told them Michael was a good kid, really tryin' to make his daddy proud. But he had his hands full with his sister." Ken leaned back in his chair, as if he'd delivered some sort of revelation.

"Yeah, yeah, yeah! We all know all that, Ken! Get to the part about the argument ya heard." Maybe it was my imagination, but Shorty seemed determined to show off his private investigator skills.

Ken pushed his head towards the center of the table again, then dropped his voice to a whisper. Maggie's customers would have a hard time eavesdropping. "Yeah, so a bunch of us were in a buddy's backyard the night before the murder. We'd gotten off work and were lettin' off some steam. You know, drinkin' a coupla' cold ones, visitin' and such. Well, my buddy's backyard shares a fence with the Cook place, and we all heard a buncha hollerin' comin' from the back o' the house."

Ken sat back again, satisfied he'd pleased Shorty.

Apparently, this was the end of Ken's story. "Hmmm...did you hear what the argument was about?"

Avery appeared with drinks and a smile, like a fairy coffee mother. "Here ya'll go–let me know if ya'll need anything else." She turned and flew away, but without gossamer wings

Ken shook his head. "No ma'am, not really. But it was so loud Bubba stopped tellin' his story about the time he saw Randy Travis in the French

Quarter." The other three bobbed their heads in unison. It must take a lot to interrupt Bubba's story.

Let's try another direction. "Okay, Ken. Could you tell whether the people were both male? Or both female? Maybe one of each?"

Ken shook his head. "No ma'am. But it was definitely two people yellin'."

Thanks Ken, for explaining that to me. I never knew it took two people to have an argument. Doug would probably confirm that, because he used to say I would argue with a brick wall. And win.

Shorty nodded his head in Bobby's direction. "Bobby's girlfriend used t'wait tables with Faith Dixon. Go on, tell Doc whatcha' know."

Bobby's eyes glistened with excitement, probably like they did on the opening day of deer season. "Yes ma'am! My girlfriend Amy Beth, she and Faith used to be good friends, until Amy Beth started datin' me. See, I asked out Faith awhile back, oh, a coupla' years ago and..."

Funny how Shorty could scurry down a rabbit trail, but he didn't tolerate it from his friends. "Hey! Stay on topic, man!" Shorty's snapping fingers brought Bobby back from the trail. "Tell Doc what Amy Beth said."

Bobby looked startled, his eyes bulging with surprise. Ah! From Bobby's reaction, I guessed Shorty usually followed the rabbit trails. This time, he needed to prove his value as a private investigator. An investigator charging a muffaletta a day plus expenses.

"Huh? Oh yeah! Well, Amy Beth said when Michael dumped Faith, he did it in front of the diner when he dropped her off for work. The guy broke up with her right as she hopped outta' the car, then told her to find another ride home. Amy Beth said Faith stormed into the diner, throwin' her purse at the busboy. She grabbed Amy Beth and pushed her into the ladies' room, and started yellin' about how Michael couldn't do that to her in front of her place of *bizness*. Faith told Amy Beth she was goin' to get even with Michael, and he'd be sorry he treated her like dirt."

The phrase, *hell has no fury like a woman scorned* rushed to the front of my brain. Faith's words sounded like someone more angry than vindictive. Not to mention, I was hearing her tirade second-person. Maybe it hadn't been that bad. Young girls overreacted, especially in matters of the heart. What was Bobby saying about a fire? My head swiveled.

"...and Tyrone barely made it out of there with his life! Now the sheriff couldn't prove it was Faith, but we all know the truth."

Ev, you've got to pay more attention! "I'm sorry, Bobby. What was that first part? Something about a fire?"

Shorty's eyes narrowed slightly. "Doc! Y'gotta' pay attention! Bobby, I'm really sorry. Ev has trouble focusin' sometimes. You know, ever since..." Shorty lowered his voice to a stage whisper. "...her husband died in the line of duty." My table companions nodded their heads in understanding.

My stomach tightened as tears surged to the corners of my eyes. It had been three years, but emotions still ran raw. *Breathe, Ev, force your lungs to take in air. Take deep breaths, smooth out the jaggedness.* Shorty glanced at me in concern, making the situation worse. Weakly, I smiled at my audience, willing my eyes to hide the jumble of emotions.

Bobby started over. "Um, yeah, so Faith used to date a guy I worked with, Tyrone. She found an earring in Tyrone's back seat when she put her purse on the floorboards. Well, that girl jumped all over Tyrone, accused him of cheatin' on her. Tyrone tried to tell her he'd taken his little sister and her friends to the football game, but she wasn't havin' none of that. He dumped her when she showed up at his work and started hollerin' in front of the customers. Tyrone almost got fired from the Gas n' More 'cuz of her."

When would the fire come into play? "So she set fire to the Graisseville Gas n' More?" Focusing on Bobby's story helped my stomach relax and my throat lose the gagging feeling.

"Oh, no ma'am! She's crazy, but not *that* crazy! Her uncle owns the Gas n' More, and she got Tyrone that job. She wouldn't burn down her uncle's place of *bizness*. Family's family, no matter what."

Oh good! It was comforting to know the girl had a code of ethics.

"Okay, so when does the fire come into the story?" My eyes skirted down at the table as my finger not so casually touched my phone screen. How long had we traveled down this rabbit trail?

"Well, that same night, after they'd broken up, Tyrone took out Tonia Geary. Not too smart, if you ask me. But nobody asked me, including Tyrone. He'd dropped off Tonia at her place and was drivin' up the road to his house."

Bobby spotted another trail and loped down its grassy path. "You knew he was staying at his grandpa's old place, right Shorty? The one where we used to hang out in the back and shoot targets? It was pretty run down, but it was free. Tyrone's dad owns the land, now that his grandpa's passed. Tyrone's grandpa, not his dad's grandpa..."

If Shorty wandered down rabbit trails, this guy's stories took seven-mile detours to the next parish. At least they made me appreciate my PI's tales.

"Bobby, da..." Shorty tried to shut down his cuss word, but the signal didn't make it to his mouth fast enough. "...mmm in a beaver!" He tried to substitute *dam a beaver*, but the table heard *dammin' in a beaver*. Close enough. "Just finish your story, okay?"

Realizing his audience's interest had waned, Bobby shifted to rapid fire mode.

"As Tyrone drove up the road, he could see smoke comin' from his house. He sped up and pulled into the yard. Tyrone grabbed the garden hose, but it was too late. His grandpa's house, in the family for five generations, was almost gone. Tyrone ran inside—stupid, really—to get what he could. He grabbed his grandpa's Henry rifle and some clothes. Then he called the fire department and watched his home burn down." Whew! Bobby looked out of breath and frankly surprised at himself.

Curt, who'd been silent until that point, caught my attention with a slight nod of his head. "Hey, Doc, if you've got a minute, I'd like to show you somethin'."

Did Curt have actual evidence that could help us? Sometimes the silent ones revealed the most information. To portray more authority, I adjusted my glasses and straightened the slump of my back. If my third-grade teacher had joined us, she would positively beam at my posture.

"Why yes, Curt! I'd love to see what you've got." Our first real clue!

My informant began unbuttoning his shirt. "See, I've got this mole, and I think it's changing color and getting bigger. Could you look at it for me, give me your expert opinion? See, I ain't got no health insurance, so you'd really be..."

Shorty leaped from the table and put his hand on my shoulder. "Thanks fellas, we *'preciate* yore hospitality. I'll see ya'll later. Doc, grab yore *chay* tea!"

Curt's hubcap sized eyes followed us as we flew out the door. Maggie had her back to the exit, so I planned an apology text later. Top on my apology list was Curt's impromptu strip tease, and Shorty knocking over his chair as he hustled me out the door. With the best coffee in a thirty-mile radius, Maggie was not someone I wanted to offend.

"I gather Curt had nothing relevant to tell us about the case? Assuming, of course, that his mole wasn't the key to solving it."

Shorty's driving made me nervous, to say it politely. My heart stopped as he reached into his cooler in the back seat and pulled out a can of orange soda. Keeping one hand on the wheel, he popped the top and gulped down a quarter of the contents. Thank goodness Shorty's buddy, Monty, was off duty today. When Monty patrolled the streets of Graisseville, Shorty knew he could drive ten miles above the speed limit without being pulled over. Fortunately, Deputy Chris Landry, Maggie's cousin, was on duty. Chris pulled over all speeders, even those breaking the law by two miles.

"Nah, Curt ain't got nothin'. He jus' said Stella went tuh a movie in Baton Rouge the night o' the murder. But she an' Michael shared a car, an' it was in the driveway when the deputies came tuh the house. My buddy, Monty, said Michael drove it home from the bank. An' neighbors said it never left the driveway until the deputies towed it as evidence. Stella says she got a ride with a friend, but this so-called friend is layin' low. Either Stella's lyin' or she's keepin' company with some shady folks. Either way, she ain't got no alibi."

Miraculously, we pulled into my driveway unharmed. Thank you, Deputy Landry!

The next afternoon, I ventured to the coffee shop without Shorty. Scanning the cars parked in front relieved my fears that Curt might be inside. The jangling sound heard as I pushed open the door warmed my heart. This coffee shop had been a godsend to an introvert like me, a place full of people eager to invite me to their tables and share their time.

Maggie waved with one hand while handing a cup to a customer. Gosh, that woman was talented! I could barely walk to the table, holding my cup with both hands.

"The usual, Ev?" My favorite barista held up the medium-sized cup, question marks in her eyes. We both pretended I might change my habits and order something else. Like I've said, there have been times I've tried other drinks, and they all left warm happy memories in my stomach. But the chai tea latte always called to me, like a familiar friend. Like Maggie calling to me across the shop.

A handful of customers, mostly retired people, enjoyed the peace before the after-school crowd blew through the door. A perfect time to hit up Maggie for information, and she definitely would not ask for medical advice.

"Yes, please! Medium-sized chai tea latte. And how are you today, Maggie?" Can't forget Southern hospitality and politeness.

"Oh, it's been a day! My espresso machine is giving me fits! Not to mention my syrup delivery guy is sick, and his replacement forgot my pumpkin spice. It's October! How can I run a coffee shop in October without pumpkin spice?" And yet, Maggie always managed a smile, even amid disaster.

"Oh girl, I hear you! Lack of pumpkin spice could cause a riot!" My mind envisioned a crowd of coffee patrons angrily thrusting pitchforks and torches towards the doors. Maggie and her employees huddled inside, barricading themselves with tables and chairs. And the finicky espresso machine.

"Say, Maggie, do you have a few minutes? I had a few questions about something." Always up for a chat, my favorite barista bobbed her head up and down.

"Of course! Once I fix your chai tea, I'll bring it to your table and we can catch up."

Remembering my promise to Shorty, I pointed to the ice cream. "Could I get a scoop of chocolate?" My eyes wandered to the scarce baked goods. "Oh! And how about two chocolate chip cookies?"

Maggie's eyes brightened as she rang up my order. "It's good to see you with an appetite, Ev! I'll be sure and pass that on to your dad. He worries about you." Maggie's father passed away a few years ago, so it didn't surprise me she teared up.

Why do certain phrases shove us down memory lane, taking us by surprise and causing tears? Why did I order cookies and ice cream, which reminded Maggie of losing her father? Stop it, Ev! Moving on is just part of the grief process.

"Well, you'd better notify Nate and Shorty as well. Probably my kids too. Everyone seems to be worried about my lack of appetite."

As quickly as they'd arrived, Maggie's tears turned tail and fled. "Yes, well, in this town, everyone's probably got the memo already. You know, the one about Evangeline Delafose eating two cookies and a scoop of ice cream at two in the afternoon."

As promised, Maggie delivered my drink, along with her own, and sat across from me in the back. She drank deeply from her cup, inhaling not just coffee but a moment to relax.

"All right, what's up? And don't tell me you and Shorty are an item. Because I've already had his admirers prodding me for information. And if you are together, you'd better watch your back! There's at least three women in town who regularly fight over him, and I wouldn't be surprised if they ganged up and tried to take you out."

Yeah, this was why I'd fought Shorty about going to the coffee shop together. But winning an argument with that man was like keeping bugs out of the house with a screen door full of holes.

"Absolutely not, Maggie! Shorty is like a brother to me—honestly!"

Maggie leaned back slowly, searching my face for clues. "Okay, I believe you. It's just that Shorty's had four dates with Candy Cahill in the last couple of months. He's told her he's not looking for anything serious, but she's been dropping hints about him meeting her parents. After your outing yesterday, Candy thinks he's moved on to you."

Of course! What was Shorty's excuse for driving me to the coffee shop? Something about his PI license required us to ride together. That confirmed bachelor was using *me* to throw off Candy Cahill! Earlier at the Graisseville Gas n' More, she'd shared a pump with me. Even though I'd smiled and said *hi*, her daggers made for an awkward tank fill up. I'd deal with Shorty later.

"Enough about Shorty! Let me catch you up on some things." Maggie's eyes crinkled around the edges, signaling her concentration.

My case review took all of four minutes, which gave Maggie time to sip and think. "I'm happy to help you in any way I can, Ev, I really am! But all I know about the case is what I've read in the papers."

"Yes, but I'm looking for information not in the papers. What can you tell me about..." My eyes scanned the notebook. Rob's information barely filled half a page. "Rob Dugas. What do you know about him?"

Maggie took a few more sips of her drink, her eyes faraway in thought. "Well, I only moved back to town about five years ago, and Rob was several years behind me in school. But..."

Was I holding my breath? Yes, I was! Did Nate hold his breath too, when his informant gave him more information?

"My cousin's ranch is down the same road as Rob's family farm. I remember my cousin complaining that Rob brought Michael out one night, and they fired the guns until 1 a.m. My cousin was good friends with Rob's dad, so he didn't call the sheriff. He just drove over and told the guys to knock it off. He told them Michael's daddy wouldn't be too happy to know his handgun was keeping folks up at night."

Rob was aware of Michael's handgun! But he had guns of his own. If he was the killer, why not use his own gun? Duh, Ev! So the detectives couldn't trace the gun back to him!

"Maggie, when did your cousin go over to Rob's farm and chew him out? How close to the murder?"

Maggie's concentration mirrored Nate's when he played chess with his son, who usually creamed him. "I'd say a week before the murder. Why? Is that important?"

Good question! "It could be. The important thing is that Rob knew about the gun, and probably knew where Michael kept it. This is great, Maggie! Anything else?"

Not only did Maggie make fabulous caffeinated drinks, but she knew things. "Rob came into the coffee shop after your brother questioned him. He told me he'd admitted to being at Michael's house the night of the murder. He begged Michael for money, but the poor kid didn't have any. Rob said he first tried threatening, then broke down in tears and begged his friend to help him. According to Rob, Michael told him this was the last time. He agreed to pawn his father's handgun the next day after work and give Rob the cash. But of course, he didn't have that chance." Maggie clicked her tongue in disapproval. "If you ask me, Michael let that relationship go on too long. You've got to know when to cut the cord on friendships." She tipped her cup towards the back wall and let the last drops slide down her throat.

That was my cue. "Maggie, I really appreciate everything you told me, and I will keep it all in confidence. Promise!" My arms instinctively wrapped themselves around Maggie's shoulders, and she returned my squeeze.

"My pleasure, Ev! And don't worry..." Maggie's voice dropped low, causing me to tuck my ear closer to her mouth. "I won't tell anyone you're working on this case. The killer's still out there somewhere. So be careful."

On my way home, I spotted Candy Cahill's car in the post office parking lot. Her bright red Volkswagen Bug filled the only slot, so I pulled in and parked right beside her. Hopefully, Candy and I could bury the hatchet, as long as she didn't want to bury it in my chest.

As I pushed open the doors, I spotted Candy opening her PO box. What did Shorty see in these women? Bright red hair, clearly out of a bottle, poking out of a baseball cap. Her claw-like pink nails clashing with her hair, but they fished several envelopes out of the box. I mentally gave her credit for devising a workaround.

Let's just get this over with. "Candy, I think there's a misunderstanding between us. I've known Shorty since I was four years old. He's like a brother to me. We have never dated, and never will. The reason he spends so much time at my house is that he's doing my brother, Nate, a favor."

Candy's eyes softened as she put away her daggers. A good sign!

"Nate asked Shorty to look after me ever since I moved back. My brother has a family and a job, and they keep him pretty busy. He knows Shorty has time on his hands and can stop by and check on me."

I took a breath. "Look, Candy, Shorty just comes around from time to time to fix my loose screen door or take my car to get the oil changed. It's really so Nate feels comfortable, and he knows I'm doing okay." I strategically placed myself outside of Candy's nail scratching range, which also gave me room to gauge her reaction.

Candy threw herself at me, claws sailing past my neck. Whew! My would-be rival was hugging me, not attacking me.

"Oh, Miss Ev, you can't imagine how that makes me feel! I know Shorty sees other women occasionally, but he told me I'm his special girl. I'm not too worried about the other women. But *you*! You're not like the others. Shorty's always bragging on you, and your *doctor-ite*." Candy's moon shadow blue eyelids drooped slightly, and her cherry red lips puckered. "I can't compete with no doctor."

Step back, Ev. Unwind yourself from this poor woman's arms, but take care not to damage her claws. I mean nails! Take one of her hands in yours, as a gesture of friendship. Watch those nails!

"Candy, you have nothing to worry about from me. In fact, I'll do you one better. I'll keep an eye on Shorty, and if he mentions any other women, I'll be sure and report back to you." Smiling my widest *let's be friends not foes* smile, I took yet another step back.

"Oh, Miss Ev! Thank you so much!" Candy hesitated, her wide brown eyes reminded of the old Kewpie dolls my grandmother collected. This woman could be attractive if she'd stop applying her makeup with a spackle brush.

"Michael Cook and I worked together at the bank, and Shorty was asking me if I knew anything about him. I couldn't think of anything, but now that I've thought about it..."

Candy's smile revealed perfect pearls as her eyes projected warmth. Author Lailah Gifty Akita's words floated into my brain. *Smile is the beauty of the soul*. If Candy's smile was any sign, her soul was breathtaking.

"Could you pass this on to Shorty, please? I stopped by Michael's cubicle at lunch one day, about a month before his murder. His computer screen had a bunch of browsers up, all real estate listings in Alaska. When I asked him if he was planning to move there, he hemmed and hawed and changed the subject. That same afternoon, he came by my desk and asked me not to tell anyone about the listings. He said he was in some trouble and he couldn't go to the sheriff. Michael said he was going to have to get out of town for a while, maybe permanently."

Whoa! What had Michael gotten into? Was he planning to take Stella with him? Maybe they had fought because he was going to leave her to deal with the fallout. Thank goodness I made peace with Shorty's girlfriend.

"Thank you so much, Candy! I will pass this on to Shorty." A peaceful scene crashed into my thoughts. Candy, Shorty, and I, sitting around a fire on Shorty's farm. Where did that come from? Not my idea of a fun Saturday night, but better than slashed tires.

Candy and I pushed through the post office doors and strolled six feet to our cars. My navy Volvo took on a wallflower vibe as she sat parked next to the belle of the ball. Could I see myself in a bright red car?

Candy waved one last goodbye, then doubled back to my side. Was this one last farewell, two sisters from another mister? Please don't ask me to go shopping, Candy. I'm just not there yet.

"Miss Ev, since we've smoothed over our misunderstanding, I should probably let you know something. When you get to your house, don't open the screen door. You need to get a broomstick or a hoe. Something to pull it open." Her caterpillar lashes fluttered at me, framing her sorrowful eyes. "There may be a dead rat ready to fall on you when you open the door. Toodles!" She waved again and fled to her car.

Yeah, we're definitely not going to be besties.

Chapter 4

Shorty got an earful as I sat in the post office parking lot. Most likely two earfuls. My car was not touching the gravel in my driveway until he'd taken care of his girlfriend's gift. Anyone driving by scratched their heads wondering which poor soul was on the receiving end of Ev Delafose's hissy fit.

Shorty promised he was just down the road at the Gas n' More, and begged me for ten minutes. He got five. No surprise when I reached my block, an F150 crookedly occupied my driveway. Observers might wonder if the driver had been in a great hurry to park.

Graisseville's resident Romeo perched on my porch swing, desperately trying to convey an air of casual coolness. Despite my suggestions, I didn't see a broomstick or a hoe. Probably because he feared what I might do with them.

As I exited the car, Shorty sprang from the porch swing, words of apology spilling all over himself. "Oh, hey, Doc! Listen, I'm real sorry about Candy. She didn't mean nothin' by it—honest! She's a sweet girl. I know you two would geehaw. It was just a misunderstandin', that's all. I already took care of it, don't you worry."

Geehaw is a Southern term meaning to get along or to see eye to eye. As Shorty held up the expired creature from its tail, I resolved to geehaw with Candy, no matter the situation. Nose to tail, that dead animal hung down a good ten inches. My brain processed the lengths this woman went to so she could get rid of a potential rival. Candy actually found this creature *on purpose* and strategically placed it over my door to scare the daylights out of me. More and more, I was thankful for my stop at the post office to make peace.

"Shorty, I appreciate you flying over here and saving me. But don't you *ever* use me again to fend off your admirers, okay? If I hadn't seen Candy at the post office and made friends, you'd have to call an ambulance right now to whisk my dead body to the morgue." The alternate ending didn't seem farfetched. I was never good with dead animals.

"Ev, it won't happen again. You have my word as a gentleman and a scholar." When Shorty used my actual name, I knew his words were sincere. As for the phrase, *a gentleman and a scholar*, our high school history teacher, Mr. Willis, always used it. He'd praise a male student by saying, "Sir, you are a gentleman and a scholar!" For young ladies, he'd simply change the pronouns. He told us the phrase originated in eighteenth-century England, when scholarly pursuits and noble manners were important characteristics among society. Mr. Willis reminded us that these characteristics still marked the measure of a person, even today. Shorty took to heart Mr. Willis' words and adopted them as part of his promises. If the guy told me I had his word as a gentleman and a scholar, there was no way he'd break that promise.

My breathing eased and my wild eyes relaxed, which Shorty observed. "Besides, if you'd uh been dead, the *am-bu-lance* wouldn't o' whisked ya to the morgue. Them *am-bu-lance-suz* don't go fast for dead people."

The wild eyes returned with a vengeance, and I lunged forward to choke my guest.

Shorty sidestepped my grip and wisely changed the subject. "Say, Doc, now that we've made peace, do y'think ya could invite me in and make me a muffaletta? Ya know, as payment for yesterday?"

Was this subject any better? "Shorty, I haven't had time to go to the store. Tell you what, come on in and I'll heat up some gumbo. Bonnie made it for me, and I need to finish it off." Telling Nate I ate his wife's gumbo had been the truth. I never said I ate *all* of it. Shorty's eyes perked up at the words, *Bonnie* and *gumbo*. Everyone knew my sister-in-law placed second in the state fair for her culinary perfection.

"Well, maybe jus' one bowl won't hurt me." Like a puppy hearing his meal drop into a bowl, Shorty practically plowed over me to get through the door. Once inside, he eagerly sniffed the air.

How could I have gumbo warming up if I just got home?

"Yer gonna join me, right Doc?" His eyes signaled memory of my promise to gain some weight.

"Yes, I will have a bowl with you. I never ate lunch, so I should eat something."

A promise is a promise, Ev. You could eat one bowl with an old friend, even if your heart wasn't in it. Glancing fondly at my dining companion, I watched his father staring back. Mack Cormier and my dad had been thick as thieves, and we'd all mourned the loss of a dear man. Shorty had inherited his father's looks and his compassion. The size of his heart rivaled Atchafalaya (pronounced *CHA-fuh-LIE-yuh*) Basin, even if he drove me crazy. Speaking of crazy.

"Hey, do ya have any cornbread? Y'can't eat gumbo without corn-bread."

With a toss of my hand, I directed Shorty to my pantry. "There's a package of Gladiola cornbread mix in there. You can pull it out and start mixing it up." Oh Ev, did you really think that answer would fly?

Was that a horse snorting in my kitchen, or just my PI? "C'mon, Doc! Yore mama never made cornbread from a mix! She'd be rollin' over in her grave right now." He stalked to the pantry to collar the contraband package. Waving the culprit in the air, he charged back to the island. "It jus' ain't right! My mama never used no mix, an' I know yours didn't neither! We gotta make it from scratch."

Shorty was hands-down one of the best cooks I knew. But over the years he'd realized it was easier to charm women into cooking for him, instead of doing it himself. Not this woman. "Look, Shorty, if you want cornbread from scratch, then you'd better get busy."

We faced off for five seconds before he blinked. "Okay, well, I guess this'll hafta do." My sous chef faced the series of cabinets, squinting intently to divine which one held the mixing bowl. Did he think his helpless act would fool me?

Heaving a sigh from head to toe, I waved my ladle to complete an image of frustration. "There, Shorty! Look at the middle shelf in the second cabinet." Who was I kidding? Not so gently pushing my way in, I reached up to open the cabinet.

"Yeah, yeah. I got it! No reason to get all pi...I mean all huffy. It's not my kitchen, y'know." Maybe not at the moment, but the guy was spending as much time in it as I did.

By God's divine intervention, we prepared supper and sat down to eat. After I nudged Shorty's elbows off the table, I asked him to say grace.

"Oh, Doc, y'know I haven't been tuh church since my mama's funeral. I don't think God wants t'hear from me. You say it! Yer probly at the top o' the list in His Book of Life, anyway."

So, he remembered something about church from his childhood! There might be hope for this man, after all. "All right, Shorty, I will. But I know for a fact God wants to hear from everyone, especially you." Was that a hint of a smile from my church-avoiding friend?

Not one second after the *amen*, Shorty's cornbread crumbles bobbed on top of his gumbo. His spoon hung in midair, poised to dip into the bowl. Did he mash up his cornbread during the prayer? No, he knew better. His mama wouldn't have let that habit develop. When it came to eating, this guy worked faster than Santa Claus on Christmas Eve.

Shorty's arm lifted eagerly to wipe his hand against his mouth. He should know better than to do that in front of me! Apparently, he did. His arm hesitated a split-second midair, then gracefully continued towards his ear, sliding all five fingers through his hair. Confidence flooded his face as he picked up his napkin and dabbed his mouth. Were single women so desperate in this town that they put up with bad table manners? Not this single woman.

"Say, Doc, Bobby was workin' while I was getting' gas this afternoon. He went on break so he could come out an' tell me a coupla' things."

Shorty inserted a dramatic pause to shove a spoonful of gumbo into his mouth. It was clear this farmer turned PI got a kick out of our brief investigation.

"Bobby made a few comments as he was ringing up folks to see what people would say. You know, stuff about how the Cook case was cold, and the sheriff was stumped. Well, one customer told Bobby that the sheriff should be lookin' into Michael's girlfriend."

"Faith Dixon? I thought they broke up?" Where was my notebook and teal pen?

"Nah, Doc, not her! This guy claimed he and his wife had supper at the Cajun Frog in Zachary, and they saw Michael havin' supper with some blonde woman about his age. They went over and said, *Hey*, but Michael didn't introduce 'em to his lady friend. Truth is, he looked like a fox caught in a henhouse, all guilty and such."

Could this woman have something to do with Michael's interest in Alaska? Flipping pages, I started a separate section just for this mysterious blonde.

"See if you can find out more about this woman, Shorty. She might be our best lead."

"Will do, Doc. Oh, and everyone in the Gas n' More agreed Rob hit Michael up for money more times than y'can shake a stick at."

What did that even mean? "Well, that's not news, Shorty." At least we had the blonde angle.

"Yeah, but Rob says first he was threatenin' Michael, then he begged for help. Rob claims Michael was gonna' pawn his father's handgun, but died before he could do it." Shorty paused for dramatic effect. Instead of irritating me, I chuckled in amusement. Maybe we both needed something to occupy our boring lives?

"What if Rob lied? What if Michael pulled out the gun to pawn it, then changed his mind? Or maybe he had the gun with him because he knew Rob was gonna' ask for money again. Either way, Rob kills Michael, then leaves the gun. He can't pawn it, cuz it's not his, and now it's a murder weapon." Shorty gobbled up gumbo, making up for the lost bites while laying out his theory.

"It makes sense. Not to mention, Rob's car was seen in the neighborhood. Yeah, it definitely tracks." We had motive and opportunity, and even means. Maybe. Puzzling over my notes, I concluded we still had a lot of holes.

"Let's divide and conquer. You go back and talk to your sources—you've got a lot more than I do. I've got church tomorrow, which probably won't give me an opportunity for investigating." It was a long shot, but one I had to take. "Would you like to come with me to church tomorrow, Shorty? I know several people who'd love to see you." Keep it nonchalant, Ev. No pressure. Just a friendly invitation. "I'm headed over to Nate's for lunch afterwards. Bonnie's making jambalaya." Would food be worth sitting still for an hour?

"Uh, that's mighty kind, o' you, Doc, but I got things to do. That farm don't run itself."

It's okay, Ev, you tried. Just keep trying, but don't be pushy. And keep praying. "Well, why don't you come over for lunch, anyway? Bonnie always makes enough to feed an army, and I know she'd love to see you." Only a half-lie. Bonnie didn't dislike Shorty, but he wasn't on her top ten list of favorite Graisseville residents.

"Mebbe. But God prob'ly wouldn't want me eatin' Miss Bonnie's *jahm-buh-lie-uh* iffin' I didn't go tuh His house that day. Say, could I take somma' this gumbo t'go?"

He'd already wrapped the cornbread in aluminum foil. Apparently, the baker got all the leftovers.

Before I'd finished my head nod, Shorty found a mason jar for his gumbo. Good thing I didn't say no.

"In fact, just take the entire container, and leave me the mason jar."

Shorty's eyes sparkled, showing off his toothy grin.

"Thanks, Doc! Y'know, workin' the farm and helpin' you out sure takes a lot outta' a man. When do ya think you'll have those muffalettas ready?"

Nice to know I'm so exhausting. "Monday's grocery day, Shorty. I promise to get the ingredients and have a plate for you that evening. Unless you have other plans?" Not that I wanted a play-by-play of Shorty's love life, but I was curious if he and Candy were still an item.

"Oh yeah, Mondays are always good for me! My lady friends and buddies stay home on Mondays cuz they're still *ree-coop-errr-ay-ting* from the weekend. If you know what I mean." His left eyelid dropped slowly, then back up, framing his pearly whites. Mack and Madie Cormier must have spent a fortune on that grin.

While walking Shorty to the entryway, I hid my smile. The guy expertly balanced a quart of gumbo and a brick of cornbread while opening the door. Instinctively, my eyes raised towards the top of the screen door. Nope, no dead varmints there.

"I like your idea of dividin' and conquerin'. Real smart. I'll be playin' poker Saturday night, so I'll talk tuh my buddies. An' you talk tuh yore church ladies an' see what ya can find out." He slid easily through the screen door and moved down my stairs. The man could carry food like a boss.

"That sounds good, Shorty. But I don't think people at church are going to know anything." Wrong answer, Ev!

My PI set his food on the hood before turning to eye me skeptically. Shorty was squinting again, which meant I'd said something not quite accurate.

"Doc, if there's one thing I learned by goin' tuh Sunday School an' church all those years, it's that church people gossip jus' as much as the rest o' us. They jus' hide it as prayin'."

My head cocked to the side—it was my turn to squint. "What are you talking about?"

The truck door swung open, and Shorty deposited his food into the passenger seat.

"Oh, ya know what I'm talkin' about. They call ya up an' say they wanna' pray for ya', but they jus' want ya t'tell 'em yore secrets. Then they tell everybody else on the prayer chain."

Shorty inserted air quotes around *prayer chain*. "How do y'think every-one found out my daddy almost lost our farm? Some lady at the church called my mama 'bout prayer requests. She broke down cryin' that we was about to be kicked offa' our farm."

He snorted again, reminding me of his horse, Festus.

Just like that, Shorty's disposition returned to carefree mode. "But, hey! Ya can use that to yore advantage. Just keep yore personal stuff quiet."

With a wave and a grin, he backed out of my driveway, then stopped. "Oh, one more thing."

Aww, was my friend getting sentimental? Perhaps he wanted to speak an encouraging word, or tell me something that had been on his mind?

"Candy said she didn't hafta' go far t'find that dead rat. Said she found it in yore backyard, next to yore woodpile. You'd best call the *ex-ter-muh-nay-terr*—ya might have a rat *in-fess-tay-shun.*" With a wave and a smile, he puttered down Pecan Street.

Chapter 5

Nate knew at 4 p.m. on a Saturday afternoon, a call from his sister meant she had a problem. "I need you to come over right now! I have a rat infestation."

A long sucking sound on the other end signaled my brother, drawing his breath slowly into his lungs, contemplating my dilemma. If I'd been beside him, I would have watched him run his fingers through his high-top fade, super short on the sides but a good four inches on top. He kept it just short enough to satisfy the sheriff's department regulations, mourning the good old days. Those good old days when he wore a mullet and played bad lead guitar in the garage with his buddies. Bonnie and I never looked back on those good old days.

"Uh, Ev, extermination isn't really part of my skill set. Especially since I can't discharge my firearm unless it's in defense of myself or others. And I don't think we have any rat poison."

Where did defending his sister against a murderous horde of rats fall, exactly? It sounded like the defense of others to me.

Before I'd called Nate, I performed some extensive research on rats. My phone's search browser returned several bits of information, which in today's world qualified as research. For instance, these creatures scurry around in a cluster called a mischief. The name definitely fit my wild imaginings and kick-started my gag reflex. These rat clubs are also called packs, plagues, colonies, and swarms. Every one of those names seemed appropriate for the unwelcome residents of my home.

As I scrolled my browser, the hairs on the back of my neck stood at attention. This last bit of information gave legitimacy to my panicked call. There was one other group name based on a unique context: a *rat king*. I'd been deep in research on my phone when I came across this little-known piece of trivia, waiting for my kettle to whistle so I could enjoy a soothing cup of lavender chamomile The kettle's chirping echoed merrily in my kitchen as I bolted out the door for the sanctuary of Pecan Street. No doubt Mrs. Owen was standing in front of her picture window, scratching her head at her neighbor standing in the middle of the road. Next would be the phone call.

"Louella, this is Linda Owen. You'll never believe what I'm looking at! Why, Evangeline Delafose is standing in the middle of Pecan Street, yelling something about a rat king into her cell phone! I tell you, Louella, those people from New Orleans are all certifiable."

Later I'd knock on Mrs. Owen's front door, apology brownies in hand. When I explained exactly what a rat king was, she'd smile in sympathy and endorse my antics.

The first documented occurrence of a rat king, also referred to as the horrendous wheel of animal suffering, took place in Germany. A miller discovered this disgusting phenomenon in his fireplace. Years later, I'd still ponder whether the miller had been married at the time of discovery, and if so, did she stay or move in with her mother?

A rat king is not one large rodent. It's much more horrific. This disgusting blight against humanity forms when several rat tails bind with a sticky substance. The article mentioned sap or gum, but concluded hair or natural oils from the rats could also keep the tails together. The result is a wheel of rats, squealing and biting and wreaking havoc in my home. Or so I imagined.

Nate patiently endured my rant describing a rat king formation and my conclusion that I had at least half a dozen in my home. His hair most likely stood tall as a cotton field just before harvest. Even as a kid, my brother thought best while combing his hair with his fingers.

"Ev, I think you should call Bruce. The guy is an exterminator and has all the poisons and traps." Wrong answer Nate.

"Bruce is fishing on Lake Pontchartrain with his boys! Don't you remember he told us that last week at church? He won't be back until Monday." Nate's hair might not survive the phone call.

"Call Shorty, then! He has a farm. He'll know what to do."

"Okay, I'll call him. But if he can't help me, then I'm calling you again." My back was hurting, and I wondered how long until Mrs. Owen called the sheriff.

"9-1-1 what's your emergency?"

"I'd like to report that Evangeline Delafose has finally gone off the deep end! She's standing out in front of her house on Pecan Street yelling."

"Yelling? What is she yelling, exactly?"

"Something about rats and kings. She's threatening someone too, on the phone. You better send a deputy or two out here immediately. Oh, and bring a straitjacket."

Yeah, I didn't have time for a trip to the detention center, and my kitchen wasn't big enough to bake apology brownies for the entire neighborhood. Shorty would have to fix this.

"Oh hey, Doc! Are ya' missin' me already?" Missing him like my 1981 Chevy Citation.

Dad brought home that car for me when I was sixteen, claiming he got some fantastic deal. We discovered later that car experts described the Chevy Citation as a rolling pile of garbage. They weren't wrong. My Citation broke down at least twice a week, leaving me and Mad and Nate on the side of the road. Fortunately, in a small town, some kind soul would pick us up and deliver us to school. Then we'd ride the bus home, and Dad would get off work and coax the car home. After six months, my father admitted he'd been ripped off. He sold the Citation for parts, bought a Ford F-150 SuperCab, and gave me his 1970 Ford Bronco. That was the car I missed.

"Shorty, I need you to get rid of my rat infestation. Bruce is fishing on Lake Pontchartrain, and Nate said to call you. I'll be at the coffee shop." Hanging up the phone before Shorty could reply worked best in these situations.

Dang it! My purse was in the house. But the gift card Nate and Bonnie gave me for my birthday was in the car! Crisis averted. Did rats prefer cars over houses? My brain shoved the thought-provoking question deep down into my subconscious as I backed out of my driveway.

Maggie's coffee shop reflected an air of vacancy, reminding me she closed early on Saturdays. Small towns didn't offer much in the way of nightlife, or late afternoon life. I didn't have many choices. Ten minutes up the road to Zachary, population 19,000, boasted the Cajun Frog and Señor

Sombrero. Since I'd had gumbo less than an hour ago, my choice was simple.

Squinting at the menu reminded me I needed new glasses. Were those fajitas for two or fajitas del pollo? Tossing my menu to the side, I lived dangerously.

"Good evening and welcome to Señor Sombrero! My name is River. What would you like to drink?"

Who names their child after a tributary?

"What do you recommend, River?" My new friend studied me with deep blue eyes. He'd never had a customer who cared about his opinion. This could be interesting.

"Uh, well, most people start with water. But it *is* Saturday night, or late afternoon anyway. How about one of our Señor Sombrero margarita specials? We have the cucumber-cilantro margarita, the strawberry sriracha margarita, the smoky watermelon-jalapeno margarita, the roasted blueberry basil margarita, the..."

"Let me stop you right there, River. As you can see, I am dining alone in a small town. If I order an alcoholic drink, word of my order will beat me home. I'll just have an iced tea with a bowl of lemons."

My neighbors already considered me borderline cuckoo, so I didn't need them worrying I was also drowning my sorrows.

River studied me again, probably calculating the statistical probability of how small his tip might be. Women definitely tipped better than men, hands down. But he might have offended me, so all bets were off.

My cheeks pushed themselves as close to my ears as humanly possible to maintain the appearance of being ready, willing, and able to tip. If River even suspected his window had shut, my service for the evening would be dismal. My smile must have satisfied the kid, because his lanky strides carried him across the dining room without a word. Yes, River, silence was golden.

As I pretended to study my menu, I thought about the case. We were no closer to a break than the sheriff's department. My notebook was in the car from when I left the coffee shop. After River took my food order, I'd run outside and get it.

As if on cue, River appeared with my tea and my bowl of lemons. This dining relationship might work out. Should I ask his opinion on my meal, since the drink ordering experience had gone so well? No, better to keep it simple.

"Thank you, River. I'm ready to order. I'll have a grilled chicken salad, fajita style. That's it." Smiling innocently, I handed him the menu. Hopefully, this smile seemed less...well...creepy. The kids always told me that I try too hard with waitstaff, and I end up creeping them out. Children never sugarcoat their opinions, do they?

River's eyes studied me again, but he said nothing. His dirty blond hair needed a trim, even by Shorty's standards. He pushed up his sleeves, probably a nervous habit. River's right forearm caught my eye. Two twisty strands wove themselves towards his palm. No colored ink, but the artist had talent. Two rivers perhaps? No, they resembled vines more than water. My waiter caught me looking at his tattoo and shoved his sleeve back down.

Not even a smile. I'd ask for the check as soon as possible so I could pay and flee the premises. This kid had not cracked a smile since our margarita fiasco.

Now, how to leave my table to go get my notebook but let everyone know I was coming back? Put my tea glass in the spot my plate would sit? My napkin laid over the chair? Spell out BRB (the texting abbreviation for Be Right Back) with lemon wedges? In the end, I told the bored hostess as I scurried out the door to my car. Why was I sprinting to get back to my seat? Who was I trying to please? *Slow down, Ev. River isn't going to give away your food. Look, there he is, carefully placing your meal on the table.*

My waiter's long legs had carried him far away by the time I got back to my seat, and I didn't call out a *thank you*. My restraint would have pleased Matty and Ellie, because they considered it weird to thank the waitstaff for bringing out the orders.

What was that white piece of notebook paper peeking out from under my napkin? Obviously, River placed it on my table in secret, so I stuffed it into my purse. Could I wait until I finished supper and got back to the car? Oh, who was I kidding?

With my salad waiting patiently on the table, I felt confident everyone would guess I would return. My purse and I arrived in the ladies' room in record time, and I dashed into a stall. Opening the paper, I read the cryptic words: *I heard you're trying to find out who killed Michael Cook. Meet me at The Dirty Pelican at 9:30 p.m. I have some information.*

Suddenly Garth Brooks' "I've Got Friends in Low Places" belted across the restaurant. Shorty had the worst timing, but I'd given him the best ringtone.

"Hey, Doc! Look, I borrowed Candy's dog Tiffy t'find out if ya have an *in-fess-tay-shun* problem. That dog's uh *Yorkshur Terr-ee-ur* an' he hunts rats and mice fer fun! I bring 'im out to the farm all the time, an' he's better than those dumb ah...I mean dumb dang cats that live in the barn." Good catch, friend. "Well, good news! Tiffy curled up an' fell asleep on yore front porch. Which means you ain't got no rats! I called Bruce down on Lake

Ponch-uh-train, and he said that was prob'ly a sewer rat. Those critters live in woodpiles, but they ain't in yore house so far. So ya can come home now."

If it was a sewer rat, then why was it in my woodpile? Never mind, I didn't want to know that badly. "Okay, I'll get my food to go and I'll head home." Wrong answer, Ev.

"Food? What food? Where are ya?"

"I'm at Señor Sombrero, but don't come down here. I don't need Candy mad at me again."

"Oh, y'don't need t'worry about her! She's at her mama's tonight. They're drinkin' Bloody Mary's an' watching Steve McQueen movies. I'll be right there—I'm jus' ten minutes away. Order me a Bud Lite an' the number three combo plate with extra beans an' rice." Chasing down rats didn't spoil that man's appetite.

As I exited the ladies' room, I nearly collided with my waiter. River studied me again, his dark eyes gazing intently. I knew he'd left the note. But did *he* know I knew he'd left the note? Did I really know he left the note? My head ached from my circular logic.

"River, I have a friend joining me."

Nodding solemnly, he observed. "So, I should bring another menu and place setting?"

This kid must be some kind of genius.

"No, just a Bud Lite and a number three with extra beans and rice." My body flopped into the chair. Supper was much less frustrating in my home.

"So now that you're not dining alone, would you like an adult beverage?"

Oh River, when you meet Shorty, you will probably want an adult beverage too.

"Sold! How about a glass of the house red wine? And another glass of water, please."

About halfway through my salad, Shorty slid into the seat across from me and grabbed his Bud Lite. He took a swig, then lifted his hand to wipe his mouth. Once again, his fingers sailed past his face, combing through his hair. Just as if he'd planned that move all along. The guy was good.

"I'm guessin' ya already said grace, right Doc? I can dig in?" His fork hung motionless eight inches above his plate, poised in anticipation.

"I did, and you are welcome to begin. I also said a prayer for you and your adventure this evening with Tiffy and the rats. Thank you for taking care of the situation so quickly."

Shorty accepted my thanks between mouthfuls. "Ain't no thang, Doc. Candy was glad t'lend out Tiffy an' said t'tell ya this time was free o' charge."

Keeping on Candy's good side was proving harder than I'd imagined.

"Okay, well, please extend my thanks. Now on to other business. I received this note with my chicken fajita salad."

How does one covertly slide a note across the table? Why didn't I ever sign up for spy school? My hand covered the note awkwardly as I manipulated it around the chips and salsa. There was no clear path across the table.

"Doc, have ya lost yore mind? Yer 'bout half a bubble off plumb." His eyes followed my hand, zigzagging through the salt and pepper. "Jus' give it to me, for cripes' sake!" He snatched the note and spread it out beside his beer.

"I think River gave it to me. But I can't be sure. It's definitely something worth checking out."

Shorty finished the note and glared at me. "Who the heh.... who's River?"

His head swiveled around the room, but our waiter was missing in action. Shorty didn't care if anyone noticed his fervent searching. But I did.

"Stop looking around! River is our waiter, and he took a substantial risk giving me that note. Don't endanger his life by blowing his cover!"

My eyes roamed the tables, casually searching for our five suspects. Maybe the actual killer was in this room, dining with us? Shorty brought me back to reality at Señor Sombrero.

"Okay, so our waiter gave ya a note an' disappeared? Don'tcha' think that's pretty suspicious, Doc? An' yer not goin' anywhere near The Dirty Pelican, at least not without me. Ladies don't go to that place!"

Didn't Shorty meet Candy at The Dirty Pelican? Stay on track, Ev!

"Okay, fair enough. Then let's go together."

My PI's dirty brown eyes darkened, but he shrugged in agreement. The hostess appeared with the check, and I fished out my credit card. No one had to remind me the meal was part of Shorty's *plus expenses* pay. When the hostess swung by to return my card, I asked about River.

She rolled her eyes. "He developed a smoking habit about fifteen minutes ago. Told me to take care of your bill cuz he had to take a smoke break." Her shoulders swept up, then down as her head cocked to the side. The familiar *whatcha' gonna' do* shrug and head tilt. Then she turned tail and sprinted towards her hostess station. Señor Sombrero was livening up. My phone showed 6:30 p.m.

Chapter 6

After supper, we hung out at my house, reminiscing about our fathers. Shorty told some stories I'd never heard before, including a night spent in jail. Around 9:15, we headed out the door, my PI insisting on driving. "If we take yore Volvo, someone might break *intuh* it. No one'll mess with my truck. They all know better." Hard to argue with Shorty's logic.

We then discussed River's tattoo.

"I ain't nevuh seen that kinda design before, but that don't surprise me. Kids that age ink themselves all the time. There ain't nothin' wrong with it. When you and I waz kids, only military and the rough crowd got inked. Nowadays, lots of folks have 'em. When ya go tuh church *tomorrah*, I betcha you'll be sittin' within three feet o' half a dozen people with tattoos."

Shocking me made him chuckle.

As we pulled into The Dirty Pelican's potholed excuse for parking, my lungs emptied in a gush of relief. We'd once again survived Shorty's bat out of H-E-Double-Hockey-Sticks driving. My eyes inventoried the parking lot, forcing me to appreciate my PI's street smarts. He was right—my car would have stuck out like a sore thumb at this fine dining establishment. Aside from being clean with no dents or scratches, my car couldn't drive over potholes and broken beer bottles. Shorty's truck knew this lot like a familiar friend, missing all the craters and most of the glass.

Shorty shoved the gearshift into park. "Now, let's get a few things straight here, Ev."

Oh boy. Calling me Ev clued me in that this guy meant business. My knees swiveled towards my driver, displaying my interlaced my fingers upon my lap. My teacup saucer eyes stared into his squinty ones.

"Yes, sir. Give me the rules."

My friend paused, looking at me like I'd grown a second head. "Y'mean yer not gonna' argue with me? Well, let me call my *cuzzin* at the *Graisseville Gazette*! Ev Delafose ain't gonna' argue. It'll be front page news."

Was that a twinkle in his eyes, or the glint from the moon?

"No sir, I am not. This is *your* area of expertise, and I'm going to follow your lead."

My plan included being Southern belle sweet, so he didn't leave me in the car. I shouldn't have stressed.

"Well good, cuz I can't leave ya' in the truck—who knows what kinda' *prop-uh-zi-shuns* ya'd get! Yer gonna' hafta' come with me. Stay right behind me an' whatever ya do, don't touch *anythang*."

What invitations could I receive hanging out in the parking lot of The Dirty Pelican? Ev, you definitely didn't want to know.

The words *darkened the doorstep* didn't apply, because the bar had no light to darken. Shorty nodded at the bouncer, who did a double-take when he spotted me. My friend didn't normally bring women sporting glasses and tennis shoes. Glancing down at my black cotton cardigan with pink flowers, I wondered, *did Candy own one of these?*

We turned our sights toward the bar, and I paced my steps to tread just behind Shorty. Who was tapping on my shoulder? My head pivoted toward the wall behind me.

"Why'd you bring someone with you? I was hoping you'd come alone." River's soulful eyes gazed down at me.

My would-be protector had his back to me, flirting with the female bartender. This would be my only chance. Linking arms with River, I guided him further from the bar. Was there any quiet place in this dive?

River took the lead and motioned towards the hall to the bathrooms. Yep, Shorty had his face towards the bar, and the bartender's head tilted back in laughter. What a girl had to do for tips!

"Okay, River, we've got to be quick! What did you want to tell me?" My notebook was in my car, so I'd be relying on memory. Not one of my best attributes since I'd turned fifty.

Oh, those eyes! The eyes of a poet, Doug used to say. Deep as Lake Charles and full of sorrow. At the restaurant they'd seemed more, well, thoughtful. Searching closely, I glimpsed a sadness.

"Stella is one of my best friends! We met at rehab, and we've been helping each other out ever since. Mrs. Delafose, I know she's clean and I know she didn't kill her brother." Now it all made sense! River had seen a lot of pain, but he was a fighter and he'd survived.

"First, why are you telling me this?" How much did River know about my investigation?

Again, he studied me, calculating how much he should share. This guy had trust issues.

"Well, I know your brother is the lead detective on the case. My mom works at the sheriff's department and she heard the sheriff gave the go ahead for you to review the case files. She tried to get me to talk to the deputies, but I was afraid to tell them anything. They automatically think Stella did it, because she's a recovering addict. So am I, and my word means nothing. But my mom said I should tell you, because you're not a cop. So, when you sat in my section tonight, I knew it had to be fate."

At last, a smile from those tight lips.

"Okay, let's hear it." My neck craned towards the opening so my eyes could peek at the bar. When Shorty got to talking, he developed tunnel vision. The guy still hadn't noticed my absence.

"You know the murder weapon? Mr. Cook's gun? Michael told Stella their father gave it to a cousin moving to New Orleans. He never mentioned which cousin, but Stella bought the story. In fact, I'm not so sure Michael even had the gun. One time when I was over at the house, Stella left to go to the bathroom. I asked Michael if he'd lied about giving the gun away. Michael said no, he'd gotten rid of the gun because of Stella and her drug habit. He didn't want her to be tempted to pawn it. Stella frustrated him a lot, but he was always supportive of her road to recovery."

Interesting. Michael lied to River about the gun, so Stella wouldn't know he still had it. Or, possibly, the killer brought the gun, used it to kill Michael, then left it at the scene. Rob Dugas knew about the gun, but he may not have been the only one.

"One more thing. Stella told me she noticed Faith Dixon's car driving down their street several times a week after the breakup, including the night of the murder. Stella believes Faith was stalking Michael. She tried to tell your brother, but he didn't believe her. Since Michael never filed a report, he thought Stella was wrong or lying." River stepped backwards, disappearing into the line for the men's bathroom. Did he have a sudden urge to use the facilities?

"What the Sam heh…hill o' beans are ya doin' in the dark? I thought I told ya t'stick with me! Did ya touch *anythang*?"

Was that Muriel Bergeron coming out of Shorty's mouth?

"Please don't talk like my mother. It's unsettling. I'm fine. I just had to go to the bathroom." Wrong answer, Ev.

"Son of a bi…scut! Son of a biscuit!"

Shorty restated his cleaner version, to prove he wasn't cussing.

"Don't *ever* go tuh the bathroom in here! I would've taken ya down tuh the *Chev-Ron*—they have nice bathrooms there."

Good to know. "Don't worry, the line was too long, so I didn't go. Can we leave now?"

My short-yet-memorable visit to The Dirty Pelican needed to end. My hair and clothes stank like cigarettes, and several men and women were giving me curious looks. I wasn't hanging around to satisfy their curiosity.

"Sure, let's go. Sorry yore *in-four-mant* didn't show." Shorty took my elbow while we made our exit, most likely to ensure I didn't touch anything.

As we peeled out of The Dirty Pelican, I relayed River's information. The road had no lights, so I couldn't read Shorty's face.

"Well Doc, it sounds like Stella's innocent. If this kid is tellin' the truth anyway, an' why would he lie? Let's get ya back home an' we'll keep tuh our plan of dividin' and conquerin'. It's a good plan."

"One question, though. Being a recovering drug addict, should River be frequenting places like The Dirty Pelican?"

The choice of location put holes in his story.

"Nah, Doc! My buddy Dino, he's the owner. He don't let drugs in there. He's a recoverin' addict himself, so he keeps an eye on the crowd, an' he don't put up with usin' or dealin'. He's one o' the good ones."

Shorty's eyes narrowed slightly as he turned his head to face me squarely. "But don'tcha ever go back there without me, ya understand? Dino may be a law-abidin' citizen, but he don't share the same morals ya do." Shorty faced the road, inching his speedometer well past the posted speed limit. "An' ya don't want those church ladies waggin' their tongues about Ev Delafose hangin' out with *diss-rep-you-tuh-bull* people." The big brother I'd never had.

As we said our goodbyes in my driveway, I realized Shorty missed his boys' night.

"Hey, I'm sorry you didn't make your poker game." My phone said 10:30 p.m., well past my pajama time.

"Whatcha' talkin' about, Doc? It's not even eleven! I'll be parkin' my truck jest in time for the first hand."

Touching his right temple with two fingers, he gave me a quick salute.

First order of business was a shower, and a quick prayer that I wouldn't smell like cigarettes tomorrow. A twenty-minute shower with large portions of lavender shampoo and body soap, and this girl was ready for bed.

After Shorty's revelations on my brothers and sisters in Christ, I had a hard time focusing on Brother Tom's sermon. When I moved back to Graisseville, sweet Ava Guidry baked me delectable browned butter oatmeal cookies and delivered them on a plate skillfully covered in cling wrap. I invited her inside while I fixed a pot of coffee, and we curled up on the front porch to visit. Ava told me wonderful stories about going to school with my mother, most of which I'd never heard. Three months later, she continued to ask after me and my kids. Shorty said the number of people with tattoos would surprise me. Did Miss Ava have one somewhere on her person? What did it look like? Maybe a mixing bowl with the words, *Bakers Gotta Bake*?

How could I investigate at church, anyway? Talking about dead bodies and murder suspects would be awkward. Brother Tom never specifically warned against discussing such things, but I'd hazard a guess he was not a fan. Shorty might be right—the church ladies could have the best intel. But I just didn't feel right bringing up the case:

"Good day, Miss Helen! I enjoyed Brother Tom's sermon immensely!"

"Oh yes, Ev! I agree. It certainly lifted my spirits! What was your favorite part of the service?"

"Well, Miss Helen, I'd have to say the music. Do you suppose it was as good as the music at Michael Cook's funeral? Speaking of which, have you heard anything about the case? Who do you think killed him?"

No matter how I twisted and turned the conversation in my head, the result was always the same. Miss Helen avoided me for the rest of her life, along with the other sweet little ladies at Graisseville Baptist Church. Also in my version, Brother Tom paid a courtesy visit to inquire about my mental health and wellbeing.

Where could I find a group of people already sharing information? A group that wouldn't mind if I tagged along? There was one such group who made no secret they gossiped, to keep Graisseville moral and upstanding, of course.

The Graisseville Ladies' Book Club began when Lila Trahan redecorated her home and needed an excuse to show it off. Twenty years later, the club met under the disguise of a monthly book discussion, but everyone knew it was a chance to exchange gossip. The book club was by invitation only. Members included the families who founded the village and their special friends.

Graisseville's founding families ran the village, although their power had waned in the last few generations. Honestly, most of us didn't have white gloves in our closets or fancy dishes just for hosting extravagant parties. More and more of us departed Graisseville for jobs and education, never to return. The old guard hoarded their power closely, realizing their time was drawing to a close. I'd tried to explain it to Doug and compared the families to the royals of England. They had no actual power, but they still wielded influence.

My maiden name of Bergeron granted me access to all the founding family hoopla—the lavish birthday galas, bridge parties, and various teas and socials. And Lila Trahan's book club.

After church, I mulled around in the lobby, waiting for Lila. The woman sat on this side of seventy, and she was a talker. Doug's favorite quote floated into my head. *Fortune favors the bold.*

Marching up to Lila was the straightforward part. Catching her attention proved difficult. Could Lila be upset with me? Hard to tell. Be bolder, Ev—stand right beside her!

"Excuse me, dear, but you're touching my shoulder. Could you stand back a little?"

At least she was talking to me. "Miss Lila, I regret my earlier decision to decline your gracious invitation. Could I still join your book club? I could bring my grandmother's lemon sandwich cookies."

Always sweeten a favor with a bribe.

In her former life, Lila was a high school English teacher. Old habits die hard. Her icy stare inspected me up and down. At last, she graced me with words.

"Well, I suppose in honor of my friendship with your aunt, Louise, I will accept your apology. Yes, you may join, but you should probably wait until next month. I doubt you'll be able to finish the book by Wednesday morning."

Challenge accepted lady. "Oh, I'm sure that won't be a problem. Which book is it?" How hard could it be? And from what I'd heard from my mother, they never discussed the book, anyway.

If smiles were street signs, Lila's would say, *wrong turn.* "*East of Eden* by John Steinbeck. 601 pages. I expect you to discuss the book with the rest of us, or else you're wasting our time. See you at 10 a.m. at my house on Wednesday. Don't forget the lemon sandwich cookies, dear." Class dismissed.

Lila limited her book club to a list of classics, her master reading list from her teaching days. Fortunately, Lila had been my high school English teacher, and I'd read every book on her list. Mrs. Trahan forced me to read John Steinbeck, George Eliot, Charles Dickens, Jane Austen, and many more. She was the reason I'd earned degrees in English Literature and Creative Writing. I should credit her for my Detective Lou Bergeron series too, because she'd given me the love of writing. Seeing her reaction reminded me I'd never shared my gratitude for her influence. Maybe the book club would give me that opportunity. At any rate, I'd read Steinbeck's novel at least three times. Bring it on, Lila!

After church, Nate asked me to run to The Market Basket in Zachary. "Sydney reminded Bonnie this morning that it's Tucker's birthday. Could you go get a cake to bring for lunch?"

Tucker was Syd's turtle, who couldn't even eat cake. Neither could Bonnie and Nate, who were still watching their sugar and carbs. "How about some cupcakes? Whatever the kids and I don't eat, you can take to work on Monday." The things we do for family!

Choosing cupcakes for a turtle's birthday proved tougher than I'd imagined. Did Tucker prefer vanilla or chocolate cupcakes? Mulling over my choices distracted me. The tap on my shoulder shot my heart rate up a good twenty beats. Who in the world scares people in the grocery store?

The man standing behind me peered at me through wireless rimmed glasses, like my high school boyfriend wore. It was his full head of hair that captured my attention. Most men in their fifties attempted the comb over or gave up and shaved every bit of hair. This guy rocked the salt and pepper look, which I'd always found attractive. His smile revealed straight white teeth, like a sexy picket fence. His dentist was worth his weight in gold.

"Sorry about that! I didn't mean to scare you. I'm Josh Fairchild, the owner of Best Dry Cleaners. Well, as of a few years ago, when I moved here."

Deep pools of blue, magnified slightly by his lenses, gazed at me sincerely.

"You're Ev Delafose, right?" Josh scooped up my hand in a warm greeting. "I've met your brother, Nathan, when he came to see me about Michael Cook's death. I hear you're working on the case now?"

Josh's head cocked to the right, like my sister's parakeet. He studied me carefully through his glasses, but his smile continued to cover his face like a soft blanket. Like a warm chocolate chip cookie? Well, anyway, his smile was really nice.

"It's good to meet you Josh. And I'm not really working on the case. Nate just asked me to review it with a fresh set of eyes. But I'm not seeing anything he hasn't already found." Josh's smile relaxed a little, along with his shoulders. Smiling can take a lot out of you, I suppose.

"It's such a shame, really, Michael's death. He was always our star! Wonderful grades, excellent athlete. With Stella being the oldest, you might think *she'd* be the golden child. It just took her longer to find her stride, I think. But I'm so proud of her!"

Josh's smile positively glowed, reminding me of a cozy campfire on a cold fall evening. Which in Louisiana would be about forty-five degrees.

"Yes, well, sometimes it takes people a little longer to find their way. I understand you and Michael Sr. were good friends?" Let's redirect this conversation to something useful.

The campfire burned more brightly.

"Oh, Mike and I were great friends! I miss that guy every day. Being single, the Cooks invited me over almost every week for a home-cooked meal."

Hard to miss the single comment, but was it directed at me? Or was he just explaining why he spent so much time at his friend's house?

"With both parents gone, I've been spending even more time with the kids. Of course, I couldn't replace their parents, but I try to be a role model. Now that it's just Stella, I make it a point to get over there as much as possible." The guy wasn't giving off a *hello I'm a murderer* vibe, but he couldn't stop telling me how great he was. Maybe he was hitting on me? Gosh, it had been so long! What did that even look like? "Well, I'll leave you to your baked goods. Have a great day." With a wave, my murder suspect pushed his cart towards produce.

Did murderers eat fresh fruit and vegetables? I'd always pictured them eating junk food. Thank goodness Josh witnessed my black skirt and silk purple shirt with matching flats! For my twenty minutes of effort, I wanted as much mileage as possible.

"You having a birthday party?" The stubbly teenager with bed-head hair couldn't just ring up my purchases in silence.

"Sort of. It's for my niece's turtle." This conversation wasn't something I wanted to pursue. Maybe Bed Hair would let it go.

"Yeah? I didn't think turtles could eat cupcakes?" Mr. Hair eyed my frosted baked goods suspiciously.

Would he call Animal Control?

"Hello? Yes. I'd like to report turtle abuse. I just rang up a woman's items here at The Market Basket, and she admitted to purchasing cupcakes for a turtle. Yes, I'll hold please."

Hopefully, my misdemeanor would go unreported.

"The turtle won't be eating the cupcakes. They're just for the guests, who are all human."

Best to clarify the guests' species, since this guy had taken an interest.

Mr. Hair shrugged and went silent as he rang up birthday plates, napkins, and plastic ware. No comments, so I assumed he didn't spot any more potential crimes.

Josh waved at me as he pushed his cart out the door. While I'd invested another ten minutes debating over birthday paper goods, he'd completed his produce choices and checked out.

"You know him?" Who *was* this kid? Perry Mason?

"Uh, I just met him. He seemed nice."

Bed Hair halted in mid checkout, his eyes reaching the size of my grandmother's casserole dish. Remembering he was on the clock, he restarted his motions.

"Maybe. All I know is what I heard. And I heard he was at that Michael kid's house and they got into a fight. The day before he died."

Hold the phone! Michael confronted Josh? About what? And was that the same fight Ken heard at Bubba's house? Both were the day before the murder. How many fights could there have been at the Cook home? Suddenly I had respect for Bed...I mean...what was his name? The tag on his shirt said Leo.

"Well, Leo, do you know what the fight was about? And was it definitely Josh? Because I understand there was a fight the night before the murder, but no one could tell if it was two men or two women. Or one of each."

Leo's head shook like a dog drying off after a bath. "No, ma'am. My sister was picking up her boyfriend from Bubba's house. You know he lives next door to the Cooks?"

Actually, I do, Leo, thanks to Ken. "Yes, but Bubba and his backyard buddies said they couldn't tell if the people arguing were men or women. How could your sister?"

Leo stared at me sympathetically. Obviously, I wasn't the fastest mule in the barn.

"Well, Bubba and his buddies were in the backyard, keeping the music up pretty loud. My sister came up the front porch, and she said the people having the fight were in the front part of the house. She guessed the living room or the entry hall."

Leo bagged my groceries and placed them in my cart. The line behind me had reached four shoppers, but I needed one more answer.

"Okay, but how does your sister know it was Josh fighting with Michael that night?"

Leo pushed my cart a few feet, as if to get it started. He bent down to ear level, almost as an afterthought. "Because Stella told her."

Chapter 7

My brain pondered Leo's words while I attended Tucker's birthday party. Celebrating a made-up birthday for a pet with cake and presents was nothing new to me. I'd thrown parties for dogs, hamsters, even a lizard we'd discovered on the front porch. It's just what mothers do. But solving an actual murder case? Definitely something new, and something that occupied my thoughts.

"Aunt Ev! What did you bring Tucker for his birthday?"

"Sydney! We do not ask people what gifts they've purchased! Besides, Aunt Ev brought the cake and the paper goods. That's better than a gift." My sister-in-law was the best.

Sydney reminded me so much of Mad when she was six. Fortunately for all of us, the good Lord didn't favor Syd with her Aunt Mad's temper. My niece stared up at me with her teardrop swimming pool eyes framed with wispy ringlets of curls. Coal black, just like Nate's. Yeah, in ten years (maybe less), my brother would sit on the front porch cleaning his shotgun. Just like my father before him, patiently waiting for his daughter's date to make curfew. Thank goodness Nate only had one daughter!

Wasn't it just yesterday that I was hosting a birthday party for Harry the Hamster? Ellie had also been six.

"Syd, hand me my purse."

My niece scurried over to the door where I'd dropped my purse. Six-year-olds scampered and scurried, didn't they? She carefully handed me the bag, then fixed her eyes on mine. We faced off, preparing for our little game.

"Oh, thank you! I just needed a piece of gum. Would you like some?"

Out came the Juicy Fruit, but Syd shook her head.

"Don't you have something else in there, Aunt Ev? Maybe something for Tucker?"

Her eyes crinkled down into a cajoling position as she wrapped a wisp of curls around her finger. Her chin tucked down towards her chest, forcing her eyes to wander upward. She kept a steady look in my eyes at all times. Nate had his hands full with this one!

My eyes signaled defeat by looking toward Bonnie, and I broke into laughter. Syd always won.

"Yeah, kid, I do."

A few years earlier, when we'd begun this game, I would try to gain control. Even at three, Syd knew she had the upper hand. Part of being an adult is knowing when you've lost. But this aunt still had a few tricks up her sleeve.

Fishing into my purse, I feigned a horrified look. "Oh, Syd, I'm so sorry! I remembered the cake and plates, but I totally forgot to go down the pet aisle and pick up something for Tucker. Oh sweetie, I'm so sorry!"

Who was the master, and who was the student? Syd's mouth drooped, like a magnet pulling her facial features towards the ground. Cue the waterworks!

Amidst Sydney's wails, I wiggled my hand around the depths of my purse. Where was the blue bag covered in sparkles with white tissue paper peeking out? My hand caught the tissue paper, then pushed farther down to grab the bag. Triumphantly, I grasped the bag, waving it like a moon pie caught in a Mardi Gras parade. Syd flashed a smile as she twisted the valve. Her pipe of tears shut off as she ran to put Tucker's Happy Turtle Hiding Cave into his tank.

Bonnie frowned. "She's just started that, crying on cue. I'm not sure what to do about it. If you have any suggestions, I'd appreciate it."

"Great question Bonnie. Ellie favored temper tantrums actually, throwing herself on the ground and pounding her fists while screaming at the top of her lungs. But I'll put a little thinking and a lot of praying into it and let you know."

What did my friend, Nicole, always say? Girls were fun and boys were easy. Nicole was a pretty smart woman.

Bonnie brewed a pot of coffee and we relaxed in the living room. Jack, at ten, excused himself to get some neighbor kids and play football in the backyard. Sydney's spirit animal was a bookworm, like me. Her tears had dried a while ago, and she was deep into a story. Coffee with adults completed my Sunday afternoon.

"So, how's the case going, Ev? Any revelations you'd like to share?" Ah, an interrogation of a different sort. At least my brother stopped inquiring after my social activities.

"Uh, not much headway, I'm afraid. But it's keeping my mind busy."

Good Ev, vague but positive. "Oh, and I changed my mind about the book club. I spoke with Lila Trahan today, and she invited me to the meeting this week."

Not really the truth, but definitely not a lie. More like a nicer way of speaking the truth. Bonnie's eyebrows arched up as she gave me an *oh really now?* stare. This tenth-grade history teacher spotted lies for a living. Her students loved her but knew better than to stretch the truth. Being married to a sheriff's deputy couldn't hurt her reputation, either.

"Oh? I thought the book club was a den of gossiping busybodies."

Her eyebrows swooped back down, slanting toward her nose. Yep, the alarm had sounded. Evangeline Delafose was stretching the truth. At home, Nate hung up his detective skills, along with his gun and badge. Bonnie, however, never switched off the teacher radar. It came in too handy as a mother.

What about striking an alliance? "I've changed my mind—that's all. My first meeting's on Wednesday. How about I pose Sydney's waterworks issue to the group? Keep your names confidential, of course. Those women have collectively raised a parcel of kids—I bet they've got some ideas."

Bonnie's eyebrows shifted closer to home base as we came to an agreement. Yes, I'm not telling you everything, but you'll get something out of it.

Shorty arrived promptly for supper on Monday evening, just in time to watch me spread the olive salad over the bread. The Market Basket promised genuine muffaletta bread early Monday morning, so I'd camped in the parking lot to get two loaves.

Shorty's mouth curved up in delight as he let himself in the front.

"*Ooh wee*, Doc! Them *sand-witches* look jus' like yore mama used t'make! Bet they taste jus' like 'em too!"

For a man with a prosthetic leg, he moved faster than my nephew, Jack, on the football field. Before I could stop him, Shorty was smacking his lips in delight. He'd already dipped his index finger in the olive salad and stuck it in his mouth.

"That's disgusting! Where has your finger been? Never mind, I don't want to know. Here!" Shorty took the wide knife I thrust in his hand. "You can finish spreading the olive salad on the bread while I stack the meat." Shorty always washed his hands before eating, but not before tasting.

My PI shrugged his shoulders and maneuvered his knife over the bread. My mother's olive salad contained thirteen ingredients, including pimento-stuffed green olives, black olives, and pepperoncini peppers. Normally I'd buy a jar of pre-made salad, but Shorty would catch my shortcut. No way I was going to spend the rest of the evening hearing him complain that we might as well serve my muffalettas to his hogs, and that my poor mother was spinning in her grave.

Fifteen minutes later, the sandwiches perched on a platter, except for one lone sandwich on a dessert dish. My sandwich I'd prepared before Shorty arrived and stuck his finger in the olive salad. Two glasses from the cabinet filled with iced tea and a bag of *Zapp's* kettle style potato chips completed our meal. Or so I thought.

"Hey, I'm gonna' run down tuh the Gas n' More an' get them spicy Cajun Crawtators kind, okay? That's my favorite flavor o' *Zapp's*. I'm gonna' get some orange soda too."

We were making progress! He didn't expect me to keep my pantry stocked just for him.

"I'll be right back." The mop of dishwater blond hair disappeared down the hallway towards the front door. Then reappeared. "Oh, an' don't feel bad y'didn't have the right food. You'll remember next time."

By the time Shorty returned, I'd polished off my muffaletta and half the bag of *Zapp's*. My stomach gurgled its happiness that I'd regained my appetite. As my friend consumed one sandwich after another, I sipped my tea.

"I tell ya', Doc! That poker game was a goldmine of *in-four-may-shun*! Sam Hughes' *cuzzin* was there, an' he said no way did Sam kill Michael." Shorty paused, taking a swig.

"See, Sam was late for a doctor's appointment—that's why he tore outta' the parking lot the day Michael died. He argued with Michael, but the guy was being a donkey's rear. He told Sam he was gonna' report 'im for leavin' early without clearing it with their boss." Shorty shoveled a bite into his open mouth. The fourth sandwich, by my count. Not to worry though, as he popped open his second soda to wash it down. How that man didn't weigh 300 pounds was by the grace of God.

A loud burp signaled he could continue. "My buddy Monty was there too—'member he's a corporal in the sheriff's department? He did some diggin' and found out somethin' interestin'." Shorty took another swig, then polished off his bag of *Zapp's*. The man had a flair for the dramatic.

"Okay, I'll play. What did Monty find out?" Had to admit, this investigating stuff was pretty cool.

"Well..." Shorty leaned in, as if a dozen nosey neighbors had their ears against the wall. He even lowered his voice.

"What? I can't hear what you're saying. We're the only people in the room—speak louder!"

Was that a horse in Shorty's pocket, or was he snorting to advertise his irritation?

"I said Monty did some diggin' an' found out Josh's full name. Turns out it's Robert Thomas Joshua Fairchild, from Texas. Monty called a buddy, an' he ran the name through some databases. Nobody on the case, includin' your brother, did that."

Was that the slightest hint of a grin?

"Robert Thomas Joshua Fairchild, aka Josh Fairchild, has a *joo-vuh-nile* record. These Fairchilds have deep *conneck-shuns* an' even deeper pockets.

For a small fortune, they got the records sealed. Monty's guy couldn't tell '*zactly* what the charges were, but they were a lot more than bustin' windows or shopliftin'. Monty thinks it was armed robbery, definitely somethin' to do with a gun."

He eyed my half-empty bag of *Zapp's*.

My stomach cried silently as I tossed Shorty the bag of chips. So much for a late-night snack.

"Okay, so Josh isn't as nice as everyone says he is. Or maybe he made a mistake, and he's a changed man." My mind wandered back to our encounter at The Market Basket. He came across as sincere. "I remember from Nate's file neighbors saw Josh's car in the neighborhood the night of the murder. But Josh said it was a mistake, that he was with his girlfriend Shannon at a restaurant. An' Shannon even confirmed his alibi." Was he still seeing Shannon? That was over a year ago. Focus, Ev!

"Yeah, well, once a *crim-null* always a *crim-null*."

"Yes, well, you thought Stella was guilty because once an addict, always an addict. Now you're convinced she's innocent. So, make up your mind."

More horse snorting. "Anyways, Crazy Faith knew 'bout Michael's gun. In fact, he'd let her shoot it a few times at the gun range in Baker."

"Let me guess. You've got a buddy who works at the gun range in Baker." This guy had a buddy everywhere.

Shorty glared at me. "As a matter o' fact, Miss Smarty Pants, I don't." Another snort. "He *owns* the gun range in Baker."

"Okay, my mistake." Best not to tease my PI when he was working so hard. "So, let's do a quick review: Stella can't or won't account for her whereabouts the night of the murder. My source says Josh and Michael fought the night before the murder, but Josh has an alibi. Sam argued with Michael the day of the murder. Nate's report says he'd called his girlfriend to say he was running an errand after his doctor's appointment, then heading home. That was right before the time of death." Thank goodness for my notebook! "Let's not forget the blonde Michael had supper with in Zachary. We're no closer to discovering her identity." My favorite pen carefully circled that clue in teal.

Shorty crushed his soda can. "Crazy Faith didn't take the breakup so good, but her grandma claims they watched TV all night. Rob still seems the most likely suspect, cuz he needed money. An' he admits t'being at Michael's house the night o' the murder. He can't come up with an alibi, cuz he fell asleep when he got home." Air quotes accompanied the words *fell asleep*, along with another snort. "Josh has some skeletons, but a mighty solid alibi. That Shannon chick is a *librarian*, for Chri...Chrysler Town and Country's sake. If ya can't trust a librarian, who *can* ya trust?"

Interesting logic, but hard to contradict. All the librarians I knew were stand-up citizens of the community. *For Chrysler Town and Country's sake*? At least Shorty was using names other than our Lord and Savior's. Did referencing a station wagon count as cursing? I needed to run that by Brother Tom.

Chapter 8

When United States Marshals look for secure locations to hide a witness, they avoid small towns. Why? Because small town living means everyone knows who you are, where you live, and why you're living there. The government would have to create the most perfect alias, and the witness would need to memorize the details completely. Far better to hide a witness in a big city where no one cares who your second cousin's daughter married.

Lila Trahan moved into her house the day after she married Mr. Arnold Trahan, and forty-five years later she still called it home. It was the same house my best friend Donna Jo Griffith, and I visited one Sunday morning at 2 a.m. Donna Jo and I planned our prank for weeks, visiting The Market Basket several times to purchase toilet paper. When Lila and Arnold awoke, Lila called my mother immediately.

"Muriel, this is Lila Trahan. Do you know where your daughter was all night?"

"Yes, Miss Lila, I do. She spent the night at Donna Jo Griffith's house." That was my mother—always cool as a cucumber.

"Well, those two snuck out at some point and covered my magnolia trees with cheap toilet paper! They didn't even use Charmin, or Northern, or some other respectable bathroom tissue! It's the cheap and tawdry kind that gas stations use! I demand your daughter come over this morning before church and clean it all up!"

My mother could hardly contain the laughter. Why was Lila more upset about the quality of the toilet paper than the deed itself? "Well, Miss Lila, let me call Mrs. Griffith and I'll call you right back."

Mrs. Griffith swore up and down Donna Jo and I never left the house. My mother had her suspicions, but what could she do? Plenty, it turned out.

"Mrs. Griffith. Let me talk to my daughter."

Uh-oh. "Hello, Mama! How are you this fine morning?" Mother was having none of my syrupy sweet charm.

"Evangeline, I'm not going to debate whether you did or didn't lavish toilet paper all over Lila Trahan's magnolia trees. But you will go over there this morning and clean it all up. Whether that Donna Jo goes with you is between you and her. But you, young lady, better get dressed and march your happy self over to the Trahans' home. Pronto."

Mother had spoken, and Daddy backed her up. Donna Jo went with me, and we cleaned up our toilet paper creations. Under the watchful glare of Lila, of course.

Cleaning up the mess proved that I was guilty, in Lila's mind at least. Relationships were strained between my parents and the Trahans, although my dad didn't care.

"Those uppity Trahans need to remember we are a founding family, too! Clement Bergeron farmed right beside Willie Trahan, and we are just as good as Willie's descendants!"

Dad would go off for a good ten minutes, but I never remembered the rest of the rant. Except for the last sentence, "And that Lila married into the Trahans, so she doesn't even count."

My parents breathed a sigh of relief when Donna Jo's father took a job in Mississippi the next year, and my small-town shenanigans came to a screeching halt.

All this to say, I definitely knew where Lila Trahan lived. As my car slowed in front of her *Southern Living* home, I surveyed the Nissans, Lincolns, and Cadillacs. My navy Volvo fit in nicely. The lemon sandwich cookies reclined on my robin's egg blue platter, like sunbathers poolside. After three failed batches and a frantic call to my aunt, I'd achieved perfection. These were the times I missed my mother the most. Muriel Bergeron put Julia Child to shame.

Anna Dunbar opened the door just before my index finger pressed the doorbell.

"Hmm...so you made an appearance." Her stare, emphasized by ice blue orbs, caught me off-guard. Was the front porch chilly from the open door, or Anna's attitude?

My mother taught me to smile through the awkwardness. "It's so good to see you, Miss Anna! Where should I put these cookies?" Anna stepped aside to allow me passage.

Was that snow by the hall tree? The entryway resembled Antarctica, with a temperature hovering near negative seventy-two. Okay, maybe closer to sixty-five. Thank goodness I'd brought my sweater. Louisiana in October fluctuated between seventy-five and eighty-one degrees, which meant respectable Southerners kept their homes between sixty-five and seventy-two.

"Well hello, Evangeline. I'd offer you a tour as a first-time guest, but you've been here before. On the outside, at least."

Nicely played, Lila. "Actually, I've been on the inside of your lovely home. When your great-nephew, Cal, got married, you hosted a bridal shower for his fiancé, Annelise. When was that? About ten years ago?"

Mmmm, Lila, if your lips stretched any tighter, they might snap like rubber bands. The shower had been another awkward situation for Lila and me. Cal's mother, Elizabeth, and I roomed together at Louisiana Tech, and she'd visited me in Graisseville one summer. I'd introduced her to the guy working for my dad at the veterinarian clinic, Cliff Trahan. Elizabeth fell in love, and a year later, I was a bridesmaid. We remained close friends, despite living hours apart. Twenty years later, I attended her future daughter-in-law's bridal shower. Lila's home temperature and her attitude had both held steady at a good sixty-five degrees. Some things never change.

Anna took my lemon sandwich cookies as Lila led me to the formal living room. That was odd—I could hear the other guests toward the back of the house, probably in the informal living room.

"I wanted to ask a few questions from the book, to make sure you'd read Mr. Steinbeck's fine novel. Being 601 pages, I'm sure you understand why I'm skeptical."

Supposedly, Graisseville's high school principal cried, and the kids celebrated when Lila Trahan retired from teaching.

"Yes ma'am. Ask me any question you'd like. I'm ready." Let's do this, Lila!

You can take the teacher out of the classroom, but you can't take the classroom out of the teacher. The woman had flashcards! But thanks to www.quizlet.com I came ready to rumble. Lila's eyebrows shot up towards her forehead, like roman candles, as I answered each question. Twice she scratched a black mark on a pad of paper. Carefully placing the stack of cards on the side table, she picked up her pad and pencil. Was she passing a kidney stone as she calculated my score? At last, she rested her grading tools on the side table and placed her hands in her lap.

"Well, Evangeline. I'm not sure how you did it, but you scored a thirty-eight out of a possible forty points. That's the ninety-fifth percentile." Gosh, Lila, you didn't have to sound so disappointed.

"That's wonderful! Honestly, I owe it all to you and your amazing teaching." C'mon Ev, let's throw the poor woman a bone.

Lila squinted at me, nostrils flaring. "How's that, dear?"

Please, Lord, don't let this information give Miss Lila a heart attack. "Well, you are the reason I earned my masters and PhD in English Literature. In fact, I completed my doctorate so I could teach. You inspired me, Miss Lila, to give the next generation the beauty of reading the classics."

Take a breath, Ev. Stop throwing up all over the poor woman.

Were those tears in the corners of Lila Trahan's steely blue eyes? Maybe her body was going into shock from her former student's confessions? In for a penny, in for a pound, Ev. Let's bring this full circle.

"You probably don't know this, but I have written a series of books. The Detective Lou Bergeron Mysteries. My books are the product of your teaching, and the love of writing that you gave me."

Was I sniffling from the chilly air, or from my *Thank A Teacher* speech?

Without a word, Lila rose from her floral sofa and glided to a corner bookshelf. Was she composing herself? She reached toward the third row from the top, the shelf at her eye level. Were those...? No, they couldn't be! Lila stacked the books on top of each other, reminding me of a librarian's delicate care of precious cargo. She turned and smiled. Why Lila Trahan, you really were stunning when you smiled! She had dimples too! Who knew? The curve of her cheeks reminded me of shiny apples I used to eat in the summer.

She strode heel to toe, the walk of someone used to balancing a load of books. Lila and her load arrived safely, and she set her treasures before me on the coffee table. Right on the top perched Detective Lou, his grim face peering underneath a gray fedora. One, two, three...my eyes traveled down the spines. All twelve Detective Lou books. My eyes met Lila's, and it was my turn to smile. Perhaps we weren't so different after all.

Lila settled back into the couch, with ankles crossed as a lady should. Her fingers scooped up the first book, bringing it to her chest like a beloved child.

"They aren't John Steinbeck by any means, but these books have given me great joy through the years. Arnold teases me that if Detective Lou was real, my husband would have some competition."

Her dark eyelashes fluttered as her bosom heaved just slightly. My high school English teacher was a fangirl!

"Miss Lila, would you like me to autograph your collection?" What could I possibly write to convey my emotions? These signings required some serious thought and prayer.

"Oh, yes, that would be wonderful! Perhaps you should take them home and sign them over several days."

More eyelash fluttering and bosom heaving. When I woke up this morning, I never guessed I would have this conversation with Lila Trahan!

Anna Dunbar poked her head inside the archway. "Lila, dear, whenever you're ready."

Her blue orbs were less frosty, no doubt because she'd been eavesdropping.

Maybe I'd gained two new friends.

"We're ready, I think. Right, Miss Lila?" I asked. Her face radiated warmth and coziness, reminding me of my favorite fleece blanket on the back of my couch. Familiar and inviting.

"Ladies, let's gather around and begin our meeting." Lila's teaching skills came in handy for the book club. "Before we discuss Mr. Steinbeck's gripping novel, I'd like to welcome Evangeline Bergeron—now Evangeline Delafose." Lila led the dozen women in a warm round of applause.

"Thanks so much for welcoming me to your gathering. I look forward to lively discussions." Hopefully, discussions about who killed Michael Cook. The ladies clapped again, just as pleasantly. Now, how to steer this meeting towards the case?

A petite lady in her late fifties raised her well-manicured hand. "Before we begin, I'd like us to pray about something." Her cherry red nail tips clicked against the double strand of pearls dangling from her neck. Were those real? In this group of women, they probably were.

Lila sat regally, a queen surveying her subjects. A royal in a Victorian wingback. "Yes, Nell, who should we pray for?" It was good to be the queen, and Lila wore it well. She'd motioned me into the chair beside her, much to the irritation of the other women. It was also good to be the queen's favorite.

Nell graduated to wringing her hands, carefully dodging the perfectly sculpted tips. "Well, the sheriff still hasn't caught Michael Cook's killer. I think we should pray that the murderer doesn't kill anyone else, and that he's brought to justice."

One of Lila's subjects poked her hand towards the ceiling, and Lila granted her permission to speak. "Well, we don't know for sure the killer is a man, do we?" Her head swiveled toward me. "Evangeline, don't you write mystery books? What's your take on this situation?" Whoops! This wasn't going down the path I'd hoped.

"Umm...well yes, I have written some mysteries. But I don't have an opinion on this case." Not a complete lie.

Nell ignored me. "Well, I heard Stella's boss gave her money and..." She leaned towards the middle of the circle and dropped her voice to a stage whisper. "...well, Michael confronted him! He accused this Josh person of keeping Stella addicted to drugs. But if you ask me..."

Nell's head jerked towards the front door. Did she think people were eavesdropping on the book club? Satisfied it was just us book lovers, she continued.

"If you ask me, it sounds like Stella's boss was just being nice. Everyone knows Michael kept his sister on a tight leash, wouldn't let her go anywhere or do anything. He said it was for her own protection. But if you ask me, I think he was controlling his sister." Nell leaned back into the floral couch, a twin to the one I'd just left in the other room.

Nell made Josh sound like a genuinely nice person and a good boss. Michael hadn't won my heart by any means, especially when he broke up with Faith at work. He dumped her heart and left her to find a ride home. This victim might *not* be the good guy Nate detailed in his notes.

A couple more hands shot up in the room. Yes, I'd definitely come to the right place! This so-called book club was a library of information. My new friend, the queen, called on first one lady, then the next.

Mrs. Lavender Dress With Matching Earrings spoke first. "My husband plays golf with Rob Dugas' father. He insists Michael Cook was no friend of Rob's. Oh sure, they were friends in high school, but Michael exaggerated about Rob's money problems. His father told my husband his son has never owed more money than he could repay. Rob and his father were close, and Rob knew he could always turn to his family. But he never asked for money, and he wasn't desperate. Not in the slightest."

Interesting. As my children's mother, I knew Matty and Ellie well enough to be assured of their hearts. Did Rob's father know him as well? He definitely believed that he did.

Lila nodded at...what was her name? A simple name that flew out of my head. Where did it go? Oh well, I'd call her Mrs. Cherry Red Dress That Matched Her Nails. These women had actual names, but for the life of me, I couldn't remember them. Ev, you've got to at least remember Mrs. Cherry Dress' name by the next meeting!

"Well, I heard from an extremely reliable source that this Josh Fairchild person has a record! Back in Arkansas, the police arrested him during his senior year in high school. He shoplifted from a Walmart, and those people don't mess around! Because of corporate policy, the store pressed charges. But Josh's dad knew the D.A. and got everything dropped to something less serious. He promised the D.A. they'd send him off to military school."

The entire circle gasped in unison. There hadn't been this much excitement since the Willard girl and the Farley boy ran off to Bossier City to play the slots and get hitched.

The book club ended with much speculation and lots of tongue wagging. Truthfully, it had been a great success, because of my reconciliation with Lila and some key clues.

While the ladies said their goodbyes, I hung back in the kitchen. My official reasons were to help clean up, but I wanted to thank Lila again for giving me a second chance. Up until that day, I'd been carrying around a pint-sized mason jar of regret in my heart. The jar had disappeared, and it felt glorious.

"Thank you once again, Miss Lila, for giving me a second chance. I promise to spend the afternoon autographing these Detective Lou books, and I'll bring them by later this week."

Lila had placed her treasured books in a canning jar box. "Here dear, why don't you carry the box? I'll carry your platter to the car, so you only have one trip." The load is lighter when shared with friends. Oh, Ev, be careful! Do not drop this box before you reach the car.

We placed our load into the backseat, then faced each other for one last goodbye. Should I hug my new friend? Was it too soon?

"Thank you again for coming, Evangeline. Your grandmother's lemon sandwich cookies were divine! I simply must have the recipe."

Such a beautiful smile—no wonder this woman still held Arnold Trahan's heart after forty years. And the Southern woman's ultimate compliment, being asked for the recipe!

"The pleasure was mine, Miss Lila! I'll get you the recipe, and I'm going to start the next book tonight."

The club's next book was *Pride and Prejudice* by my girl Jane Austen. Even if we never discussed the books during club meetings, my heart delighted in the assignment.

The top of Lila's snow-white head came just below my clavicle, and it fit perfectly when she wrapped her arms around me. How far we'd come in less than twenty-four hours! God certainly works miracles on our hearts.

It was time to hop into my car for the three-minute drive home. I'd considered walking, but knew with certainty my cookies couldn't survive the Louisiana heat. Thank goodness I didn't, since I had Lila's books to autograph. Once again, I promised to return in a few days with her books.

"Don't worry, Miss Lila! I'll take good care of your Detective Lou books. And I promise to bring them back promptly."

"Oh, sweetie, I know you will! And when you return, you can tell me more about the Michael Cook case, and how close you are to solving it." She stepped back into her yard and waved.

Definitely no secrets in this small town.

On the way home, my phone rang. Sister Sledge singing "We Are Family" signaled my sister-in-law, Bonnie. Why would she be calling?

"Hello, Ev! How was your book club?"

Whoops! My promise to gather parenting advice about Sydney's crying on demand! Wait a minute...in the kitchen I asked someone about Syd's crying. Who was that? More importantly, what did she say?

"Oh, hey Bonnie! It was fantastic. I think Lila Trahan and I made peace. I'm so glad you called! Listen, I asked for advice about Sydney turning on the waterworks, and I got some great feedback. The consensus was to put Syd in some activity that will use up her energy. Ballet or gymnastics, karate, or even basketball."

Could one person's advice be called a consensus? Definitely, all parties agreed on the solution. Yeah, that was a consensus.

"Hmm...that's not a bad idea, Ev. She's been wanting to try gymnastics or ballet. Yeah, this could work! Thanks so much, and please tell the book club ladies thank you as well."

Ev, darling, sometimes you were a genius!

Chapter 9

After signing three of Lila's books, my boredom consumed me and I wandered into the kitchen for a drink. Orange soda stared at me from the middle shelf of the refrigerator. Shorty had left his Gas n' More purchase, probably as a reminder for my shopping list.

Hmmm...a cup of tea...just enough caffeine to stir my soul but not enough to jar it. Making tea reminded me of my mother. She would put on a pot before tackling a problem or chatting with a friend. No friends in the house at the moment, so this was definitely a problem pot of tea.

My weather app vied for my attention with a soft ping, and I glanced at my phone. Rain was in the forecast all afternoon, so my pot of tea and I would stay in for the day. My thoughts turned to our dog Banjo. We'd bought him for Matty and Ellie, but he'd been my dog. The keeper of the food is a dog's best friend, and Banjo was no exception. That dog hated thunderstorms and would curl up at my feet, shivering until the storm had passed.

Who cried more when he died, me or the kids? Probably me. Banjo, at fourteen, slept more than he played, which suited me just fine. As I'd aged, I preferred sitting to running as well. We'd relax in the living room, me deep into a book and Banjo snoring at my feet. Two peas in a pod, Doug would say. At Banjo's annual checkup, the veterinarian felt lumps in his stomach. X-rays confirmed Banjo had cancer, and my heart plummeted.

As Banjo and I pulled into the driveway, I struggled with how to tell the kids. At fifteen and twelve, it would still be traumatic. Doug promised to race home as soon as he came off shift, so I shoved the bad news into a corner. The kids should have suspected something, because Doug rarely made it home for supper. But being teenagers, their minds were occupied with sports and friends and homework assignments.

After supper, Ellie and I cleared the table, but I told her to stack the dishes in the sink. Again, another clue something was amiss. But twelve-year-old girls are self-involved. The family gathered in the living room, including Banjo, and Doug broke the news. My sobs began quietly, soon rolling out of control. Matty's large brown eyes became watery, and Ellie burst into gut wrenching cries of anguish. Even Doug wiped a few tears. He dealt with death and violence every day, but this news was personal. He admitted later he cried for his children's sadness, wishing he could shield them from tragedy. Three years later, in that same living room, Nate broke the news of Doug's death as I sobbed uncontrollably. Or did I break the news as Nate sobbed? My heart still can't revisit the memories without shattering into a thousand pieces.

A new house should have brand new memories. Happy memories. But, Ev, you don't need a dog, and you're not a cat person. Dogs take up a lot of time and energy. Time piled up in every room of my house, which was why Nate gave me the Cook case. Let's get through this case and revisit the dog idea later.

Doug and the kids bought me a delicate teapot with a matching cup, so I always had a fresh cup of tea at arms' length. Have tea, will travel, he used to joke. While transporting my tea twenty feet between my kitchen and office one day, I had spilled both pot and cup.

A week later, Doug brought home a tea cart. "I want your tea to be safe," he joked. Later that evening, he'd confessed. "It's not your tea I worry about, Evangeline. If anything ever happened to you, I don't know what I'd do with myself."

Doug always called me Evangeline. Never Ev. "You're an angel fallen from Heaven, and angels have beautiful names like Evangeline. Mere mortals have names like Ev." When Doug left his dirty underwear beside the laundry basket for the twenty-fifth time, I'd push the sweet memories to the front of my brain. Or when he forgot to pick up milk. Again.

My tea cart and I trekked the five feet from kitchen to office. Truthfully, I didn't need the cart in this house, but I needed the happy memory. Sometimes I envisioned Doug looking down from Heaven, smiling as I pushed my cart. Keeping myself safe from dangerous teapots.

The cart was too beautiful to shove in a corner, anyway. The two-tiered wooden gift looked vintage, but at our income level, I knew better. Most likely, my husband discovered it in a thrift shop and bartered the owner down to a price more comparable with a detective's salary. The sudden early morning meetings made sense once I had my gift. Doug sent the cart home with his partner, along with a can of paint. Then he made up a story about meeting for coffee before their shift. Doug left early every morning for a week so he could paint my cart. Shabby chic white with just the tiniest hints of cornflower blue, to match my blue teapot and cup.

Sipping my tea gave me time to gaze out my window, watching the birds fight over the feeders in my backyard. My office was actually the breakfast nook. But with this glorious picture window, it made a better office for me. Not to mention, I rarely ate breakfast and spent most of my time in the office. Would Lila Trahan approve? Thinking of my new friend brought the tiniest of smiles to my lips.

As I took another sip, I felt peace. Mornings were for coffee, but God created rainy afternoons for tea and contemplation. Maybe I should spend more afternoons with tea and happy memories? My heart leaped at the thought, which didn't happen much anymore.

Okay, Ev, time to work on the case! My mind wandered to my encounter with Josh Fairchild at The Market Basket. How about some social media snooping? Of course, it was just for the case. I was definitely not interested in the guy romantically. Not one bit.

My friend Amy, recently single, hopped on Facebook, Instagram, and Twitter to check out her dates. She called it a deep dive. For TikTok, she had a warning: "Ev, TikTok's for kids in their twenties and thirties. If a guy our age is on TikTok, he's either younger than he represents, or he's trying to reclaim his youth. So run, don't walk if your man's on TikTok." Amy had always been clever with words.

Facebook seemed a good place to start. It was the only social media platform I used, so it was the only place to start. Matty and Ellie had Snapchat accounts, maybe. Actually, I didn't know what they used, because they wouldn't tell me.

"Mom, you don't need to be looking at my social media. If I think you need to know something, then I'll tell you."

Thanks, Matty. I appreciated your censorship.

Ellie was a little nicer. "Mom, you'd be bored with the things I post. It's just stuff like my new haircut, or a cute shirt I found. How about I just send you pictures if I think it's something you'd like?"

Still censorship, but presented in a kinder package.

All right, Facebook, let's get busy. My fingers typed in *Joshua Fairchild*, and twenty-five profile pictures popped on the screen. How many Joshua Fairchilds existed in this world? This deep dive was going to be at least two pots of tea, maybe three.

Facebook stalking proved easier than I'd hoped. Josh's posts revealed mostly clever memes and photos of him with the Cook children, mostly Stella. Definitely no drama sharing. Not super personal, but nothing alarming. Many of my male friends had similar feeds, sharing family photos and posts from other sources. A profile picture update or two.

What next? Matty? No way. Ellie? Nope. Wait a minute! Ev, you were a genius!

My cousin's son, Ethan Bergeron, maintained the village social media accounts. Being twenty-something, he knew the ins and outs of the internet. He attended LSU, pursuing a degree in Digital Media Arts & Engineering. Surely with a degree like that, he'd know how to find people on the world wide web. Now, where was his phone number?

Frantically, I scrolled my list of contacts. Ethan and I weren't that close, although I sent birthday cards. Of course, that was to his parents' address in Graisseville. Matty and Ethan were about the same age, so he probably had Ethan's number.

Hold your horses, Ev. Asking Matty for a phone number invited interrogation and criticism.

"Mom, why do you need Ethan's phone number? You're not going to ask him how to reboot your computer, are you? Why don't you ask me your questions instead? That way, your ignorance of the twenty-first century stays between us."

Ellie? Not a chance. Why not go straight to the source? Pulling up my texting feature, I typed in *Sam Bergeron*. My cousin would know his son's phone number. Two sips of tea later, my text notification *swooshed*. Sam shared Ethan's contact information without a *hi* or *hope you're well*. That was Sam—straight to the point.

How to contact a twenty-something? Matty and Ellie preferred texting, probably so their friends didn't know they actually had a mother.

Hey Ethan, it's Ev Delafose, Matty's mom. I need your technical expertise. Please call me when you get a chance.

Did it sound coherent? Intelligent, even? After reading it five times, I gave up. The words, *Mom, don't be lame*, rang through my head. Hopefully, Ethan found my text lacking in lameness.

Twenty minutes later, my first cousin once removed called.

"Hey, Ev! How are you? How are Matty and Ellie?"

What a considerate young man! He probably sent his mother flowers for Mothers' Day.

"I'm good, Ethan, and so are the kids. Ellie headed off to Louisiana Tech this fall, and Matty's starting his junior year at Tech too. How are your mom and dad? How's school?" After the proper time spent on Southern etiquette, I got down to business. "Listen, I hate to bother you, but I'm helping the sheriff's department with a case and I could use your help."

As I outlined my involvement and detailed the case, Ethan's verbal cues became more frequent and enthusiastic. Instead of *yes ma'am* and *oh okay*, I heard several *oh wow*'s and a few exclamations of, *are you serious?* My cousin wanted in on the case.

Most of us fantasized about playing detective, interviewing witnesses, and mulling over clues. Maybe even a car chase or two. Doug maintained that detective work was never as exciting as in movies and television. Still, I jumped out of bed each morning, my brain puzzling over the clues and working out strategies. My relationship with Shorty had blossomed as we texted and talked several times a day about the case. We'd added a cyber expert to our team, at least compared to my partner and me. Shorty still used a flip phone and thought Mark Zuckerberg was the weekend meteorologist on Channel 2.

Ethan asked me to text all the personal information I had on Josh, as well as the other suspects. Nate kept profile sheets of every person interviewed in the files, so all I had to do was scan them. Ellie taught me how to scan documents on my phone, so I proudly sent Ethan the profiles. My newest team member promised to have results by the end of the week.

Now what? My mind had reserved the afternoon for my deep dive. More like wading in up to my ankles. No worries, because Ethan's skill set worked better for this part of the investigation. My talents were more of a face-to-face nature. My window confirmed the forecast for rain, drops smacking the panes of glass. Maybe when the worst of the storm cleared, I could stop by the coffee shop. Time for another pot of tea!

My kettle took its sweet time to whistle, so I sat on the barstool to wait. What was that noise? My eyes traveled towards my kettle. Were we whining to signal hot water now? The kettle claimed innocence, so my ears honed in on the noise. Definitely an animal, but what kind? Did rat kings whine? Tiffy, the canine rat expert, cleared my house of rats, but my mind still registered on the skeptical scale. Should I call Nate? Shorty? No, Ev. You needed to figure this one out on your own.

Sliding my barstool out a few inches, I stood on my tiptoes. Weren't tiptoes stealthier? Should I take a weapon?

Doug's backup gun, a SIG Sauer P365, lay on my bedside table. As a police detective's wife, guns didn't scare me. In New Orleans, I'd kept my father's shotgun near the front door. Doug's long hours worried both the men in my life. They slept better, knowing Dad's twenty-gauge Mossberg stood guard in our entryway.

Here in Smalltown, Louisiana, the twenty-gauge lived in my closet. At least my tennis shoes and flip-flops would be safe.

Surveying the kitchen, I spotted my block of cooking knives. Should I run to the bedroom and get the SIG or the Mossberg? Or a knife recommended by The Pioneer Woman herself, Ree Drummond? Why weren't these life choices covered at LSU?

Compromise, Ev. How about a knife to tide me over as I grabbed the SIG? Pioneer Woman for the win! Crouching into a half-crawling, half-running position, I tucked the knife close to my arm. Nope, that wouldn't work. No way I'd make it to the bedroom without cutting my arm. New plan, Ev. Let's keep upright but hunch down to avoid detection. As my brain processed my so-called brilliance, it hit me. An animal wouldn't be tall enough to peer into the windows and see me. It wasn't human...was it? The beats of my heart rang in my ears. Deep breath in...then out. Focus, Ev. Be calm and logical. What was this noise exactly?

Four short whines, not howls. A cat? No, definitely not a cat. A puppy? Perhaps, but more like a young dog. Ree Drummond's knife and I creeped toward the front door. My ears picked up the whine as I inched towards the hallway. Peering through the window on my front door, I spotted a medium-sized dog. Definitely male and absolutely terrified of thunderstorms.

Oh, goodness, Ev! Hadn't you just reminisced about Banjo? What words had I used? *I don't need a dog—they take up a lot of time and energy. Get through this case and revisit the dog idea.* And yet...

As if on cue, the dog scrunched up his midnight eyes to study me. The word, *pushover* flashed across my head in bright neon lights, causing my trespasser to shake from damp head to soggy tail. His pleading eyes locked onto mine. *Stop being so cute!* Leaning closer, I took stock of my visitor. Definitely less than a year old, golden brown except for his muzzle, which was coal black. As my father the veterinarian would say, *Heinz 57.* A little of this and a little of that, much like hobo stew.

"Those dang pedigreed dogs, just breeding amongst themselves. Ev, you need to shop the shelters, get a good Heinz 57. They need a home more than those pedigreed dogs. Cost less too! And they come from all different breeds, so they're healthier. Fewer ailments and problems."

Did this dog need a home? Maybe he was just lost. My right arm reached for the door handle as my left wielded the knife. Being left-handed made everything so awkward!

Thankfully, my guest tumbled inside, eager to get away from the crashing and the wetness.

"Okay, young man, let's set a few ground rules. First, I'm going to do everything in my power to get you back to your home." What happened to the hair on his back? Why was his skin all flakey? Oh boy, this dog had mange. As I reached down to touch his back, the animal hunched away from my hand and shivered. Oh my goodness! This dog thought I was going to hurt him!

I'd hung out in my dad's office since I could walk and chew gum. In high school, Dr. Skeeter Bergeron actually paid me to hang out in his clinic, to administer shots and soothe pet owners. We had our fair share of animals that people had found on the side of the road. I was no stranger to animal abuse.

No way, Ev! This dog wasn't going back to an owner who beat him! My heart stepped up to the plate. So, he's yours, girl. In sickness and in health. What was that smell? Yeah, this dog and my bathtub had big plans.

Chapter 10

Why don't dogs enjoy bath time? Soothing music, bubbles, peace and quiet. Honestly, I spent more time cleaning up *after* the bath than I did giving it to the dog. Calling the veterinarian's office for an appointment proved the easiest of all. And the driest. Dr. Cliff Trahan had an opening that afternoon. Yes, that vet tech I'd introduced to Elizabeth graduated vet school and purchased my father's practice.

"So, Ev, you're right. This dog has mange. He also has fleas, hookworms, malnutrition, and kennel cough. Not to mention a bunch of emotional issues." Cliff's curvy smile widened towards my frown. "Don't worry. You'll get the discount reserved for the person who introduced me to the love of my life. Just the cost of the medication."

My grin matched his pearly whites as we stood eye to eye, understanding each other. Finally! Wearing that ridiculous orange jumpsuit with white fluffy feathers in his wedding had paid off. One of life's unanswered questions was why my best friend made her bridesmaids wear feathers and jumpsuits.

"So how long, Cliff? How long will he be here, and how long until I get him back?" The cowering canine's eyes stared deep into my soul. *I'm so sorry...whatever your name will be!*

"A week, maybe less. Oh, and by the way," Dr. Cliff's eyes danced in anticipation, "if you have a friend who's twenty years old or so, have I got a vet tech for you! Hey, isn't Ellie about that age?" His smile practically burst from his mouth.

"Nope! My matchmaking days are over." Oh, that guy! Thank goodness Elizabeth loved goofy grins and big hearts.

What to do until my new sidekick was ready for action? I couldn't spend an entire week worrying about my furry new friend. Kids and finances kept me busy enough with worry. My brain shifted towards more caffeine. Maggie's Coffee Shop! A place open and full of information!

Maggie welcomed me with a grin and questioning eyes. She held up a medium cup and tilted her head. *Your usual?* My head bobbed up and down, like my dad's fishing pole when he had a bite. Thank you, Lord, for friends like Maggie!

Sipping my chai tea latte, I relished the sights and smells of the shop. Maggie slid into the seat across from me, eyes wide and engaging.

"I've been keeping my ears open and I've heard a few things. For instance, Faith Dixon is afraid of guns. She's never fired one in her life!" Maggie's eyes reminded me of birthday candles on a cake. A cake with a large number of said candles.

"Guess what else I've learned!"

"Goodness, Maggie! Tell me!"

My informant leaned forward on her elbows. "Rob Dugas' drug dealing friends claim his luck ran out, and he owed people more money than he could beg, borrow, or steal."

My brow furrowed as I pondered this news. Maybe Rob's father was wrong. Maybe Rob owed a lot of money and couldn't face his father.

"Maggie, how do you know these scumbags are telling the truth? And how do you know Rob's friends?"

Shaking her head like a teacher disappointed in her student, Maggie set me straight.

"My friend's brother is one of the so-called scumbags."

Oops!

"Ev, he has no reason to lie! Larry says Rob owed money, and he said he'd be going to the one person who always bailed him out. Larry said he thinks this time Michael said no. Well, Rob has a terrible temper, so Larry thinks he became violent when Michael refused to loan him money. Most likely, Michael grabbed his father's gun to scare Rob into leaving. Rob wrestled it away and shot Michael. It's not that far-fetched!" Maggie's eyes shone brighter. Someone had added candles to that birthday cake.

"Also, let's not forget Stella!"

My heart sank. Was this woman really guilty? As a sister, I just couldn't imagine anyone capable of murdering a sibling. Yes, they are annoying, but they are still family.

Maggie's theory could be right, though.

"The sheriff's department arrested Stella a few years ago for using drugs. Only, they dropped the charges, thanks to the Cook family's influence. Her parents sent her to rehab back in Mississippi, near family. Once an addict, always an addict."

Why did people keep saying that? It wasn't always true.

Shorty arrived just before 6 p.m., eager for muffalettas and a strategy session. I'd gotten more efficient making my olive salad spread, so I greeted my PI with a platter full of sandwiches. His stomach rumbled in appreciation.

"Good job, Doc! Yer gettin' better at cookin'! Yer actually on time."

Should I point out that nothing about these sandwiches involved cooking? Or that he was darn lucky to be eating so well? He could always go eat at Candy's, or get food from the parade of other women eager to cook him anything his heart desired. No, better to just keep quiet.

"Thank you, Shorty. I appreciate your kind words." Did he hear the sarcasm? No, this man was too busy eyeing the muffalettas and *Zapp's*.

"I see y'got my *fave-rit* chips. I 'preciate that, I really do."

We said the blessing—or I did anyway—and settled into muffalettas and *Zapp's* potato chips. Kettle style for me and Spicy Cajun Crawtators for my PI. Shorty had already popped the top on his orange soda from my fridge.

"Okay first, Shorty, I called in a cyber expert of sorts. My cousin Sam's kid, Ethan, is at LSU, majoring in Digital Media Arts & Engineering." What a mouthful!

Shorty's eyes immediately hunkered down into his eyelids, a sure sign he had trust issues. "We don't need no stinkin' kid tellin' us what t'do, Doc! We're uh doin' jus' fine without some *snaw*...I mean, whiny kid, that's spongin' off his parents."

Shorty stopped short at the first syllable of *snot-nosed*, which I appreciated. Although not a curse word, still not an accurate description of Ethan. As for sponging off his parents, Shorty considered anyone over eighteen still taking money from their parents a blight on humanity. We'd avoided the discussion of my parents paying for my college, and my kids still receiving money at ages eighteen and twenty.

"Look, I understand your point of view. I really do. But here's the problem. You and I just aren't skilled enough in technology to perform internet searches. *Ethan* has that expertise, and probably more resources than even the sheriff's department." My elbows scooted across the table as I leaned in. Our new team member had a major advantage over the sheriff's department, and I needed Shorty to understand that. "Ethan can find information the sheriff's deputies can't. Because he can use alternative sources. Know what I'm saying?"

Shorty's eyebrows raised up then down, like someone opening a window shade then closing it. "So, this cousin Ethan *dudn't* need a warrant t'see what our suspects are browsin' on the internet. An' he can find information that's against federal, state, an' local laws. Not t'mention he can search the dark web."

Hmm...apparently Shorty understood.

"Okay, then it sounds like we can use 'im. Let me know what he finds out." The munching continued. "By the way, Doc. I think we need to be talkin' with the suspects. Which one should we start with, and who do y'want to do it?"

For once, Shorty and I agreed on our investigation. "I think Stella. Since she's Nate's prime suspect, she'll be the most willing to talk to us. We can pitch it as we want to help clear her name. In fact, let's both talk to her. I'd like us to form our own impressions."

Shorty nodded, just like my Elvis bobblehead, a gag gift from the kids one year. "You wanna' set it up, Doc? Jus' let me know the date an' time, an' I'll come pick ya up." Always the protector.

"Sounds good. Oh, we have more addition to our team." Why couldn't I stop smiling?

Again, with the hunkered down eyelids. "Doc, we don't need no more people!"

My hand reached towards Shorty's arm, and I placed my fingers lightly on his wrist. "I found a dog. Or rather, a dog found me. He's at the vet clinic right now, getting fixed up." When was the last time my heart felt warm and gushy? Gosh, it felt good!

Shorty's eyes wandered out of their caves. Surprised but not irritated. "Whatcha' talkin' about? A dog wandered up tuh yore property? I can't tell ya' the number o' dogs that wander onta' my farm."

My fingers tightened around his wrist, and Shorty hesitated. "Please don't tell me about those dogs! I don't want to know. All I want to focus on is that *this* dog needs me, and I need him. It's been too long since I had someone who needed me." Wow, Ev! You actually said that out loud.

Shorty gingerly placed the palm of his hand on top of my fingers. Sometimes this dear friend really got me. "Funny that dog found ya'. Cuz, ya know what? I've started prayin' again. An' I've been prayin' that God will take care of ya. It wouldn't surprise me iffin' the good Lord sent that dog to keep ya' safe."

My arms wrapped around Shorty's neck, surprising both of us. Of all the friends I considered dear, this man leaped to the top two. Strong contender for number one. If only he'd kept his mouth shut.

"Whew, Doc! When's the last time you brushed your teeth? Cuz your breath stinks! Seriously, mebbe that worked fer ya' in New Awlins, but here in Graisseville, y'gotta' brush yore teeth at least once a day." He took another whiff closer to my mouth. "Mebbe in yore case twice a day."

Not to worry, Elizabeth Trahan. You were definitely still number one on my friends list.

Setting up an interview with Stella Cook proved easier than I'd thought. "Hello Stella, this is Evangeline Delafose. I'm working with the East Baton Rouge Parish Sheriff's office to solve your brother's murder. I'd like to drop by, when it's convenient, and talk to you. I mean, if that's okay. If it's not, then that's fine. But I really don't believe you did it, so I'd like to help clear your name. If you're available, I mean. Not to be too much trouble, but it would be great if I could stop by soon. If that's okay. If it's not, that's fine too." Way to give away the farm, Ev!

Fortunately, Stella sensed my sincerity. Or felt sorry for me. Frankly, I'd take anything at that point.

"That's fine—anything to help clear my name! I'm free most evenings after 7 p.m. What works best for you?"

Stella and I coordinated our schedules for 7:30 p.m. the next evening and I mentioned my plus one who'd be coming along. Shorty was at home around females, so they'd get along well. It was me who needed to practice my people skills.

As we turned onto Stella's street, I stared at the houses. A typical older neighborhood. Several homes kept their elegance from when their wealthy owners created them, and a few could be called genuine mansions or even estates. Unfortunately, several houses featured chipped paint, broken stairs and dirty windows. Unruly grass and weeds framing abandoned cars created the look of neglect or possible abandonment.

Shorty took the lead, knocking three times on the front door. Even though I didn't find Shorty attractive, I enjoyed watching him work his charms on other, more receptive women. Would Stella find Shorty good looking?

"Oh, please do come in! Miss Ev, it's so nice to meet you. And, Mr. Shorty, is it? Welcome!"

Our hostess led us into her spacious living room, waving a hand towards a navy upholstered sofa with red floral accent pillows. Shorty made himself comfortable immediately, balancing an accent pillow in his lap. Stella waited for us to settle ourselves before continuing her hostess obligations.

"Would any of ya'll like something to eat? I've just baked some brownies. Would you like one? With vanilla ice cream?"

Had Shorty ever turned down food? "Why yes ma'am! I'll take a coupla' brownies with ice cream. Whatcha' got to drink?"

While my PI placed his order, my eyes scanned the room. Built in the early 1900s, the spacious living area featured ten-foot ceilings painted pearlized cream, matching walls with chair rails, and carefully shined hardwood floors protected by oriental rugs. The Cooks had spared no expense maintaining their home. Upscale furniture coordinated perfectly with the rugs. Had I accidentally wandered into an Ethan Allen showroom? No, two dozen framed family photos hung neatly on the walls, and another half-dozen sat on side tables. It was definitely Stella's home.

Our hostess returned with a square lacquered tray showcasing a plate of brownies and a bowl of ice cream shaped into perfect scoops. She'd also scared up some orange soda in a crystal drinking glass. A pitcher filled with ice tea and lemons completed the display, with twins to Shorty's glass standing side by side in front of the pitcher—Waterford crystal, the Lismore pattern. Lila had served us with the same pattern, and I'd asked her about it. She received the pieces as wedding gifts, and forty-five years ago, the glasses alone cost fifty dollars each.

The dish pattern looked familiar too, and I gasped when I recognized it. Doug and I had looked at Old Country Roses by Royal Albert for our china pattern. When we realized no one could afford $70 a plate, we chose something more affordable.

Stella smiled at my gasp as she set the tray on the cherry oval coffee table. "It's nice to have a reason to break out my grandmother's Old Country Roses. The pattern is just breathtaking, and it seems a shame to hide it in the china cabinet." She seated herself on a brown leather club chair, then leaned forward to fix a bowl of brownies and ice cream.

"Here you are, Mr. Shorty. Please enjoy." Stella fixed another bowl and offered it to me. "Let's not make Mr. Shorty feel like he's eating alone."

Oh, honey! Shorty could never care whether he was eating alone or in a crowd, as long as he was eating. "Of course, Stella. Thanks so much."

Several questions rolled around my brain. What did Stella know about Michael and Rob's relationship? What exactly were Josh and Michael fighting about? Did she know anything about Josh's sealed records? Why didn't she have an alibi? Would we ever get to the actual interview? How much would my private investigator actually eat?

Chapter 11

My PI focused on the task at hand, which was not interviewing our suspect. The task at hand was consuming his bowl of brownies and ice cream, balanced in his lap. Shorty gauged the contents of the lacquered tray, calculating the time ice cream takes to settle into a white pool of goo.

Obviously, it was my job to put our cards on the table. "Look, Stella," I began, "The detectives are at a standstill. Your brother's investigation is circling the drain, and the next stop is the black hole of unsolved cases. Shorty and I are the last-ditch effort to solve this murder. We don't think you did it, so we'd like to find the real killer."

Please, Stella. Look into my eyes. This whole excuse of 'once an addict, always an addict' doesn't fly with me. Let me help you!

Our hostess eyed me carefully as she licked her spoon. "Okay, what would you like to know?"

Shorty fixed his gaze on the tray, his share of brownies long gone.

I shoved my portion toward his eager hands. "Here, why don't you eat mine? I'll start the interview."

No arguments from my PI—he was too busy dropping brownies and ice cream into his open mouth.

"Okay, Stella, I spoke with your friend, River. Did he mention our discussion?"

She dropped her chin slightly. "Yes, Miss Ev, he did." Those wide green eyes reminded me of a cat. A cat who never stopped staring at me.

"The murder weapon, your father's gun. Michael told you that your father gave it to a cousin, correct?"

Again, Stella's feline eyes never wavered, and she dropped her chin another inch or two.

"Okay, good. You never realized Michael had the gun, then?"

Miss Cat Eyes blinked twice, then looked to her right. What did those detectives say in the last *Midsomer Murders* episode? Looking to the right meant lying? Or did it mean thinking about the truth? Why hadn't I paid more attention?

"Actually, that's not true. I mean, Michael told me our father gave it away. But I'd seen it in the closet, so I knew my brother lied." Stella's mouth curved upwards, and a hint of happiness warmed her cool eyes. "Michael knew guns scare me. He wanted to keep it around but didn't want me to be afraid."

My teal pen wrote slowly, so I could ponder this bit of news. What did it mean? Could Stella have killed Michael? Why tell us she knew about the gun if she'd killed him? Why couldn't the murderer just make it easy on me and confess?

"All right, what can you tell me about Sam Hughes?" My pen wavered above the notebook, waiting for her answer. Hopefully, this line of questioning would be less confusing.

"Well, I know Sam and Michael didn't get along. They'd started working at the bank about the same time, so they came up for promotions together. Sam has a bit of a temper, and he's a showoff. He couldn't stand that everyone at the bank loved Michael and that he got bigger projects. Someone complained to Human Resources about Sam—said he was rude to customers. Sam always thought it was Michael, but it wasn't. Let's not forget Sam's knowledge of guns."

That was new! "What do you mean, exactly?"

Was that a smile or a smirk? "Michael told some co-workers about going to the gun range with our father and shooting the handgun. He'd commented on how special those memories were. Of course, Sam heard the stories and had to top them! He boasted that *his* father took him to the range as well, only they had bigger and *better* guns. And no surprise, Sam's dad is still alive, so they're still making memories. Just hateful!"

My pen tapped against the paper, and Stella's eyes observed my nervous habit. Was she trying to figure me out, just as I was doing to her?

"What do you know about Michael and Faith Dixon's relationship? Did he really break up with her in front of the diner, then leave her at work without a ride home?"

An actual smile from my suspect. "Well, there are two sides to every story, you know. Michael tried several times to break up with Faith, but she wouldn't take no for an answer. The diner dump was my suggestion."

Stella paused, dipping her spoon into her bowl. "I told Michael he should let Faith close the car door, then roll down the window and deliver the news." She poised the spoon just before her mouth. "I told him to say something like 'Oh, one more thing, Faith. We're broken up. For good. So you'll need a ride home.'" The spoon glided inside Stella's mouth as her lips closed around it. Maybe she wasn't a murderer, but she found great delight in Faith's misery.

She swallowed. "Oh, Faith wouldn't kill Michael. She's someone who wants a person alive and kicking, so she can wreak havoc. Just ask her ex-boyfriend, Tyrone. You know, the one who dumped Faith, then watched his house burn down?" A quarter way through her dessert, Stella set her bowl on the tray with a light *clink*. Playing with the spoon seemed more important. A distraction, maybe? Keeping her brain engaged so she could lie with more conviction?

Shorty had already polished off my uneaten bowl, then eyed Stella's with interest. Mama Madie Cormier's upbringing must have kicked in, because he didn't reach for the half-eaten bowl. But he wasn't finished either.

"May I, Miss Stella?" Right hand already reaching for the ladle to claim the drippy ice cream scoops. Might as well add the last two brownies. Maybe I should film this event, in case the Guinness Book of World Records could use it?

"Stella, what can you tell me about Michael's relationship with Rob Dugas?"

Again, with her cat eyes, so unsettling.

"It's a complicated situation. Or was, rather." She traced an index finger around the rim of her tea glass. Pitiful cubes of ice floated near the lemon slices. "Michael always had a heart for helping others, and Rob had been his pet project during high school. But after graduation, my brother grew up and came to an important conclusion." Stella dropped her eyelids toward the floor. "Not everyone wants to be saved."

The lowering of the eyelids meant something, but what? A lie? A confession?

"Okay, so had Michael helped Rob recently?"

"Yes, the month before Michael's death. My brother told Rob that was the last time, and he needed to find someone else to believe his lies. He'd finally realized Rob was using the money for drugs, not food and rent like he had promised."

"What about you, Stella? Where were you the night of the murder?"

Stella's face lost its playfulness, and a storm passed over her eyes. Then it was gone.

"I told the deputies that I went to the movies with a friend in Baton Rouge! But my friend wishes to remain anonymous, so I can't say anything else."

Rob looked to be the murderer, and yet I had a weird feeling about Stella. Still one more suspect, though.

"What about Josh Fairchild? I understand he and Michael were fighting the night before his death. Can you tell me what they were fighting about?"

Stella's eyes shot up from her glass, willing me to meet her gaze. "Me, actually. They were fighting over me. Mother and Daddy paid off this house, but we've still got property taxes, utilities, and food. I'm supposed to be helping with everything. But that month I did something stupid. I spent my paycheck on new clothes, so I didn't have enough money for the bills. Josh advanced me some cash—told me I could work some extra hours and pay him back. Only, Michael figured out that I couldn't have *both* new clothes and money for the bills. When Josh came over that night, Michael started yelling at him. He asked Josh how I was going to manage my money if he always bailed me out? Josh defended me, and they both lost their tempers. Did the neighbors tell you that?"

Stella's question sounded more like an observation, and she didn't wait for an answer.

"Later, Michael apologized, and we were all friends again. It really wasn't as big a deal as the neighbors described. Small towns, what can you do?" With a shrug of her shoulders, Stella ended the line of questioning.

"Oh no, I get that. Tell me, though, do you know anything about Josh's sealed records?" Would she look me straight in the eyes, or down at the floor?

Straight in the eyes. "Oh, it wasn't any big deal, really. Josh was trying to impress some girl, and she dared him to shoplift a necklace at the Walmart. He got caught, and the police searched his truck too. They found a hunting rifle, which turned the situation into a mess. I mean, he'd gone deer hunting that morning. Of course, he had a gun!" She rolled those saucer eyes to accompany her sigh. "Since Josh had recently fired it, the police were off and running. Thank goodness Josh's father played golf with the D.A. Otherwise, his life would have taken a different path." Those green eyes never wavered.

"Last question. You work closely with Josh. Is he still seeing Shannon, the librarian?"

Keep your tone even, Ev, and hopefully, she will think it's part of the investigation.

Shorty was still polishing off the brownies and ice cream, but he left enough room in his mouth to snort. The daggers shooting out of my eyes ensured he stuck to his eating.

Stella's gaze never wavered, but her posture stiffened slightly. "Actually, Miss Ev, Josh is dating someone new. A lady in Baton Rouge, I believe." Her posture relaxed as her eyes crinkled in the beginnings of a smile. "Please keep that quiet, though. You know, small towns."

Stella tucked a two-inch slice of hair behind her right ear. Had Detective Barnaby mentioned anything about hair tucking in *Midsomer Murders*? Something to research for sure.

Stella rose from her chair, cuing the end of our interview. "I'm afraid I've got an early morning tomorrow. I'm going to have to ask you to leave."

Staring at the tray, I noticed only Stella's uneaten snack remained. Just how much did Shorty eat? Yet he'd contributed nothing to the interview.

"Thank ya', Miss Stella, for yore hospitality. You'll have to give the doctor here yore brownie recipe." Shorty's charm worked on women of all ages, and Stella wasn't immune.

"Oh, Shorty! I appreciate your graciousness. I'll be sure and get her the recipe. You're both welcome back anytime."

Shorty tipped an imaginary hat towards Stella as he turned for the front door. We thanked Stella again on the front porch and headed down the steps.

"Jus' one more question, Miss Stella. Didja' kill yore brother?" Oh, good grief! Had he planned that all along? And was *this* what he'd learned in his private investigator course?

Stella's green saucers narrowed.

"No sir, Mr. Shorty. No sir, I did not."

"Okay then, thank you. Oh, so if this Josh fella ain't datin' the librarian no more, do y'know if she's single?"

"Stella, thanks so much for your time." My legs flew down the stairs, putting as much distance as possible between me and that embarrassing situation. For someone with a prosthetic leg, my PI still beat me to the truck by a good minute.

Shorty turned towards my home, just a few minutes across town. "Well, I think that went well, don'tcha' agree, Doc?"

Where to start? Never mind the question about the librarian. We each used the interview to further our dating life.

"Well, I suppose so. But tell me, what was with that question on the front porch? 'Did you kill your brother?' What did you expect her to say?"

Shorty's eyes never left the road. For once, my PI focused on his driving. "Didja' notice, Doc? She never hesitated. Didn't stumble, didn't stutter. I don't think she killed her brother. And y'know what else?"

Perhaps I'd misjudged Shorty and the integrity of his private investigator course. "No, I don't. What else did you discover?"

Both of Shorty's hands rested on the steering wheel, perfectly forming the ten and two positions. His eyes narrowed, staring into the darkness. "I think she knows who did."

"Ev, darling! How are you? I hear you have a new friend. Is he replacing me?"

Was Elizabeth talking about the dog or Shorty? Since she was married to the veterinarian, I assumed she meant the dog.

"Of course not! Let's talk about you—how's your father?"

Elizabeth Trahan had been over the moon to learn I was moving back to Graisseville. We'd both admitted long distance friendships, like long distance romances, were hard to maintain. Unfortunately, just as I closed on my new home, Elizabeth's father suffered a heart attack. She packed her bags and headed for the boot of Louisiana (the southern tip of the state) to help with her father.

"Dad's doing better, but Mother's still just a basket case. She can't keep the home health care schedule straight, and struggles with Dad's medication. Oh, Ev, I'm not sure I'm ever coming home!"

Things get complicated when the child becomes the parent. "Well, don't you worry about Cliff! Your daughter-in-law has him over most every night for a wonderful home cooked meal. Please don't repeat this, but I think Cliff's gained an extra ten pounds since you've left." Was that a chuckle on the other end of the phone?

"Yes, he complained about it last month." Her voice dropped an octave as she mimicked her husband. "'Elizabeth! I've got to call Shorty to fix our dryer—it's shrinking my pants!'" Her voice trailed off into peals of laughter, resonating like a medium pitched wind chime with mellow but vibrant tones. That laugh put a smile on my face more times than I could count.. Nobody understood me like Elizabeth.

Oh, how I missed my friend! "Well, stay as long as you need, and don't worry about Cliff. Or me either. We're both doing fine."

"Yes, I hear you and Shorty Cormier are working a case for Nate. What's that all about?"

Shorty dropped me off from our trip to Stella's, just about the time Elizabeth called. Listening to her updates gave me time to hang my purse on the hall tree and head to the kitchen to brew a pot of tea. Wheeling my tea cart with both hands and Elizabeth on speakerphone, I hurried to the couch to share my new adventure.

"Honestly, I think we've narrowed it down to two suspects: the drug addicted friend, and the disgruntled co-worker. Although I'm not ruling out the sister." Stella was back on my radar, so I felt comfortable sharing that with my bestie. We talked for almost an hour, and I brewed another pot of tea. Finally, we said our goodbyes. She couldn't come home soon enough.

My eyes rested upon the picture frame on the end table. My favorite picture of me and the kids, when we rented a cabin on Caddo Lake. Our first trip without Doug, and we'd worked hard to have fun. We'd succeeded too, at least in my mind.

The frame always faced the couch, so I could see it while watching TV or reading a book. Why was it turned just slightly, so I couldn't quite see Matty's face?

The hairs on my neck vibrated, like a tuning fork. No, I always positioned the frame toward me. My eyes traveled toward my dad's Mossberg, standing guard beside the couch. After my scare with the-dog-I-hadn't-yet-named, I'd moved the shotgun downstairs.

Yeah, I needed to name that dog. But what about the picture frame? Ev, you're being paranoid.

Cliff's number popped up on my screen. "Sorry for calling so late, but your dog is doing better than expected. You can pick him up tomorrow." Good news, but he still needed a name. Cliff agreed.

"Right now he's in our system as Baby Boy Delafose. But when you pick him up, please give Debbie a name for our files." Cliff chuckled at his own cleverness.

We chatted about Elizabeth, and that we both missed her. Cliff more than me, it seemed, because the guy wouldn't stop sharing—I couldn't get him off the phone.

"Oh, I've got another call," I interjected, "See you tomorrow!" That man needed his wife back and pronto! "Ethan! Great to hear from you! Did you find anything?" Thank goodness Ethan had a life and would be straight to the point. As I sipped my tea, Ethan shared his findings.

"Well, I ran the names through some standard programs, searching for the suspects all across the net. Let's start with the victim, Michael Cook. He'd filed a report with the sheriff that someone keyed his truck."

"Hmm, well, that was probably his ex-girlfriend, Faith. Or maybe he parked sideways and someone keyed the truck." Not helpful, really.

Ethan sensed my lack of enthusiasm. "Okay, well, I discovered the victim's sister, Stella, dropped out of high school after being caught with drugs."

Oh, hey, that was news! "Wait a minute! Nate's notes don't say anything about that."

Ethan's voice grew in confidence. "Stella wasn't arrested. A fellow student snitched to the principal, so he raided her locker and found a stash of drugs. Instead of calling the cops, the principal called her parents. They hammered out a deal, and Stella entered a rehab facility in Baton Rouge.

After rehab, she lived with a relative in Mississippi and graduated high school. She moved back here, and her parents died in a car crash not long after. Then she *was* arrested for drugs, convicted, and sent back to rehab. Michael didn't have as much influence as his parents, I guess."

So, Stella's drug issues weren't just a one-time mistake. The deputies discovered drugs when they searched the house, but I'd dismissed it. Maybe I'd misjudged her.

"One more piece of information, Ev. I found a review about the bank. You know, the one that Michael Cook and Sam Hughes worked at? Here, let me read it." Ethan paused as he pulled up the information. "'Don't put your money in the First Bank of Zachary! One of the loan officers, Sam Hughes, won't give you a loan unless you slip him some cash. The branch manager even knows about Mr. Hughes' bribe process, and doesn't care.'"

"Okay, that's horrible, but why is it relevant?" My scribbling halted as my pen rested on the notebook.

"Well, someone, probably the bank IT people, deleted the review and the accompanying comments. Except, of course, the internet never completely wipes away anything. Sam Hughes commented that he knew Michael Cook posted the review. He said Michael was a liar and a thief. Michael replied to the comment, and then Sam replied, and it all got angrier and more threatening. In fact..."

Ethan's voice trailed off. Was he trying to decide if he should tell me?

"Uh, well, Sam told Michael he'd better stop spreading lies or his sister would become an only child."

As I hung up with Ethan, thoughts whirled in my head, vying for my attention. The case exhausted me, so my brain focused on something pleasant. Tomorrow, I would become a dog owner again. Shorty and I had scheduled a strategy session for the morning, after he fed the cows and hogs and I'd picked up my dog.

Brush your teeth, Ev, and make Shorty happy. His comment still irritated me! Everyone's breath stinks after eating muffalettas. Salami and onions and garlic will do that. Include Shorty in your prayers, Ev—pray for those who persecute you!

Pajamas on, teeth cleaned...this girl had a date with the bed! Reaching over to turn off my side lamp, I glanced at the SIG Sauer beside it. Why was the gun facing the wrong way?

My headboard stood against the far wall, so the bed faced the door. My nightstand sat on my left. Being left-handed, I always set the SIG Sauer on the nightstand with the butt of the gun pointing toward the wall behind me. When I reached for the gun from the bed, my left hand dropped easily on top of the handle so I could curl my fingers into position.

The butt of the gun now faced the door, making a left-handed grab impossible. Someone picked up the gun, then put it back down—someone right-handed. My brain replayed the angle of the picture frame. No, Matty's face definitely wasn't visible from my seat on the couch. Doug teased me about my obsession with neatness, but everything had a place and a reason for that place. Who had been in my house? And did they find what they wanted?

Chapter 12

Not my finest moment, sleeping in a closet with the inside deadbolt locked. Before I'd moved into my new home, I'd asked Shorty to replace my closet door with a solid core door and a deadbolt. Being married to a police officer, I'd learned the value of a safe room.

We'd replaced the door in our downstairs pantry in New Orleans, making it a safe place to take shelter in bad weather. Doug had been the lead detective on some dangerous cases, so he'd felt better knowing his family had a refuge from criminals too. We'd used it so often that I'd wanted a safe room in my new house, too.

Could I have called Shorty or Nate? Of course, and they'd have whisked me away to some motel on the outskirts of the parish. Nate might have put me up at his house, but that would endanger his family. Shorty would offer to house me as well, but that would be my backup plan after my backup plan. No, I thought it best to barricade myself in the closet with my SIG and cell phone. Shorty would get the full story in the morning and we'd go from there.

At 4 a.m. I called it morning and started the day. My SIG and I cleared the hallway and the living room. During the night, I'd had some time to think. Someone had gathered everything they needed from the case file, which meant they'd be looking for my notebook. My notebook would never leave my sight again.

My SIG, my notebook, my purse, and I made a hasty retreat. Next stop: the Trahan Veterinary Clinic. Next task: naming my dog. Normally, I had no say in naming pets because the kids handled it. This name had to be a good, solid Louisiana name, but not too cute or clever. Something personal and meaningful. Naming two kids wasn't this much trouble—was it? Matthew and Elliana? Of course, Matty didn't like his nickname anymore.

"Matty is a baby name, Mom! When you visit me at college, I'd prefer you called me Matt or Matthew."

My daughter had tolerated *Ellie* so far. Thank goodness dogs don't care what you call them, as long as it's not late for supper.

Ahhh...isopropyl alcohol and disinfectant! My father taught Cliff well, judging from the fresh smell in the lobby. Three cats in carriers, two dogs on leashes, and a young lady balancing a ferret cage. Small town vets treated a wide range of patients.

"Good morning, Debbie! So many animals in the lobby, yet it still smells clean! How do you do it?"

Debbie's freckles reminded me of the time Doug and I painted Matty's nursery. When I dipped my brush in the can of *Blue Bayou*, I'd playfully flicked it towards my husband. Specks of paint dotted his arm in a haphazard pattern. Just like Debbie's freckles. Only Debbie's spots framed her nose perfectly, giving her a girl-next-door vibe. Her strawberry blonde hair enhanced it. Why hadn't anyone snatched up that girl?

Debbie's *Tickled Pink* lips curved towards that adorable nose. "Well, Miss Ev, dogs and cats rely on their smell to know what's what. Dr. Cliff says if our lobby doesn't reflect our dedication to good health and happiness, then how can our patients trust us?" She leaned across the partition and dropped her voice a few decibels. "Let's just say our weekly shipment contains a good amount of disinfectant and antibacterial spray."

Cliff welcomed me back into a room, and his vet tech, Kimberly, brought in my dog. Was that *really* my dog? His now pink shiny back boasted new hair growth, and he'd gained a few pounds. Don't worry, kid—you and I will both work on losing our pitiful skin and bones features.

As Kimberly placed my pal on the exam table, he trembled. Oh, no! Was he frightened of me, too? Bending down so we could see eye to eye, I received a lick right on the mouth. Well played, dog, well played.

"This guy is shaking with joy to see you! That's a good sign, Ev."

Cliff turned his palm upward, to show friendship. A sniff of inspection, and Cliff passed the test. Moving his hand towards the dog's ears, he touched them just slightly. Another test passed, so Cliff moved on to the end goal of ear rubbing.

"So, Ev—do you have a name for this handsome fella? Because if you don't, I have a suggestion."

"Yes, please! My brain hurts from trying to find a good name for this guy."

Cliff nodded to Kimberly, who pulled out her phone.

"Kimberly comes in on the weekends to feed and walk the animals. She likes to play music for them—says it helps keep them calm. Of course, every animal is unique. Well, why don't you tell the story?"

Cliff's eyes crinkled as his smile reached cheek to cheek—what in the world got him so excited?

Kimberly held up her phone, right index finger paused over the screen. "This guy here, he didn't enjoy Adele or Dierks Bentley or even Phil

Wickham." Her nose scrunched up like a tossed piece of paper. "I mean, who doesn't like Phil Wickham? He's one of the most popular Christian artists right now."

We all laughed.

"Out of desperation, I tried Rosie Ledet—he loved her!"

Who the heck was that? Be cool, Ev. Hopefully someone will tell me, so I don't have to ask.

"So then I tried Terrance Simien, Andrus Espre, and Buckwheat Zydeco—he loved all of them!"

Wait a minute! Buckwheat Zydeco? Were we talking about zydeco music?

A blend of Creole, Cajun, gospel, and the blues, zydeco traditionally features an accordion and a washboard (called a frottoir). It originated in the boot, what we here in Louisiana refer to as down near the Gulf Coast. Doug and I frequented a club on Frenchmen Street in downtown New Orleans, featuring live bands playing blues, jazz, and zydeco. Amazing jambalaya too!

Kimberly's phone confirmed my hunch, broadcasting "Paper in My Shoe" by Boozoo Chavis. As if on cue, the dog's ears stood at attention and his tail wagged madly, like my windshield wipers in the last storm.

My dog had great taste.

"So what are we thinking here, guys? Boozoo? Buckwheat? Beau?"

What were the names of those other artists? Why didn't they teach this at Louisiana Tech?

Kimberly and Cliff shared a look, then turned back to me. Cliff, being the one with his name on the building, took the lead.

"Well, gosh, Ev! This dog likes all Zydeco music, at least all the music on Spotify. We think you should name him Zydeco!"

"Woof!"

Three sets of eyes fixed upon the dog, followed by a chorus of laughter. We had a winner!

"Great! I'll tell Debbie she can keep the name in the system. Truthfully, Ev, we'd all hoped you'd be okay with it." Cliff's brown eyes danced in the fluorescent lighting. "Since the entire staff's been calling him that for the last couple of days."

Debbie's precious nose scrunched at me, the center of her freckles. "That will be $298.54, Miss Ev. We take cash, checks, and credit cards."

Cliff had suspiciously vanished. "Hmm...how much would this have cost if I hadn't received the matchmaker special?"Debbie's nose flattened itself as she calculated my request. "Uh, $684.12." Nose back in scrunch position. "Will that be cash, check, or charge, Miss Ev?"

Shorty would have to buy his own *Zapp's* and orange soda. "Charge please, Debbie."

Strategy sessions with Shorty gave me a headache. My night of no sleep provided an opportunity to change our agenda. Step One involved a call to my PI explaining the situation.

"Look, this dog is costing me a lot more than I'd imagined. Could you bring your own snacks and drinks this morning?"

What? No grumbling? God works miracles every day. "No problem, Doc. Wouldja' like me t'bring ya' anything? *Mebbe* a breakfast *san-witch* from the coffee shop? An' a *chay tea lat-tay*? My treat."

Wow! God was working big miracles! Shorty offering to buy my food? Nope, that had never happened in the history of our friendship.

"Why thank you, Shorty! That would be wonderful." Wait a minute! Shorty offering to buy me food? Take a breath, Ev. Just enjoy God's blessings.

Zydeco lounged beneath my feet in the kitchen, content to sit under the bar while we finished our lunch. The dog definitely had trust issues with men, so both kept their distance.

Shorty's eyes fixed on Zydeco's paws. "That's gonna' be a big dog, Doc! At least sixty-five pounds or so! An' his head's gonna' hit yore hip fer sure! Why, look at them feet! Y'might wanna' sign up for the bulk rate dog food!"

More good news! Did pets count as dependents for tax purposes?

"Oh, Ethan called last night—let me fill you in." Ten minutes of Shorty's chewing and sipping was all the time I needed. My PI paid more attention to his food than my news, which irritated me.

We wandered into the living room for our strategy session, quarter cups of Maggie's caffeine delights in hand.

"I'd like to review the information we've gathered. We're all over the place in figuring out what's important and what's just small-town gossip." Why did I think this plan would work?

"Whatcha' talkin' about, Doc? I thought we was doin' pretty good!"

"Okay, then tell me: who's the killer?" This should be good.

Shorty's eyes stared me down. Was that pity? "Well gosh, Doc, that's easy! It's either Rob Dugas or Josh Fairchild!"

Possibly. "What about Sam Hughes? He threatened Michael both at work and on the internet. And he boasted of his gun knowledge at work. He knew about Michael's gun, and he knows how to shoot handguns."

"Okay, Doc. Keep goin'."

"He supposedly ran an errand after his doctor's appointment, then headed home. And the call to his girlfriend was near Michael's time of death."

What was that sound? Oh yes, the sound of my PI when he was wrong. The sound of silence.

"Okay, yer right. But, I don't think Stella or Faith did it. Do you?"

Poor Shorty! None of us enjoyed being wrong, and most of us had a hard time admitting it.

"No, I think you're right. I think Faith enjoys torturing her exes, and I don't think Stella did it. But she knows more than she's telling us."

"Okay then, Doc—what's next?" He glanced down at my feet, where Zydeco had planted himself. "Should I be jealous? Ya got a new bodyguard."

Did those ears need to be rubbed? Oh yes, they did, they sure did! "He's grateful to have a home. And I'm happy to have a roommate." More ear rubs? Of course!

Ear rubbing completed, Zy rested, head facing the front door. Even with Shorty, my Mossberg remained by the couch and my SIG rested on the coffee table.

Shorty had observed my new attachment to the SIG, but kept quiet. How much longer could he take it?

"Speakin' o' bodyguards, why're ya carryin' around that SIG? Is there somethin' yer not tellin' me?"

My friend listened without speaking, not always a good sign. No interruptions meant he was deep in thought, wheels turning to solve the problem at hand. Solutions were good, but Shorty felt his solution was the only one. Hopefully, we could agree.

"Well, I'm glad ya' got the dog. No way he's gonna' let anyone hurt ya, Doc." We both stared at my bodyguard. Closed eyes meant his ears were on duty. Every time Shorty shifted on the couch, those eyes popped open like a jack-in-the-box. But my movements caused no change in the guard's status. Unless I stood up.

"Mebbe y'shoulda called him Shadow, cuz ya ain't goin' nowhere without 'im!" Time for my friend to get serious. "But I'm still gonna' sleep over here, Doc. And before ya say anythin', jus' hear me out. If ya don't agree t'this, then I'll go tell yore brother about yore unwanted visitor, an' he'll ship ya off t'somewhere ya won't like. Don'tcha have relatives in Tuscaloosa?"

My body seized, as it always did when someone mentioned anything related to the *University That Shall Not Be Named*.

"Okay, Shorty, you win! No way am I going to Crimson Tide country! You can sleep in the guest room."

For the rest of our session, we created a grid of motive, means, and opportunity. As a mystery writer, I knew the killer had to have a reason (motive), a way (means), and a chance to kill (opportunity).

We'd mapped out Sam Hughes' motive, means, and opportunity. He threatened Michael both at work and on the internet (motive). He had knowledge of guns and he knew about Michael's handgun (means). His girlfriend insisted he ran an errand after his doctor's appointment, then headed home. Detectives confirmed Sam kept his doctor's appointment, and cell phone records showed he called his girlfriend around the time of the murder. Sam had no receipts to prove his errand (opportunity). Unfortunately, Stella had popped on the radar, so the detectives shifted their investigation and Sam was off the hook.

What about Stella Cook? She convinced Shorty of her innocence, but her answers were almost too perfect. She easily threw blame on Rob and

Sam. Deputies found drugs in Stella's home—she and Michael could have fought over that, or money. Definitely a motive. Stella admitted she knew that Michael still had the gun, and that Michael didn't realize she knew (means). Stella lived in the house with Michael and couldn't account for her whereabouts the night of the murder (opportunity).

Faith Dixon enjoyed torturing her exes, but perhaps she'd gone too far? Michael humiliated her in front of co-workers, and it quickly became small-town gossip (motive). Maybe she'd shot guns with her father at the gun range, but did she know about Michael's handgun? The means was weak. Her alibi was her grandmother, who claimed they watched a *Matlock* marathon all night (lack of opportunity). Of course, watching television with my father meant watching him sleep (opportunity). Also, according to Shorty, guns are a woman's preferred choice of murder weapon.

Rob Dugas checked every box on the suspect checklist! A convicted drug dealer always needing money (motive) who definitely knew his way around guns (means). He knew Michael owned a gun too (also means). Neighbors identified Rob's car the night of Michael's murder, and he had no alibi (opportunity). Again, detectives shifted their focus to Stella and left Rob alone.

Which brought us to Josh Fairchild. As much as I didn't want him to be the killer, I had to look at the facts. He definitely had some sort of past, whether it was shoplifting, armed robbery, or worse. Shorty's friend, Monty, thought it leaned toward the worse side of the scale, and Nate had some suspicions too. In the file he penciled, *Stella's drug dealer*? Josh and Michael argued the night before the murder, loud enough that the neighbors heard. Did they really argue about Josh giving Stella money, or something else? Yeah, there was something going on in the motive department.

As for means, Stella confirmed Josh knew his way around guns and was at the house frequently. Being buddies with Michael Sr., he certainly knew about the handgun.

Opportunity? Shannon the Librarian confirmed Josh spent the evening with her. Despite Shorty's theory on librarians, we couldn't verify Josh's alibi. He had the most credible lack of opportunity out of all the suspects, though. Did Shannon lie to protect her boyfriend?

"Hel...lo Dolly! They all look guilty tuh me! Maybe it's some sorta *sit-choo-ay-shun*, like that story about everybody on a train killin' the guy!"

"You mean *Murder on the Orient Express*? You've read the book?" Impressive.

"No, Doc! But I took a lady friend out tuh supper, an' she wanted t'go see the movie. Same thing."

Not quite.

Chapter 13

S horty and I prepared a list of people to interview. Lila Trahan called, reminding me to drop off her autographed books. My thoughts huddled in the corner of my mind, preoccupied with the case. But I vowed to stay awhile and visit with my new friend.

"Evangeline! Your call warmed my heart. Please come in—I put on a pot of coffee." Most respectable Southerners drank coffee and iced tea, so as a hot tea drinker I'd learned to drink dark brew and cold tea all hours of the day.

Lila's home warmed me with its charm and elegance. Although the first generation left home ages ago, her grandchildren and great-grandchildren visited most every weekend. Yet Lila never compromised style to secure her home from curious hands and busy feet. Vintage teacups lounged in locked cabinets, letting children look without touching. Bookshelves didn't offer locking doors, but Lila discovered a solution. Lower shelves housed stuffed animals and wheeled toys, an open invitation for playing. But just above Tonka trucks and Baby Tenderlove dolls, Lila's tatted doilies cradled Windsor depression glass and first edition books.

As my eyes traveled the length of her cabinets, I chuckled. My friend's life experiences had obviously taught her the exact height of a child who was old enough to leave her treasures alone. That height appeared to be four feet. My attention turned to Lila's Old Country Roses china, peeking out from the locked cabinet. Just like Stella's dishes. I was once again reminded of the case. Fortunately, my friend had information to share.

After Lila re-shelved Detective Lou Bergeron and his twelve cases, she poured the coffee and set out tea cakes. Fresh from the oven, judging from the tantalizing smell lingering in the room.

"You know, dear, I had lunch with Faith Dixon's grandmother yesterday. We had a lovely visit, and she shared some insight I wanted to pass along."

Straight to the point—oh, how I loved this woman!

"Edith practically raised Faith, and they are extremely close. Edith nearly had a nervous breakdown when deputies came to her door last year to question her. Since then, she has hardly had a good night's sleep, worrying if Faith is involved in that Cook boy's murder."

Okay, Lila, get to the good part!

"Edith heard you reopened the investigation, so she wanted me to pass along a few things." Lila sipped her sugared up coffee and took a bite of tea cake. "Evangeline, please don't use this information against the poor girl! Faith never told the detectives, but she went to Michael's home the night of the murder. That misguided young lady wanted to give him a piece of her mind about the way he ended the relationship."

Truthfully, I was on the fence about Faith. Many women killed exes, so theoretically Faith could fall into that category. Shorty's gun research hammered that point home.

Perhaps Faith visited Michael for closure?

A college memory drifted into my head...Brian Fields.

Brian Fields took me out for pizza my freshman year at Louisiana Tech. He walked me to the dorm and kissed me goodnight. Then he never called again. Two months later, I spotted him at the same pizza joint with friends and I snapped. As Brian shoved a slice into his mouth, I began my tirade:

"How dare you! How dare you take me out for pizza, kiss me goodnight, and promise to call me? Then you didn't!"

He'd committed a terrible crime, a borderline felony really. My older, wiser self finally admitted that Brian did what many young people had done before him—he changed his mind. Faith might only be guilty of being human.

"Perhaps I should talk to Faith myself, Lila. You know, so I can hear everything from her directly." Definitely take Shorty with me, so he could work his charms. Better yet, just send Shorty over there...

"That's a good idea, Evangeline. Faith is dating someone new, and she's quite happy. Edith doesn't believe her granddaughter had anything to do with the murder." Lila took another bite of teacake as she contemplated Faith's innocence. "Although Edith admits she fell asleep during the *Matlock* marathon, so she honestly can't confirm Faith never left the house."

Back to square one with Faith Dixon.

After twenty minutes, I wrapped up my visit with Lila. Nate agreed to meet me for lunch to answer a few questions. And to check up on me, of course. As I told Lila, being late to an appointment with Nate, invited both a lecture and an interrogation.

My brother suggested the Shining Stars Cafe in downtown Graisseville, and I arrived exactly at noon. Of course, Nate had already parked his department issued navy sedan squarely in the middle of a parking space. Had he measured the distance on both sides, to ensure they were equal? Knowing my brother, he had a tape measure in his car for that very task.

Nate smiled as I entered the cafe, but I knew he'd glanced at his phone. *How late was I?*

"You look good, Ev! Not so gaunt, more filled out."

And we were off to a great start! In nine words and a glance, my brother let me know I was late, by his standards, but fatter and less like a starving war refugee. Maybe tomorrow I'd do something right.

"Thanks Nate! For the record, I'm right on time. We'd said noon, and I pushed the door open at exactly that time."

"Well, yes. But really, to be on time is to be late and to be early is on time."

Only in your world, Nate—which I didn't choose to live in.

"Anyway, what looks good to you?" Changing the subject worked in both our best interests.

"I've heard the grilled chicken salad with strawberries is excellent. But the bacon cheeseburger is supposed to be fantastic too. Actually, I've not heard anything bad about this place. Gracie St. Clair, the owner, is a wonderful chef."

"St. Clair? I don't recognize that name." Less than six months back here, and I played the game without thinking. You know, the small-town name game. Who's related to whom, and where did they grow up?

"She used to be Gracie Dunbar. She graduated about fifteen years after you did, Ev. So, you probably don't know her. She moved back here with her three kids after her husband left her for someone on the internet."

Oh, good grief! Did I really need to know that? Who was I kidding? It was small-town America—of course I did.

Thankfully, Gracie appeared to take our order. "Hello, folks! What would you like to drink?"

Goodness, did she hear Nate's last comment? Burying my nose inside the menu, I mumbled, "Sweet tea with lemon, please." Leave her a big tip, Ev!

Nate's sources were correct—the bacon cheeseburger made my heart weep. Before it reached the table, the bacon and beef smell danced together with the American cheese, forming a conga line directly to my nostrils. My hunger had become less shy since I'd promised Shorty to put meat on my bones. Bacon and beef aromas shoved each other aside as they rushed to our table. My stomach uttered a low growl. Grab your tea glass, Ev, and shake it! Make some noise.

"What are you doing? You're being so loud I can't hear anything." All part of the plan, little brother. "Have you forgotten how to act in public? Settle down and eat your food. Geez, I feel like I'm talking to my kids."

And people wondered why Nate and I didn't spend much time together, just the two of us.

Once I'd consumed half my burger, my stomach settled down and so did Nate. We sipped our tea and carried on a respectable conversation. A respectable conversation about murder, killers, and my lapse in judgment to hire Shorty.

"What were you thinking, exactly? Yes, Shorty has his PI license, but he's never had a case!"

"Gosh Nate, is that what the sheriff's department told you? We're very sorry, Mr. Bergeron. Although you've passed the academy training, you've never worked on a case. Don't let the door hit you on the way out."

My brother unleashed one of his famous *that isn't remotely funny* glares.

"It's not the same at all, and you know that! You've never had a case either, and you haven't even had training. Sheriff Dupre sat me down this morning and told me he's getting phone calls about you and Shorty gallivanting all over the parish asking a lot of questions. Do you have anything to show for it?"

Gallivanting? www.thefreedictionary.com defines the word as, *to roam about in search of pleasure or amusement.* Driving around with Shorty definitely did not qualify as either. Should I continue to exasperate my brother? It was great fun, but not getting this case solved.

"Give me one more week. If Shorty and I can't crack it by then, I'll hand over everything we've learned and we'll back off."

Nate gave me a *let me decide if I should believe you* stare. Between him and Bonnie, poor Jack and Syd would never get away with anything.

"That's not my call, so let me check with the sheriff. But I guess one week might be okay."

Should I hug my brother? Definitely not at that moment, and probably not soon. Either he'd drunk some of Syd's homemade lemonade (a glass of water and two lemons—no sugar), or he was pretty unhappy. Given the choice between Syd's lemonade and finishing our meal, I'd take the lemonade.

"Okay, Nate, could you explain one of your notes in the file? Why did you scribble something by Josh Fairchild's name about how he could be Stella's drug dealer?" Maybe I could salvage this lunch date.

"I'm not sure. Josh appears to be an upstanding citizen. When I run his name through all the databases, it comes up clean. Even when I run combinations of his first and middle names, nothing pops up. But Rob Dugas let something slip in an interview—what did he say exactly?" Nate's lemonade look disappeared, replaced with crinkly eyebrows and pouty lips. That *I left my keys somewhere...where could that be?* look.

"Oh yeah! I worked an angle where Rob sold drugs to Stella. Michael found out and tried to stop him. He'd helped Rob with money issues, but when he discovered his friend was selling drugs to his sister, he confronted Rob. The problem was, we had trouble making that theory stick. We found drugs while searching the house, but Stella said they were from back when she was an addict. We arrested her, but her fancy lawyer got the search thrown out."

"Rob admitted he knew Stella, but when I brought up Josh's name, he stopped talking. Said he wanted a lawyer, and his daddy would pay for it. We had to shut down the interview." Had I ever seen my brother so burdened?

Gracie arrived with the bill and Nate grabbed it before I could protest. He offered his credit card, then waited for her to clear our space.

"Why would you bring up Josh's name to Rob? Do they know each other?"

"To be honest, Ev, I wasn't sure. But I had five suspects and nobody was talking. So I asked each person about their relationship with the other four. Stella was cool as a cucumber when I mentioned Josh, but Rob got all twitchy. Josh looked in on the Cook kids after their parents passed, and hung out with Michael frequently. It stands to reason they could have bumped into each other."

Gracie returned with Nate's ticket and we thanked her for the amazing meal. My brother walked me to my car, but I still had questions.

"How did you make the jump from Rob as a drug dealer to Josh as a dealer too?"

Nate opened my door for me and I slid inside. "If Rob had known Josh through legitimate avenues, then he would have said so. His eyes told me he knew Josh, so it must have been through something illegal."

Next on my list was Hugh Cormier, Shorty's cousin and editor of the *Graisseville Gazette*. Shorty and Hugh got along just fine, but I'd asked for the interview. Hugh used to work for *The Times-Picayune* in New Orleans. Honestly, I wanted to chat with someone from my old stomping grounds.

Hugh's daughter, Julie, met me—hands working furiously as if she was wringing out a wet dish towel. "Oh, Miss Ev, I'm Julie Morris, Hugh's daughter. My mama tripped on the throw rug in the living room, and Daddy had to take her to the urgent care in Zachary. He wanted me to meet you and apologize for his absence." That dish towel should be almost dry, if it were real.

"He left me some notes for you, which I've placed in this envelope." Julie stopped wringing long enough to hand it to me. "Again, Daddy is so sorry! He said he will call you when he's able to get in front of his calendar and reschedule."

Shorty promised Hugh knew almost as much about the goings-on in Graisseville as he did. "Heck, ol' Hugh's the *ed-it-tore* of the newspaper! If he don't know somethin', then it prob'ly ain't news, anyway!"

Well, Hugh, will you live up to your cousin's bragging?

My fingers ripped open the edge and flipped over the envelope. Out fluttered a single white sheet of paper, words neatly printed across the page in black ink:

1-Sam Hughes' co-workers confirm Sam left at exactly the same time as Michael several times over a three-month period. It appeared Sam was stalking Michael.

2-Sam called his girlfriend the day of the murder and told her he lied to the police about his whereabouts after his doctor's appointment. He'd actually driven to the Cook home to confront Michael, but changed his mind. Told her he had to run an errand, then would head home. Girlfriend couldn't reach him until the next morning.

3-Faith Dixon knew there was a hidden key under the flowerpot. She could have entered the Cook home and stolen the gun, waited for the victim, etc.

4-Michael Cook confronted Josh Fairchild the day before the murder, because Josh gave Stella drugs, not cash. Cannot verify this information with a second source.

Thanks to my two informants, I had some interesting information. Sam still didn't have an alibi, and lied to the police about where he was after his doctor's appointment. He could have been stalking Michael before murdering him!

Faith had no alibi either, since her grandmother confessed to Lila about her snoozing. Faith also had a way in the house.

Josh could be a drug dealer. One thing was certain...my case didn't look good. And neither did my one dating prospect.

Rob Dugas rounded out my interviews for the day, and I was hoping he might just confess and save me a lot of trouble. But I wasn't holding my breath.

I'd be the first to admit I didn't know what a drug dealer looked like. On TV they wore lots of fancy jewelry and sported gold teeth. Rob looked nothing like the drug dealers on *Blue Bloods*.

He answered the door and greeted me with a *yes ma'am* and a *won't you come in, please*? At five foot seven, the young man barely filled the doorframe, and his sandy hair was already receding. Couldn't a drug dealer pay membership dues to the *Hair Club for Men*?

"I'm afraid I only have water. Would you like some?" What year did I buy my leather weekend bag? Oh, my goodness, I had luggage older than this kid!

"Water would be great, Rob, thank you. May I sit?" After visiting turn of the century homes, his apartment was a change of pace. Still, someone had raised this young man to have good manners. In my book, that counted for something.

Water in hand, I began my interview. "First of all, thank you for taking time out of your busy schedule to meet with me. As you probably know, I'm assisting the sheriff's department with the murder of Michael Cook. Is there anything you'd like to tell me? Anything you didn't tell the detectives, but you've since remembered?" A long shot, but what could I lose?

Rob tapped his glass rhythmically—where had I heard that beat before? Wait, a minute! Elvis Presley's "Jailhouse Rock." Interesting choice.

"Um, well, I'm not sure what you're looking for. Stella was older than me in school, so I hardly knew her. Me and Michael ran around together but lost touch after graduation. I mean, I tried to stay in touch, but he was always busy. Sometimes I'd drop by the house, for old times' sake. 'Specially after his parents died in the car crash."

More Elvis tapping.

"Um, I s'pose you know," he continued, "Stella left school when the principal found drugs in her locker? Michael and I became closer after that."

"Well, not really. Could you tell me about the drugs in Stella's locker? Do you know who told the principal?"

More Elvis, but also shifting from side to side on the couch. Was Rob dancing? Or was he getting uncomfortable?

"Uh, well, it was Michael. Stella tells everybody that she and Michael were the best of friends. But that's not true at all. Michael loved Stella—she was his big sister. But he didn't trust her and wasn't close to her—not really."

Hmm, okay. "Tell me about your relationship with Michael. A few people think you owe money that you can't repay. That you're desperate, and you looked to Michael to bail you out."

Should I request another song? Maybe something less jangly—the poor glass looked like it would break from all the tapping. Maybe "Love Me Tender?"

"Who told you that? Huh?" Rob dropped the glass on the coffee table with a *thump*. But then what to do with his hands? The glass came back off the table for an encore. "Look, whoever told you that was just tryin' to put the blame on me! These so-called 'informed people' exaggerated, just plain lied, really!"

A pause in the concert.

"Honestly, ma'am, I've never owed more than a few hundred dollars at a time. Sure, I asked Michael for cash. You know, for old times' sake. My parents have lots of money—my dad owns Dugas Construction. If I need money, I can always go to them."

Down went the glass—the second show finished earlier than expected.

"Let's switch gears. You own several guns, correct? Do you own a concealed carry permit?"

Rob picked up the glass—Elvis' encore? "No ma'am, I don't have a permit. As you know, I'm a convicted felon, so I can't have a permit. In fact, the sheriff took all my guns when he arrested me."

No encore—did Elvis leave the building? Was it because Rob told the truth? He didn't have any guns? With no guns, it made sense for him to use Michael's instead.

"But didn't you and Michael used to shoot guns?"

Rob put down the glass, so I had a hard time working out the truth.

"Ma'am, I don't know what you've heard. But I haven't done anything that would violate my parole. Including shooting guns, or holding guns, or anything to do with guns."

His reply sounded like someone who had violated his parole and didn't want to go back to prison. Probably best to take another path, because I wasn't going to get a truthful answer.

"What can you tell me about Josh Fairchild?"

Not only had Elvis exited, but Ev followed quickly. "Miss Ev, I'm going to ask you to leave now. My lawyer advised me against talking to you, and it sounds like I should have listened to him."

To add insult to injury, I couldn't get "Jailhouse Rock" out of my head. Hopefully Shorty's day had been more productive.

Chapter 14

My PI met me for supper at Señor Sombrero. We planned to give reports for the day, and hopefully run into River. Shorty reminded me that his share of the meal fell under *plus expenses*. How could I forget?

"Welcome to Señor Sombrero! How many in your party?"

Why were the greeters always so cheerful? Doug and I joked that greeter interviews must be based on cheerleader tryouts—pom-poms optional of course. If a young person belted out a cheer while high kicking, they secured a greeter spot.

"Just two please, and a booth."

And why did they question my math skills? With a smile, of course, but most wondered if I could count without using my fingers.

"Only two, then?"

Was that a dig at my social life? Only two? Why couldn't it be a date? *Oh, good grief! Please don't think it's a date!*

"Yes, only two. And, we're just friends, nothing more. He has a girlfriend and I'm a widow. It's been over three years, but I don't feel ready to date. Yet, anyway. Although there was this guy, but now I'm thinking he might be..."

This was why the kids didn't want me talking to anyone.

The server led me to the table in silence, probably a first for her. My waitress appeared, and I ordered my standard house red wine.

"Oh, last time I had the most delightful young man named River. Is he working tonight?" My eyes scanned the dim restaurant, but I couldn't find him.

She stared at me for a moment, the smile melting from her face. "Ma'am, I have a lot of experience waiting tables. There's no reason to ask for another server."

Maybe Matty and Ellie were right. Maybe I shouldn't speak to anyone in public. Perhaps I could have a sign made— *This person is deaf and mute. Please ignore her.* Would Shorty ever show up?

My PI arrived at the same time as my wine. "Doc, how many times do I gotta' tell ya'? Never drink alone—people will talk about ya'!"

Being deaf and mute could be a good thing for our relationship.

"Then order a beer and I won't be the only one."

Our waitress' smile resurfaced—was any woman immune to his charms? She also took our food order and left us to our chips and salsa.

"All righty, Doc, who's goin' first?"

"Since you're the one with a mouthful of chips, how about I start?"

Notebook and teal pen in hand, I carefully outlined my revelations about Faith and my interview with Rob. Next, I pulled out my list of clues from Cousin Hugh.

"Yeah, I heard about Margie—poor little thing! She sprained her *ane-kull*, but she's doin' better. Hugh said Miss Ava Guidry brought over a Louisiana crunch cake when Margie came home."

Where was he going with this?

"Yeah, I was thinkin' I should go over and see how my poor *cuzzin's* doin'."

And sample some crunch cake, of course.

"Of course, yes, you should definitely do that. Now tell me about your day."

Through mouthfuls of beef enchilada, my PI gave me his version of a complete and concise report.

"Me n' Sam Hughes had a good long talk—didja' know his *cuzzin* married my best friend's sister from high school? We both went tuh the *batch-ler* party and the weddin'—ain't that a kick in the pants?"

A slow sip of wine, Ev. He'd get there when he got there.

"Turns out that *batch-ler* party that we both went to? It was at The Treasure Chest by Lake Pontchartrain. *That's* where Sam was the night o' the murder, with some buddies."

See? I knew we'd get there, eventually. "Then why did he lie about the errand and going home to fall asleep all night?"

Oh, Ev...did you really want to know?

"Oh, that's easy! Sam didn't want his girlfriend t'know he stayed out all night with his buddies. So, he lied tuh her. But then Michael turned up dead an' all, so Sam had t'keep the lie goin'. He even got his girlfriend t'lie for him by tellin' everyone he'd come over tuh her place. But he'd lied tuh her an' said he went home an' fell asleep. Man, I thought *I* was good! This guy might teach me a trick or two!"

Nope, not even going to touch that big, hot mess.

"Okay, so can Sam prove he was at the casino during the time of the murder?"

Shorty pulled up his phone and showed me his key piece of evidence. "Oh yeah, he can! Sam won big that night an' had t'fill out those *guv-err-munt* papers, so they can take all yore money."

Should I? Oh, why not? "You mean Sam had to fill out a W-9, so the casino could report his income to the IRS?" Wrong answer, Ev.

With a flick of one wrist, he dismissed my knowledge, while the other guided his fork into his mouth. "Yeah, yeah, yeah—that's what I said. He got copies o' those papers an' he let me take pictures of 'em. He says the casino can prove he was there with those timestamp things."

Another sip of wine seemed in order. "Well great! We can officially cross off Sam Hughes. Who's next?"

Shorty waved over our server. "Young lady, couldja get me a glass o' sweet tea, just as sweet as those dimples on yore face?"

Giggling, our server hustled to make Shorty's wishes come true.

"Isn't she too young for you?" *Tea as sweet as your dimples?* She had to be young to fall for that line.

"Doc, no one is too old or too young t'get a compliment. That's just a fact o' life. An' before y'keep goin' with this, I'm not gonna' ask fer her number. But I betcha' ten bucks she writes it on the ticket."

Nope, not taking that bet. "Could we continue, please?"

If I hadn't witnessed the entire meal, I'd think that Shorty licked his plate clean. Not a morsel of food remained. Growing up in the middle of six kids taught a person a few things: Money doesn't grow on trees, and eat everything on your plate. Next time, the plate might not be as full.

"It would interest ya' t'know that Josh definitely has a temper! Sam and Michael didn't geehaw, but they had mutual friends. Not t'mention co-workers. Michael didn't like Stella workin' for Josh, or him comin' over all the time. Now Josh never hurt him or Stella, but Michael heard a few *con-ver-say-shuns* Josh had on the phone. *Con-ver-say-shuns* with other folks, where he was threatenin' people. Tellin' 'em they'd better straighten up or else."

Or else what? "Shorty, what does that even mean?"

Most of the time, Shorty took great patience with my lack of street smarts. Even though our fathers had been best friends, we came from two different worlds. In my world, children always had enough to eat and the biggest worry of the week was having a date on Friday night. Shorty's world had a lot of love, but not much else. My mother sent me to school with extra sandwiches for the Cormier kids. Later, I realized why we prepared monstrous platters of muffalettas on LSU game days. The Cormiers ate one good meal that day and took home lots of leftovers.

"Look Doc, I don't know exactly what 'or else' means. But I'm bettin' it means somethin' off the books. Well, speak o' the devil!"

"Well hello, Ev, and Mr. Cormier! So nice to see you this evening!"

Ev, don't look at those amazing teeth or that wildly attractive salt and pepper hair. Murderer, Ev—this guy was a murderer. Well, he was probably a murderer. Actually, he might be a murderer. Maybe he just knew who the murderer was. Did that make him a bad person? How far was the state prison? Focus, Ev—no need to be on the next season of *Love After Lockup.*

This was the one time Shorty focused better than me. "Well, hello there, Mr. Fairchild. Why don'tcha' join us?"

Josh's face lit up. He might be a suspect, but he sure was easy on the eyes. His smile alone could get him on the cover of...well, the cover of some magazine that featured extremely good-looking men.

"It would be my pleasure, it truly would! This place is my standard pickup meal joint when I've got nothing else going on. Let me pay for it and join you."

Shorty leaned across the table. "This is great, Doc! We need to interview him anyway, and this looks less *uh-fish-ull*. Keep yore notebook an' that *ri-dik-you-luss* green pen outta' sight."

Probably not the best time to mention it was a teal pen.

Josh casually slid into the chair beside me. Did my heart skip a beat? Maybe I should actually watch *Love After Lockup*, to see how people handled relationships with felons. Stop it, Ev!

My active imagination kept my sanity in check—and produced some fine mystery fiction books. No, I would never date someone in prison. But joking about it gave me a release. Yes, I had a bizarre sense of humor.

Josh pursued. "How's the investigation going? Any new insights?"

What did murder suspects eat? From the grocery store, I learned that my suspect consumed fresh produce. When dining out, however, choosy suspects preferred chicken fajita salad with dressing on the side. Oh yes, the investigation...

"We was jus' talkin' about that Josh. What kin ya' tell me about Rob Dugas? Do y'know 'im very well? He claims he hardly knows Stella—jus' Michael." Thank goodness for Shorty.

Our suspect chewed as his steel blues wandered to the right, then the left. What did that mean? Since Stella's interview, every morning I'd recall there was something I needed to research. My notebook yielded nothing. After three days I'd remembered to research which way eyes gazed if someone was lying. Google informed me that looking to the right meant someone was not telling the truth. The right side of the brain handled the creative side, so the liar glanced right to access that side and create the lies. Two days later, I'd remembered which way Stella had looked (right), but couldn't remember what she'd said while looking right. In the future, I would write down which way the interviewees looked as well as what they said. My fifty-year-old memory and I didn't hang out together much anymore. But what did *both* ways mean? Dang it, Ev! And dang Shorty for making me put away my notebook.

"Rob hardly knows Stella? That's not true—exactly. Well, maybe it is. You see," Josh paused to take another bite of salad and swallow it.

This guy might be a suspect, but he had the best table manners I'd seen in a long while.

"Rob and Stella know each other through me. Rob helps me out now and then, when I need someone to pick up dry cleaning supplies or deliver orders. You see, at Best Dry Cleaners, we offer a mobile service serving a thirty-mile radius. Let me give you a card."

Shorty waved off the card, but I took one and placed it on the table. Josh smiled through his eyes, as if to say, *we both know this guy hasn't seen the inside of a dry cleaner for quite some time.* Truthfully, I hadn't seen one in a while either. Our cleaners in New Orleans picked up Doug's uniforms for cleaning, so I understood the words, *mobile dry cleaners.* My clothes rarely required cleaning, and it wasn't in the budget, anyway.

Josh continued. "But to answer your question, are they friends? Probably not."

"Next question then. What's your relationship with the Cook kids?" Shorty definitely saved all his charm for the ladies.

Josh found my gaze and locked in. "As I've mentioned, Michael Sr. was my best friend. When he and his wife died, I did the best I could to pick up the pieces and hold their kids together. Stella wouldn't mind me saying this, I'm sure, but she's always thought of me as a surrogate father. Michael too, I think. Let me tell you something. Those kids grew up practically in front of me, and I loved them like my own. Stella and Michael were the best of friends—we were a loving family, much like that old show. What was it called? With Brian Keith and that large, jolly man?"

Josh loved *Family Affair*? The perfect man...except for potentially killing someone.

"The show was *Family Affair*—Brian Keith, Sebastian Cabot, Kathy Garver, Johnny Whitaker, and Anissa Jones. It ran for about five seasons."

Josh snapped his fingers. "Yes! That's right! Thank you, Ev!"

Shorty's horse snort reared its ugly head, but Josh's perfect smile made it all worthwhile.

My PI kept his rapid fire steady, like his M-16 during the Gulf War. "So, didja know anythin' about Rob's money issues? We keep gettin' different stories, an' since ya was his boss, mebbe y'know somethin'."

Such perfect manners—*maybe Josh attended cotillion?*

Graisseville didn't have a program for young people to learn social skills and dancing. For us, that was high school social events. It wasn't pretty. Matty and Ellie attended cotillion in New Orleans, although I'd find empty bait buckets in the trash from Cochiaras Marina. Along with empty soda cans and wrappers from their famous bacon cheeseburgers. Doug didn't always support my efforts to teach our children proper manners.

"Oh, Rob's official story is that people exaggerate, or misunderstand. Sometimes he calls them out-and-out liars. The truth is, he loved gambling, but wasn't good at it. My sources tell me Rob had some serious lowlifes after him for the money he owed. It wouldn't surprise me if he turned up one day with his face rearranged. Or worse."

Our suspect placed his fork on the table. The guy hadn't even asked for metal tableware, but used his plastic fork and knife included in the to-go bag. Yet, he still ate more politely than any man I'd ever met. What a pity!

"Thank you for a delightful supper! The food here is top-notch, but tonight the company kicked it up a few levels."

Was he talking about me? Josh's compliment came straight toward me—right? After the way Shorty treated our suspect, why wouldn't those delightful words be for me? The compliment sent a warm flow of happiness into my heart and put a smile on my lips.

As soon as Josh left the restaurant, I grabbed my notebook and pen. *Research why people look both left and right when speaking.* There! Shorty snorted again.

"Geez, Doc, didja offer anythin' tuh the interview? Other than yore eyelashes flutterin' an' yore breath gaspin' in *adj-you-lay-shun*?"

How did he know that word, adulation? And did he wake up mean, or did he pull it out of the closet and put it on for the day?

"Let me pay for our supper and we can talk later." Yes, the ticket confirmed that I would have lost ten bucks. Right on top, with a pink heart, the server wrote her number. This night totally stunk!

Shorty smoothed the server's ruffled feathers. Even so, I wanted to apologize.

"Here's your tip—Charlene, isn't it? Look, you did a great job tonight—thank you so much! Let me be honest."

Gently cradling Charlene's elbow, I guided her back a couple of steps.

"Does River still work here? He's not a friend exactly, but he shared some concerns about a mutual person we know. Since I don't have his contact information, I hoped to see him tonight and follow up on our mutual friend. Do you know how I can get in touch with him?" A twenty on a thirty-dollar meal made for a friendly server.

"As far as I know, River still works here. He had the 6 p.m. shift tonight, but never showed. And so, I had to work a double. You might talk to the manager, though." She pointed a bubble gum pink nail toward a kid not much older than her.

Inner Circle's "Bad Boys" blasted from my phone. Nate hated the theme song from the TV show *Cops*, so it had to be his ringtone. *Bad boys, bad boys, whatcha' gonna' do, whatcha' gonna' do when they come for you?* Strangely enough, he liked the show itself.

"Excuse me, Charlene. I need to take this call. Thanks for your help."

Did she even hear me? The back of her head accepted my gratitude.

"Ev, do you know a man named River Woods?"

Truly, how many male Rivers could there be? And what was his middle name? Maybe *In-the*? If so, did the mother of River In-the Woods really love him? Why would someone burden their child with such a name?

"Um, probably. I know a *River*, but I'm not sure what his last name is."

"Okay, call Shorty and tell him to meet you at a place called The Dirty Pelican. Do you know where that is?"

Definitely a trick question. "Well, I have a GPS on my phone, so I'm sure I can find it."

"Sounds good. Get Shorty to meet you at your house, then drive there together. You won't want to subject your car to the roads."

You're telling me!

My brother—always the last word. "Oh, and Ev?"

"Yes, Nate?"

"Be prepared to identify a body. And please don't tell my wife I asked you to do that. Or Dad either."

"Of course, Nate."

Okay...I'm so sorry, Lord, for poking fun at River. That was not my finest moment, and I didn't realize he was dead when I made fun of him. Oh, and his parents! Please forgive me for criticizing his parents' naming talents. Lord, You gave me a quirky sense of humor for a purpose and a plan. Help me use it to further Your Kingdom, not tear down Your children. Amen.

Should I call back and ask...what does one wear to a crime scene? Yeah...probably not.

Chapter 15

A s I approached Zy's crate, his tail whacked the floor rhythmically. No barks to greet me, but that would come. Hopefully, he wouldn't need me much longer to supervise his yard duties either. Watching a dog sniff and lift a leg for twenty minutes hadn't hit my list of favorite activities.

My shadow escorted me to my closet, where I dug out a pair of hiking boots. Had they ever been on my feet? Oh yes, once—when I tried them on. After their crime scene adventures, my boots would beg to stay in for a while.

Zy returned to his crate. I laced my boots and locked the front door behind me. My PI sat in his F-150, headlights cutting a path for my trek.

"Doc, why does it take women five seconds t'change their minds, but an hour t'change shoes? Can y'explain that tuh me? Huh?"

Shorty pretended irritation, but I sensed his excitement. Our first crime scene! If only it could have been someone I didn't know, or even didn't like. Could I look at River's dead body?

"Seein' as how I know women so good, I went back tuh Señor's an' asked 'em t'brew a pot o' coffee for me an' a pot o' tea for you. Then I went tuh the dollar store an' got us a coupla' those big travel mugs. Figured I'd have time t'kill waitin' for ya', so I made myself useful."

He did indeed. "My tumbler is the pink glittery one, right? The picture of a garden with the words, *butterflies are self-propelled flowers*?" What did that even mean? "Yours, of course, is purple and gold with the LSU logo on it. The school I actually attended."

"Look, Doc, there wasn't a lot o' choices! Geez, why do I even bother?"

Why was I pushing Shorty's buttons? Normally I'd not even care what tumbler he bought me. "I'm sorry. Please forgive me. It's just that identifying a dead body isn't how I planned to spend my evening."

A grunt confirmed my apology had been accepted.

River's death yanked the case down yet another path. Faith Dixon seemed a less likely suspect, unless I could prove she and River knew each other. No, River's drug history made the other three suspects more, well...suspect-y. Suspect-ish? Pretty darn guilty looking.

Sam's solid alibi took him off the list for good. As for Stella, River claimed they were good friends—would she kill him? As I thought back to our interview, I realized Stella lied about at least one thing. She'd claimed to have forgotten about the drugs found in her home, but did that make any sense? Addicts don't forget their stash locations.

Don't forget Stella looking to the right as she spoke. Why hadn't I noted the direction she'd looked, and what answers she'd given? Still, according to Google, Stella lied during her interview. But why?

In many ways, the crime scene resembled my favorite TV shows. People gawked behind crime scene tape, probably patrons from The Dirty Pelican. Sheriff's deputies stood with arms crossed, grim statues guarding the evidence. No TV cameras though—this small-town crime registered a tiny blip on Baton Rouge's radar. My eyes scanned the spectators, looking for

Hugh Cormier. Nope, the editor of Graisseville's paper snoozed away in his cozy bed. Tomorrow morning he'd stop by the substation with a plate of Maggie's baked goods and a tray stacked with lidded coffee cups. Then, within the comfort of four gray walls, he'd sip and nibble as he collected the important details.

My phone vibrated, singing the theme from *Murder She Wrote*. Angela Lansbury's theme song signaled that I hadn't assigned a special ringtone to my caller. Glancing down, I saw Ethan's name. Might be time to find him one.

"Hey Ev, sorry to bother you so late at night. But I scored a piece of news you'll want to hear."

"Uh, sure Ethan. But make it quick. I'm at a crime scene." Was there pride in my voice? Ev, really? Your mother taught you better than to enjoy someone else's misery.

"Oh, wow! Okay, well, you'll have to tell me all about it later. I'll keep it brief. A buddy of mine is better at digging up dirt on the internet than I am, so I asked him to look into your suspects. He found a way around Josh Fairchild's sealed juvie records—a way to unseal them so to speak."

No way! Nate's department couldn't even do that. Well, not without a warrant, anyway. Might be best not to mention how I'd learned this news.

"Please don't tell anyone where you got this, okay? Let's just say it violates several federal laws and my friend might never see the light of day."

Already way ahead of you, cousin. "Of course. You have my word."

Ethan spoke in a news reporter voice, probably reserved for delivering important information. "The stories on the internet say the local police in Arkansas arrested Josh for shoplifting in his senior year of high school. The family got the charges dropped and sent him away to military school. But that's not what happened, not at all."

Ooh, this sounded important!

"The truth is, the police received a tip that Josh was dealing drugs at his high school. He had quite an operation going, in fact. The police sent in an undercover officer to infiltrate the ring and discover the ringleader."

"Oh, my gosh! Just like *21 Jump Street?*" Did the officer look like Johnny Depp or Peter DeLuise? Maybe even Holly Robinson or Dustin Nguyen?

"Oh, I saw both those movies! Jonah Hill is hilarious!"

Wait! There were movies? Who's Jonah Hill?

Focus, Ev! "What happened next? And please hurry—my brother is giving me the evil eye."

Ethan coughed. "Sorry, I thought we were talking about Jonah Hill. I never knew you were a fan."

This conversation had taken a wrong turn down a dead-end street. "Back to the drug bust. What happened? The one with Josh Fairchild, not on *21 Jump Street.*" Or with what's his name—Jacob Hall? Jordan Haynes? Never mind.

"The undercover cop identified Josh Fairchild as the leader, with eight other dealers working for him. They arrested everyone, including our guy. But his dad flashed some cash and called in some favors. The other eight headed to prison, but Josh finished his senior year at a military academy in Alabama. He graduated a year later and went to college. Despite the severity of the crime, Josh was seventeen and the judge treated him as a juvenile. That included sealing his records."

Wow...just wow! Did Stella know the truth? According to her, Josh had been arrested for shoplifting. It was all a misunderstanding, and the charges had been trumped up. If she knew the truth, she might not be so loyal. Perhaps Michael had discovered the truth, and paid for it.

"Thank you so much Ethan! Now, I'd better go see the dead body. Bye!"

Wow! Never thought I'd say that to anyone.

My brother's glare barged into my line of vision. Was that a vein poking out of his forehead? Why was it throbbing?

"If you're done with social hour, Ev, could you saunter over to the crime scene? Unless you need to make another phone call? Perhaps share a recipe?"

Sarcastic much Nate? "No, sir. You have my full attention." How did one saunter? Teal pen and notebook appeared and I turned to the inside cover. *Look up what saunter means.* Then I crossed it out. Probably best I didn't know.

My new boots made crunching sounds on the gravel as we crossed the parking lot. Dang, these boots looked good! Angela Lansbury needed some of these when she filmed *Murder She Wrote*. The woman always looked stylish in her tweed and earth tones, but these boots would have kicked up her wardrobe a notch or two.

We stepped behind the building to the yellow tape, and my PI greeted me.

"Oh good! You brought your notebook and green pen. Now you're actually going to work."

Et tu, Shorty? "Yes, I am. Now what have we got?"

My pen scribbled another note: *Watch Angela Lansbury and observe what she says and does at a crime scene. Look at her shoes too. Check out Detective Baez's wardrobe as well.* Between *Murder She Wrote* and *Bluebloods* I should be covered next time.

"You're writing. Does that mean you've got something to share?"

Definitely not! "Not yet Nate. Just taking some notes about the scene right now."

My heart warmed with pride as I watched my little brother do his job.

"Dispatch received a call around 8 p.m. An employee named Artie Miller stepped outside to the back of The Dirty Pelican to take a smoke break. Poor guy discovered the body instead."

"River never showed or called in for his shift, which began at 6 p.m. What time was he killed?"

Two heads snapped towards my voice, like wipers swooshing to the other side of the windshield.

"What? How do you know River missed his shift?"

Why imagine that! Miss Sauntering Suzy had something to contribute.

"Well, I spoke with my waitress at Señor Sombrero's. She told me River was scheduled to work tonight, beginning at 6 p.m. But he never showed, or called in."

Did Shorty really shake his head? Was it in disbelief? Or did I impress him? Yeah, I'd go with that.

Nate glanced at his official memo pad. It was so tiny! Maybe I needed one like that—did they come in purple?

"We're thinking time of death is between 7 p.m. and 8 p.m. Employees come back here for smoke breaks pretty regularly. A different employee took her break from 7:15 to 7:30 and didn't see a body. That means the killer dumped the victim back here between 7:30 and 8:00, but this is definitely not where he was killed."

"The owner of The Dirty Pelican identified the body and stated that River has not been inside the building this evening. He says the victim always seeks him out and says hello. Interviews with customers confirm the victim did not go inside the bar tonight."

Nate pocketed his memo pad and crossed his arms. "Since you're not officially with the department, I can't let you cross the yellow barrier. In fact..."

Here we go.

"We have no evidence this crime is tied to Michael Cook's murder. Honestly, I jumped the gun by asking you here. But Shorty mentioned you'd spoken with someone named River about Michael's murder. When we found a driver's license with the name River Woods, I figured chances were good he was your River. My apologies for dragging you down to this place—you've probably never been somewhere like this before."

How many lies had I spoken to my brother tonight?

"Oh, yeah, well that's true. But I appreciate you thinking of me." Not to mention, I got to wear those comfy boots!

On the way home, I mentioned my call from Ethan.

"Well, I'm sure glad ya' *wazn't* making a *so-shull* call! Cuz I've been tellin' Nate how *pro-fess-shuh-null* you've been. Y'know, dressin' up, wearin' some makeup. Even fixin' yore hair a bit. Course I didn't mention the bad breath that one night."

If I strangled my driver, could I do it fast enough to take control of the truck? Make sure I only killed him and not both of us? No, too risky.

"Thank you, Shorty, for your concern about my well-being. Warms my heart really, to hear such kind words."

Truly, sarcasm went over my PI's head. Probably a good thing though, since it would keep me from completing my strangling plan. That strategy needed more thought and preparation, anyway.

Time to turn back to our case. "Once Nate and his team process River's crime scene, maybe something will point to Josh Fairchild. In the meantime, let's keep our focus on sorting out our suspects. How are you feeling about Faith Dixon? We haven't interviewed her yet, but I'm really leaning towards the suspects involved with drugs."

Shorty opened his window and dumped his travel mug, only not all of the coffee made it through the opening. My PI took his shirt sleeve and rubbed it along the door, wiping away the spill. *Oh, Mama Madie Cormier, please don't be watching your son from up in Heaven!* The glove compartment! Many people kept napkins or wet wipes in there. At least we did, if our compartments actually opened.

"What're ya' doin', Doc? That glove compartment hazn't opened in a coupla' years."

Well, of course not. Should I bother with the console between us? Let it go, Ev.

"Anyway, if yer done with the nozin' around, I'll answer yore question."

At least both hands remained on the wheel.

"We should interview her, see what she knows. An' her alibi's crap...I mean scrap! Her alibi's full o' scraps."

Nice save, my friend. "Wonderful! I will call her tomorrow and set up something. Want to tag along? You always do better than me with the ladies." That came out so wrong.

"Hel..lo no, Doc! That woman's bat shih...tzu crazy!"

Hmmm...have you met Candy Cahill?

"No problem. Faith and I will have a chat, woman to woman."

Could I survive the next ten minutes home? Could Shorty?

Most people form opinions before they have all the facts. It's human nature—we can't help it. For Faith Dixon, my mind pictured a tiny young lady in her twenties, five-foot nothing. Her hair color came straight out of a bottle called White Trash Blonde, and she flashed nails (toes and fingers) painted *Flaming Orchid*.

We met for coffee at Maggie's, and my friend promised she'd have her cousin, Deputy Landry, on standby in case things got crazy.

When my feet hit the coffee shop floor, my eyes locked with Maggie's.

"The usual, Ev?" Her eyes shifted to the figure in the back, scrolling on her phone.

"Yes, please. Here, let me pay you." Kind of obvious but my goal of appearing casual conflicted with my pounding heart.

"That's her, in the back. The tall girl with the brown hair and glasses."

What?

"Thanks, Maggie. Just let me know when my order's ready."

Breathe, Ev. Why so nervous? Faith had no reason to burn my house down—I wasn't a single man in my mid-twenties.

"Faith? My name is Evangeline Delafose. We spoke on the phone."

This girl was dressed in ripped jeans and a Kane Brown concert shirt. Kane Brown? How scary could she be? Why, I'd faced a dead rat, a house break-in, The Dirty Pelican, and a dead body. Well, I saw the yellow plastic tarp from the coroner's office but still...

"It's so nice to meet you, Mrs. Delafose. Please join me."

So far so good.

"As I said over the phone, I'm consulting with the sheriff's department to solve Michael Cook's murder. In your opinion, who killed your ex-boyfriend?"

Faith blinked several times, her wide framed glasses giving her an owl-like appearance.

"Look, Mrs. Delafose, I know I've been a suspect from jump, and my eighty-year-old grandmother isn't the best alibi. Probably anything I say is going to be suspect. But since you asked..."

Faith's breathing picked up speed, giving me a sense she had something to fear.

"Michael and I fought over a couple of big issues, and that's why we broke up. Number one source of our fighting was his sister. Long before we dated, when Michael's parents were alive, they kicked Stella out of the house. They also refused to help her with any bills or anything. Stella couldn't keep a job, so Michael would slip her cash and food. When he couldn't afford to do that anymore, he begged Josh Fairchild to give Stella a job. Josh would never fire her, so she had a steady paycheck. But it was never enough."

Interesting! "When did Stella start working for Josh?"

Faith's eyes, like full moons, crinkled a bit around the edges as she looked left to access her memory. "About two years ago, six months or so after coming back from rehab. Michael never told his parents that he gave Stella money, but he figured they knew. Or suspected anyway. When they passed, he let Stella move into the house with him. He wanted to have closer access to her, and to make sure she always had food and money."

Faith's shoulders rose towards the ceiling, then sank slowly as she let out a sigh.

Maggie arrived with my drink and I waved her off. We'd made a deal that I would share later, and a hand wave meant she should leave us alone.

"So why do you think Stella killed Michael?"

Faith glanced over my shoulder to the seats in the coffee shop. At one hour before closing, it was just the two of us.

Satisfied she could share her thoughts, Faith continued.

"It's no secret that the Cook family has money, although Stella's is locked up in a trust. Mr. Cook was smart to do that for his daughter, but not smart enough to do that for his son. With Michael gone, his money is sitting in investment accounts. From what I've heard, Michael didn't have a will and Stella was his only living relative. She now has full access to his share of the money."

"Faith, you mentioned you and Michael fought over a couple of major issues. What was the other issue?"

Faith tipped her cup so the last drops hit her throat. "Michael wanted to move to Alaska. He was tired of Stella and dealing with Sam Hughes at the bank. He wanted to get away. You know, looking back to before our breakup, I had the impression Michael was afraid of something. Or some*one* maybe, but he'd never share with me."

Maybe he was afraid of Josh? The guy seemed nice, but I wouldn't want to make him angry. "What can you tell me about Rob Dugas?"

Faith performed a decent hair flip. "Oh him? Why, he's a blight on humanity—that's what he is! Mrs. Delafose, it wouldn't surprise me one bit if Rob had his grubby hands all over Michael's murder! But Stella's definitely involved."

Why did my murder suspects constantly point fingers at each other? To my list I added, *What did Jessica Fletcher do when her suspects blamed each other?* Zydeco and I needed to make some time for a *Murder She Wrote* marathon.

Chapter 16

My canine roommate had adjusted more easily than my human one. "Don'tcha have shampoo that doesn't smell like a flower garden?"

"Why don't you use the liquid soap by the bathroom sink? You know, the one for washing hands."

"Is that what that is? Well, it smells like flowers too! I've been washin' my hands in the kitchen with the bottle o' Dawn."

Which explained the almost empty bottle next to the dish drainer. At least he was washing his hands, though—his mama would be proud.

"After I feed the cows an' hogs, I've been takin' a shower at home. But I need t'take one now—got a date with a lady friend. An' she don't want me smellin' like no flower shop either!"

Was that nerves making his voice tremble? Could Shorty be nervous about his date?

"But you said you weren't leaving me home alone, except to feed the animals. How's this going to work?"

Oh, Ev, why'd you ask?

"Cuz Annabelle's comin' over here. By the way, add another plate for supper, an' what're we havin' anyway?"

"What happened to Candy Cahill? She was such a lovely young lady." Stop being mean, Ev. "And you two seem so well suited for each other. I'm sorry it didn't work out." No sarcasm that time, but not exactly truthful. At least I was trying.

My PI appeared in the kitchen in...was that my bathrobe?

"Honestly, Doc, she got too clingy. Textin' and callin' all the time, wantin' t'know what I was doin'. Can't a guy just do nothin'? An' she thinks you an' I are a couple, since I'm stayin' over here. Even though I told her there ain't no way in...well, no *sit-choo-ay-shun* that put you and me together like that. But she's convinced we're datin'. Ain't that the dumbest thing ya' ever heard?"

Lord, please keep my tongue in check.

"Yes, yes, it is. Should I expect another dead rat? Or something worse?"

Shorty grabbed the Dawn dish soap and headed towards the guest bathroom. "Nah, not while I'm here, anyway. Besides, my buddy, Curt, asked for her number. Y'don't hafta' worry about that girl no more."

Ah, Curt. The buddy with the mole. Those two were a match made in Heaven.

Should I ask about the bathrobe?

Shorty spun back towards me. "Y'never answered my question, Doc. What's for supper?"

Probably best to start off right with Annabelle. "How about chicken parmesan and a side salad?"

Shorty's mud brown eyes squinted a little as he mulled over my suggestion. "Yeah, that'll be fine. Not too fancy-schmancy but better'n beans an' weenies."

Indeed. "Do you want me to bake some brownies? We've got some vanilla ice cream in the freezer."

"Yeah, that'd be real nice, Doc. I 'preciate that."

One more comment before my PI and my bathrobe headed to the shower. "Oh, an' after supper, could y'head to yore bedroom? Me 'n Annabelle wanna' watch a movie, an'...well, ya know...three's a crowd."

Smiling sweetly, I nodded. As Shorty padded to the bathroom, I gritted my teeth. Lord, please remind me that my bodyguard was just as inconvenienced as me. It was hard for my friend to shuffle between two houses, trying to keep up with farm chores while maintaining a watchful eye on me and the house. Help us catch this killer so we can restore our lives to normal. Amen!

Zydeco and Shorty had reached an understanding. My dog was my main protector, but Shorty could guard the rest of the house. We called Zy my primary security detail and my human roommate my secondary detail. My primary allowed my secondary to feed him hot dogs, and granted him access to the house. If Shorty came closer than two feet to me, Zy warned with a low *Grrrrrr*. My secondary detail had chased down a bull to de-horn it, but he refused to mess with the primary detail.

"Y'know, Doc...anyone who tries t'tangle with ya is just plain stupid! That dog don't trust nobody 'cept you. If I were you, I'd let 'im roam the house when yer gone, cuz he'd take a chunk outta' anybody that broke in."

Zy opened his eyes long enough to eye Shorty suspiciously.

"In fact, he might take a chunk outta' someone even if ya let 'im in."

That evening, primary detail whined pitifully in his crate. We didn't want Annabelle to become a chew toy.

My plan for the evening hinged upon resting quietly in the shadows. If Candy Cahill was the poster child for Shorty's girlfriends, I wouldn't spend any more time with his date than necessary.

The doorbell echoed through the house.

"Now that's Annabelle, Doc! Ya look real nice tonight. I shore 'preciate ya' dressin' up for my guest."

Was that a vase of flowers perched on my hall tree?

As Shorty welcomed his girl, I remained on my couch. After discarding several options, I'd settled upon sipping a cup of tea. Pretending to read a book communicated indifference, as if I'd forgotten Annabelle's visit and started a chapter. Drinking a cup of tea conveyed coziness and hospitality. Which was why my teacup was nestled in my hands, ready to be slipped on the side table as I rose to meet Shorty's girl. No tea cart though, as that would be too fancy—according to Shorty. But what to say? *Hi, I'm Ev—Shorty's casual yet friendly temporary roommate.* Yeah, this wasn't weird at all.

"Ev, it's so nice to meet you! Shorty speaks highly of you. It's wonderful to get to know you at last!"

Was I looking into a mirror? As we faced each other and shook hands, I noticed we stood at the same height. Looking down, I recognized gray pointed ballet flats. Didn't I own something similar? Training my gaze upwards, I noted her no-name jeans, a pumpkin-colored t-shirt, and...yep, a brown cardigan. Oh, I definitely had a similar sweater in my closet. And I would have to ask where she bought her shirt because it went perfectly with our cardigan!

Just a thin silver necklace with a charm on it, and matching earrings. Again, my jewelry box contained similar bangles. Annabelle's shoulder-length hair flowed evenly from a brown headband. Straight, not wavy like mine, but almost the same color. Annabelle's hair reminded me of Kate

Jackson's when she starred in *Charlie's Angels*. As memory served, Shorty always had a crush on her...the brainy Sabrina Duncan. His friends hung posters of Farrah Fawcett in their rooms, but Shorty kept Kate Jackson's photo tucked under his pillow. The only reason I knew that was because his sister, Dottie, blurted it out at school.

Annabelle's glasses caught my attention. The blue cat's eye frames didn't distract from her features—they emphasized her eyes. Was I just hungry, or were they the color of my brownies? Dark brown, with flecks of black.

"Supper is ready, if you are. Shall we go into the dining room?"

As the meal progressed, I came to a startling conclusion. My first impression of Annabelle scared me into thinking Shorty had a crush on me. If the old saying is true, *boys tease you when they like you*, then Shorty was madly in love with me. Annabelle dressed the same, was the same height, similar hair color and style, and we both wore glasses. Shorty didn't want to ruin our friendship, so he did the next best thing. He found someone who looked just like me, or almost anyway.

After freaking out and wondering how I could let Shorty down easily, I'd realized my mistake. Shorty crushed on Sabrina from *Charlie's Angels*, but I'd aspired to *be* Sabrina. For a while, I'd even cut out pictures of the character and asked my mom to buy me similar clothes. Shorty didn't have a thing for me—he still had a thing for the smartest of Charlie's angels. Thank goodness!

My mind wandered back to the conversation.

"And the guy says to me, 'Oh I don't want to borrow the book—I want to buy it!' For the next thirty minutes, I tried to explain that you don't buy books at the library. But he insisted. 'Why do you have all these books if you aren't selling them?' It was so hilarious!"

Shorty laughed until he snorted. He really liked this girl!

"Excuse me, Annabelle. You're a librarian?"

Another snort from my roommate. "Geez, Doc, where ya' been for the last five minutes?"

Don't ask, Shorty...don't ask.

"Gee, I'm sorry, Annabelle. Ev gets distracted real easy. See, I've tried t'talk her into goin' tuh the doctor. Y'know, t'see if they can do a brain scan or somethin'. But she's pretty stubborn."

Yes, I was the stubborn one.

"Forgive me, Annabelle. What branch do you work in?"

"The branch in Zachary. Shorty came in a week ago looking for Shannon Adams. He told me about your case, and asked me about Shannon. But she'd resigned and moved away a few months after the murder. So, I told Shorty what I remembered from my conversations with Shannon. We had been friends, even though she worked for me. Then Shorty asked me out, and here we are."

Here we were, indeed. Why did it irritate me that Shorty attracted women even while investigating a murder? Come to think of it, Jessica Fletcher had a male admirer in almost every episode of *Murder She Wrote*. Maybe Shorty was right—maybe I should wear more makeup and pay attention to my hair. A new style perhaps? What was the name of that beautician down at the Bristle n' Blush? Hannah maybe?

"This was a lovely meal you prepared, Ev. Again, thank you so much for inviting me to your home." Despite my grouchiness, I really liked this woman.

Please Lord, please don't let Shorty screw up this relationship. And please don't let Annabelle have any jealous tendencies, or an affection for dead rats.

As we cleared the table, Annabelle offered to load the dishwasher.

"Oh, don't bother. They can wait until morning. You should join Shorty in the living room for your movie."

"Ev, please! We can't kick you out of your own living room! Stay and join us."

Yes, that would go over well with my roommate. "It's your first date, so you should enjoy each other's company. But maybe sometime we can meet for coffee. Graisseville has the best coffee shop in a thirty-mile radius."

Annabelle's eyes shone like candles burning behind a pool of chocolate. "Oh, yes! That would be wonderful!"

Mmmm...chocolate. Didn't we have some leftover brownies?

Zydeco, my brownie, and I settled into my bedroom with the door closed. As I munched on my bedtime treat, I sorted out the new clues in my notebook. Were we any closer to solving the mystery?

Stella had lied during her interview, but about what? Concentrate, Ev. How many times had Stella glanced right? As I reflected on the interview, I decided she'd only done that once. All other times she stared straight into my eyes. No, one time she looked down at the floor. When was that? *Not everyone wants to be saved.* Ugh—what did that even mean? Trying to remember things gave me a headache, not to mention struggling to analyze someone's eye movements.

Time to focus on the brownie. My guard snoozed on the braided rug, nose pointed towards the door. Thank you, Lord, for bringing me this dog! As my consciousness enjoyed my chocolate delight, the back part of my brain puzzled on the clues. Slowly, the pesky details crept back into the front of my brain, disturbing my brownie time.

Why couldn't Nate solve this crime? He had more resources than I did. Yet Ethan discovered the real reason Josh had been arrested. Shorty cleared Sam Hughes as a suspect and discovered Annabelle. That woman could prove a good resource into Josh's life, and she had no reason to protect him.

My guard and I padded to the bathroom, and I continued my mental conversation. Shorty had shifted into Romeo mode, so his interview with Annabelle couldn't be trusted. Tomorrow I would ask my roommate for his girlfriend's phone number and schedule an interview. Maybe I should just drop by the library? Better plan, and then I wouldn't have to involve Shorty.

As soon as my human roommate left for the farm, I headed to the library. To speak with Annabelle privately, I needed to leave after my PI.

Shorty's words sounded in my brain, reminding me he'd had a good idea: Leave Zydeco loose in the house to warn off unwanted visitors. My guard whined as I headed out the door, but his shiny eyes told me leaving him out was a nice consolation prize. Five seconds later, I doubled back to peek in the window. Zy rested on the hallway rug, nose pointed towards the front door. No one would come in the house without regretting the decision.

"Why, Ev! It's so nice to see you! Tell me, what brings you by?"

Red tennis shoes with bling, khaki skirt, red tee with white cardigan, gold necklace and matching earrings. Yes, we needed to go shopping together sometime—this girl had my taste in clothes.

"Actually, I wondered if you had a few minutes to talk. If not, I thought we could have lunch together. Which do you prefer?"

"Could we do both? I can spare some time right now, and I'd love to have lunch with you later!"

Annabelle ushered me into her office and closed the door. "My guess is you'd like to talk about Shannon Adams and her relationship with Josh Fairchild. Am I correct?"

"You are! Shorty hasn't told me anything that you've said, and honestly I'd like to ask my own questions."

Annabelle jumped up, almost knocking over her swivel chair. "Tea! Would you like some? We have a break room with a single serve coffee and tea maker. We have Earl Grey, breakfast, and chai. Are you interested?"

Do Rougarous prowl the swamps of south Louisiana? "Yes ma'am, that would be fantastic! Chai please."

A few minutes later, I had my chai and Annabelle sipped on her strawberries and cream flavored coffee.

Start simple. "Tell me about Shannon. What kind of person is she?"

Annabelle took a long sip.

"She was a hard worker, extremely dedicated. The first to work and the last to leave. Her family lived in Mississippi, and she was saving up to move closer to them."

Another sip.

"Shannon was a good friend too, loyal and caring. She knew all our birthdays and baked a cake for each celebration. She also snuck small gifts on our desks for the various holidays—Christmas, Mardi Gras, Valentine's Day. Even St. Patrick's Day. Such a thoughtful woman. We all miss her."

"Annabelle, what can you tell me about her relationship with Josh?"

My new friend stared thoughtfully into her cup before speaking.

"Honestly, he seemed like a really great guy. Constantly sending flowers, surprising Shannon at work with small gifts, taking her out for lunch. There had been some rumors, but he struck me as a genuinely nice guy. A few times we chatted while Shannon finished up a project, and he always asked about my kids or my parents. He even donated money to our children's summer reading project."

The question remained unanswered: was Josh Fairchild a good guy or a bad one? Maybe a little of each, like most of us?

"Sorry I'm not much help, Ev. About Josh anyway. But I can tell you something about Stella. Oh, excuse me—I need to take this call."

Annabelle waved for me to stay seated as she answered questions from another branch manager. Oh, Shorty, please keep this one around. She was fabulous!

"Sorry about that! Where was I? Oh—Stella! She was at the library the evening of the murder. Her browser history showed she applied for spring admission to East Baton Rouge Parish Community College. Shannon wasn't working that day, but another librarian remembered greeting Stella as she entered the building. That was about 4:00 p.m., a couple of hours before we close."

On the day of the murder, Michael Cook's boss said that Michael left the bank at 4:30 p.m. He'd had some sort of personal situation to deal with, and received permission to leave early. Nate hadn't discovered any errands or stops that he made, so Michael probably arrived home at 4:45 p.m. Neighbors reported a gunshot at 5:00 p.m.

"What time did she leave the library?" Stella lived approximately five minutes away, twelve if she walked.

"That's the problem, Ev. We can't confirm when Stella left, because no one noticed. Her computer was still logged on the next morning. We have no idea."

"Annabelle, did you ever mention this to the police?"

My new friend stared at me for a split second then shook her head. "No, because I didn't think it was helpful. But Shorty told me that all information is relevant, so I thought you should know."

Probably not the information about Curt's mole, but all the other information certainly could be.

Did someone pick up Stella and take her to the movies in Baton Rouge, as she claimed? Or did she go home and witness her brother's murder, possibly killing him herself?

Chapter 17

G arth belted out, "I've got Friends in Low Places"...my signal that Shorty was trying to track me down.

"Doc, where are ya'? When I came back from the farm, you was gone. You *know* yer not s'posed t'go anywhere without me!"

Truthfully, I knew this conversation would take place, and I was prepared.

"Oh, I just ran to the post office—no big thing. In fact, I'm on my way home."

True statement—except for the post office part.

"Doc, don't lie tuh me! Y'didn't go tuh the post office, an' I know that fer sure cuz I was jus' there. Brad hasn't seen ya' all day."

You know you live in a small town when the postal worker rats you out.

"All right! No, I didn't go to the post office. If you must know, I went to the library to have a chat with Annabelle."

Ugh! How mad would he be?

"Really? That's great, Doc! Did y'all have a good visit?"

One of my many issues with Shorty was that he couldn't recognize my sarcasm, but he dished it out freely himself.

"No need to be sarcastic about it, Shorty! We didn't talk about you at all—just the case." Should I mention our lunch plans starting in forty-five minutes? Probably not.

"What sarcasm? I was serious! It's great you an' Annabelle are gettin' t'know each other. My best friend an' my best girl."

Which one was I? Best friend? It couldn't be his best girl. But, *best* friend?

"Umm, well...thank you?"

"Yeah, I'm real sorry I didn't tell ya' about goin' tuh the library last week. Honestly, I jus' planned t'stop in an' talk tuh Shannon. But Annabelle said the lady quit, an' then wanted t'know why I was lookin' for her. Well, I jus' told the truth, an' I told her all about the case. Then we got t'talkin', but she had t'get back tuh work. So, I asked fer her number. Y'know, so I could continue our *con-ver-say-shun*. We never talked 'bout Shannon, so I didn't think I needed t'mention all that to ya'."

Should I look out the window to see if the world was ending? Ladies and gentlemen, Cleophas Alphonse Cormier was falling for the local librarian! If he told this woman his real name, I'd know things were getting serious.

"Not a problem, Shorty. Annabelle also had to get back to work this morning, so we're meeting for lunch. Would you like to join us? She answered my questions about the case, so it's just a friendly lunch. You are more than welcome to come."

A pause as his brain mulled over the situation. If he came with me, then he could make sure I didn't say anything embarrassing about him. But would his presence seem like he didn't trust us? Or maybe that he was smothering Annabelle?

A hard decision for my friend to make—uh, best friend, apparently.

"Uh, no—that's okay, Doc. You gals go an' have some fun without me. Me an' Zy'll hang out an' do some bondin' of our own. I'll run tuh the Gas n' More. Get some hot dogs an' a coupla' cans o' beans."

Ugh! Shorty and beans didn't enjoy each other's company. And about an hour after eating them, people around Shorty didn't enjoy his company either. Hopefully Zydeco wouldn't have the same problems, or he'd be sleeping alone. Or with Shorty.

Annabelle met me at the Shining Stars Café. Gracie's menu had captured her interest, and my new friend insisted she could make a ten-minute drive for the best bacon cheeseburger this side of Heaven.

After popping my head into Maggie's shop and saying *hey*, I wandered twenty feet over to Shining Stars. Gracie welcomed me in with a smile and ushered me to a table.

"My friend, Annabelle Brochet, is joining me. She's the branch manager of the Zachary Library. When I told her about your bacon cheeseburgers, she wanted to taste them for herself."

Gracie smiled at the compliment. "Thank you, Ev, for giving me free advertising! That will have to go on my Facebook page for the café: People come all the way from *Zachary* to sample the food!"

Annabelle chose that moment to enter the café, and I waved her over. She introduced herself to Gracie and asked for water with lemon. As we studied the menu, I noticed the special of the day: Crawfish Monica. Be still my heart!

"You know, Annabelle, after seeing the special..."

"Oh my goodness, Crawfish Monica! Well, I know what I'm getting!"

Yeah, we would get along well.

"Gracie, two specials please!"

As I leaned back in my chair, I realized I had one more question about the case.

"Annabelle, let me ask you something. Shannon is Josh Fairchild's alibi for Michael's murder. Did she ever talk to you about that? Do you think he was really with her that night?"

My dining companion studied her lemon carefully, then squeezed it into her water.

"Honestly, Ev, I don't know what to think anymore. Shannon insisted that she and Josh met for an early supper around 5:30 p.m. He'd brought takeout food from The Fried Won Ton and they ate in the park. Then they went to her house and watched a movie. You know, that movie that came out last year about sharks. The one with the guy and the girl on the boat."

Definitely not. "Uh, no. Sharks terrorizing people isn't something I like to watch."

Annabelle shrugged. "Anyway, she's never struck me as a person who'd lie. Shannon was definitely in love, but I don't think she'd lie to protect her boyfriend. She is the most honest, ethical person I've known. But then again..."

But then again?

Gracie arrived with steaming plates of Crawfish Monica. The aroma whisked me back to Christmas Eve as a child, any Christmas Eve. My mom went all out for Christmas Day, so she put my father in charge of supper the night before. Dad had never been much of a cook, but he'd perfected Crawfish Monica over many years. Picture macaroni and cheese taking a road trip to Cajun country, down in the boot of Louisiana.

Dad started the sauce early Christmas Eve, folding in lumps of crawfish meat, plenty of butter, heavy cream, and spices. The divine mixture simmered all day, with our father sitting close beside it. He'd pull up a bar stool and flip open the *Graisseville Gazette*, one eye reading and one eye watching the pot. His diligence proved necessary because his children devised countless ways to sample the sauce without detection. We tried distraction, misdirection, even blatant lying—all to no avail. Dad's right eye never strayed from the simmering pot.

One year Nate faked a head injury, with me and my sister Mad's help.

"Dad! Nate fell down the stairs and he's bleeding all over the carpet! Come quick!"

We felt certain if Nate's medical condition didn't rouse our father, the potentially ruined carpet definitely would.

"Nate, go wash off in the tub right now! Ev and Mad, go clean up the mess! You kids owe me and your mother $2.00 for all the ketchup you wasted! And if we have to get the carpet cleaned because of your shenanigans, then you're paying for that too!"

Another time, Mad saved up her money and bought a fake plastic finger from the dollar store. Then she worked up a batch of tears.

"Daddy! Oh, Daddy! I was slicing potatoes for Mama, and I cut off a finger!"

Mad even wrapped up the artificial digit in some toilet paper and squirted a packet of ketchup from the school cafeteria. She'd learned her lesson about wasting food from home.

Mom took one look and ran to the bathroom.

Our father was made of stronger stuff. "Why, I remember when I was in Vietnam. We were sloshing through a swamp, guns held high above our heads. All of a sudden, our sergeant started hollering! One of those Vietnamese crocodiles bit his leg clean off! Let me tell you, we'd never seen so much blood in our lives. My buddy, Rodney, took off his shirt and made a tourniquet, and wrapped it around Sarge's leg. Me and Rodney, well we carried Sarge and his gun the last fifteen miles to camp. Then they flew ol' Sarge to a MASH unit in a helicopter. Child, that little dab of blood is nothing compared to what poor Sarge went through. You lost a finger?

Baby girl, get on your knees and thank the good Lord that you've still got both legs! Not like poor Sarge." My father wiped a tear from his eye.

None of us three kids ever got a taste of that crawfish delight before supper.

Next, my father would boil corkscrew rotini pasta, then pour it into the pot of Heaven and turn down the heat. By that time, he'd switched to *Field and Stream Magazine* and was three-fourths through it. Just as he closed the cover on the last article, our supper was ready.

Gracie's Crawfish Monica came pretty darn close to my father's, maybe even a little better. Did her children dream up tricks to taste her sauce before meal time? That was a question I'd definitely have to ask when the café wasn't so crowded.

"Annabelle, you said that you didn't think Shannon would lie to protect her boyfriend. But then you changed your tune, so to speak, and said, *but then again...* what did you mean by that?"

In the short time I'd known Annabelle, I'd noticed a couple of things. First, she was open and honest. The second was that she put a lot of thought into everything she said, especially if she felt her words could change someone's opinion. This woman never blurted out something she would regret or retract later. But what was she struggling with?

After staring into her Crawfish Monica for a good five seconds, Annabelle met my eyes.

"Have you ever loved someone so much that you'd do anything for them? Even if you knew it was wrong, and that it went completely against your belief system?"

Hmmm, good question. "Maybe. Well, probably. Why?"

Annabelle stirred her meal slowly, moving her spoon in a counterclockwise motion. Was she cooling her food, or stalling for more time?

"It's just a feeling, really. Shannon never told me she lied, and neither of them ever gave me reason to think she had. But one day, after a deputy visited the library for the third time to interview Shannon, she seemed rattled. At first, I thought the deputy had been rude to her, maybe accused her of being in on it all. So, I took her into my office, shut the door, and insisted she tell me what was going on."

Annabelle dropped her eyes and began stirring again. Without looking up, she continued. "After several minutes of getting nowhere, I told her my door was always open and dismissed her. She twisted the handle, then glanced back towards me. As if she needed to say just one more thing. *Annabelle*, she said. *Relationships are about sacrifice, and that's okay.* Then she turned and went to her desk. When I questioned her later, she said it didn't mean anything specific. Just a general comment about love and relationships."

She took a bite.

"If this dish isn't waiting for me at the pearly gates, I might have to rethink my options!"

Her joke broke the tension between us, and I definitely felt she didn't want to discuss Shannon anymore. The rest of our lunch was spent exchanging fashion ideas and making plans to go shopping at Annabelle's favorite store in Baton Rouge.

My report to Shorty didn't include Annabelle's comments about Shannon and Josh. But I no longer believed that Josh's alibi held water.

After lunch with Annabelle, I stopped by the coffee shop for tea and a chat.

"Maggie, I need to interview someone about Faith to clear up a few questions. Who do you suggest?"

Afternoons at the coffee shop were slow, so Maggie didn't mind my loitering at the counter. It gave her a chance to catch up on the case.

"What about Faith's grandmother, Edith? She was pretty forthcoming with Lila Trahan. With her urging, Edith might be honest with you, too. Why don't you give Lila a call and see how it goes?"

Not a bad idea.

The call to my former English teacher proved encouraging.

"Evangeline, dear! Always wonderful to hear from you. What's on your mind?"

"Lila, do you think your friend, Edith, would speak with me about her granddaughter? I've talked to Faith already, but I have some questions best answered by someone close to her."

"Well, I guess we won't know until we ask! What are you doing this afternoon? Let me call Edith and invite her over to talk with you. My house would be best, I think—a neutral place to chat. I'll bake some Ooh La La sugar cookies and put on a pot of coffee. Let me call Edith and get back with you."

What does one serve when conducting a murder investigation? Of course Lila knew! She'd probably seen it in a past issue of *Southern Living*. An article entitled, "Five Best Desserts To Serve During A Murder Investigation."

My interview took place later that afternoon, after Edith's knitting group. Lila had to bake Ooh La La cookies and brew the coffee, anyway. Detective Lou Bergeron hadn't had these scheduling conflicts, so it was all new to me.

Notebook and teal pen in hand, I arrived at Lila's and rang the doorbell.

"Come in, dear! Edith is sitting in the living room. She's just a bit nervous, but I told her I wouldn't leave her side. That's all right, isn't it?"

"Of course, Lila, of course! Shall we?"

In many ways, I saw Faith when I looked at Edith. She was also tall, with brown hair and glasses. Edith's frames reflected the taste of the Boomer generation, instead of a Millennial.

"Thank you for meeting me, Edith. Really, I just had a few questions. Shall we begin?" Small talk was never my strong suit.

Edith stirred her coffee and I noticed her hand trembled just a little. Was that her age or her nerves? A cautious smile—most likely nerves.

"Did Faith have any experience with or knowledge of guns?"

Edith picked up an Ooh La La, then returned it carefully to the silver tray.

"Evangeline, I really don't know if this is a good idea. The last thing I want to do is cause Faith any problems."

More stirring.

"Honestly, Edith, I think your answers will help clear your granddaughter. You're confirming what she's already told the sheriff, and verifying her alibi."

A deep breath, and the stirring halted.

"Well, I certainly want to do that! I can tell you that Faith's father has a lot of handguns and rifles. He loves to hunt, and would take Faith to the gun range. He'd always tell her that a prepared young lady was a safe young lady. He even gave Faith one of his handguns for her protection, and paid for her concealed carry license."

Oh, boy! Maggie heard that Faith was afraid of guns, and had never fired one in her life. Just smile, Ev, and take some notes. Look pleased with the answer.

"Fine, fine! That's wonderful. Next question: what can you tell me about Faith's love life, currently? Is she dating anyone? Lila had mentioned someone, but I wanted to ask you directly."

Edith's nose crinkled, like a piece of paper crumpled for the trash can.

"Uh, well, let me think. Right after the murder, Faith told me she was dating someone new. She'd met him at work and he treated her much better than that Michael ever did. But when I mentioned inviting him over for supper, she became awfully vague about the relationship." She shook her head. "Come to think of it, I never met the young man. After the paper announced the case had stalled, Faith told me they'd broken up."

Edith's hands started to shake, and Lila leaned in to encircle them with hers.

"Oh, Lila! I think I was wrong about Faith! She just may be involved in this awful situation. If my granddaughter had really been over Michael, why would she have confronted him?"

Edith glanced toward my direction, tears welling up.

"She never said so, Evangeline. But I think Faith made up this boyfriend, hoping it would make her look less guilty."

With the coffee table between us, I couldn't comfort Edith except with words. Faith looked even more guilty, so what words would offer comfort?

"Oh dear! Evangeline, I didn't help Faith at all did I?"

No ma'am, you did not. Don't say that out loud, Ev!

"We still have more investigating to do, Edith. Don't be too concerned just yet."

Edith's tears became a full-blown storm of sobbing, and Lila lifted her hands to embrace her friend. Would it be inappropriate to eat an Ooh La La? What would Jessica Fletcher do?

Chapter 18

"Don't feel too bad, Doc. If Faith is a killer, you're just gettin' her granny prepared. Didja walk her through the steps t'visit someone in Angola?"

Was Shorty teasing me or completely serious? In a momentary lapse in judgment, I'd researched the Louisiana State Penitentiary in Angola, LA. It was about fifty miles away, so visits were definitely doable. Unfortunately, the prison only allowed each guest two visits per month. By then, I'd come to my senses and closed the browser.

"Shorty, I don't even know how all that works!"

My PI shot me a sideways glance and delivered a horse snort. Had he snooped through my browser history?

"Could we steer this conversation back to Faith, please?"

A shoulder shrug confirmed that was possible.

"Great! So, I'd like to talk to some of Edith's neighbors. Maybe they can confirm whether Faith left her grandmother's house that evening."

The theme from *21 Jump Street* (the TV show, not the movies) blared from my phone. Shorty grabbed his chest.

"Geez, Doc! If you're gonna' listen tuh music, then keep it at a *rez-peck-tuh-bull* level! What kinda crazy music is that, anyway?"

"It's a ringtone, Shorty! It's Ethan Bergeron. Here, let me put it on speakerphone."

Could Ethan have some more dark web intel?

"Hey, Ethan! I've got Shorty here with me. Do you have some news about the case?"

Shorty gave a two-finger salute to my phone. Did he understand the concept of speakers and telephones?

"Hey, Ev! Hey, Shorty! Yeah, I do. My source discovered a couple of things. We're not sure if they're relevant, but I wanted to report back to you, anyway."

Shorty motioned me to the kitchen. Sleuthing created an appetite, at least for my PI.

"Did you know Michael Cook was getting ready to sell his house? He'd been talking to a realtor and had signed a contract."

Interesting.

"We knew he wanted to move to Alaska. But we thought it was just a pipe dream. What else can you tell us?"

Ethan's voice deepened slightly, encouraged by my interest.

"There is a realty company in Baton Rouge that specializes in low-key home sales. You know, where you don't put a sign in the yard and people don't come by and look at the house. Michael definitely wanted to sell his home quietly. He must have signed a contract, because we found the listing on a few exclusive real estate sites. The agent had been looking for buyers."

We knew our victim wanted to move to Alaska, and had browsed some homes on the internet. He'd wanted to get away from Stella and Sam. That wasn't just a dream—our victim had been trying to make it a reality. Wait a minute! Was the realtor...?

"Ethan, do you know what this agent looked like?"

"Sure, Ev. The realtor is Mona Whitman. Do you want her picture, or should I just describe her?"

"Oh no! Just tell me what she looks like."

"Well, she has blonde hair…"

Of course! The woman having supper with Michael in Zachary wasn't a mysterious girlfriend. She was his realtor.

"Thanks Ethan! We had a mysterious blonde on our list, but no leads. You solved that mystery."

Did Josh discover Michael was leaving town? Or maybe Stella figured it out, and went to Josh. Either way, Michael's desire to leave town could have contributed to his murder. But why?

"One more thing, Ev. Josh did not have the loving close-knit relationship with Stella and Michael that social media portrays. Stella used to have another account on Twitter. Same IP address as her current account, which is how we found it. The tweets are about two and a half years old, so they were posted about a year before the murder."

Okay, that was strange but not unusual. "What did they say, Ethan?"

"Stella tweeted a lot about how Josh was trying to replace her father, always telling her what to do. He pretended that he cared about her and her brother, but it was all an act. She also said Michael was afraid of Josh, and she probably should be too."

Shorty nudged me, but I was too stunned to speak.

"Hey Ethan, this here's Shorty. Thanks for all the good intel—y'did great! We'll talk to ya' soon."

Shorty drove me to Edith's neighborhood—I was too rattled to do anything but stare out the window. Why was this latest piece of news freaking me out?

"Doc, are ya' okay? Mebbe y'should stay in the car. But I hate to leave ya' by yoreself."

The lids of Shorty's eyes fluttered down just a little as he studied my face.

"Y'look a little pale. Say, I've got some whiskey in the glove compartment—mebbe ya should have some."

Yes, day drinking would solve everything.

"You told me that glove compartment hadn't opened in years!"

A chuckle from my PI.

"Well, mebbe I fibbed a bit. There's stuff in there y'don't have no bizness puttin' yore fingers on. Like my friends, Jack and Diane."

That would be his .38 Special named Diane and a bottle of Jack Daniels.

"No, Shorty, I'll be fine. It just hit me hard that I had supper with a murderer."

Both of Shorty's hands encircled my left, making a sort of hand sandwich. His palms felt leathery and firm, like Italian bread. My hand was on the inside, soft like chicken salad. Was I hungry or just weird?

"Darlin, what'd ya' think we've been doin' for the past few weeks? One o' those folks has t'be a killer. After this little interview with the neighbors, we're gonna' bring in Nate. We'll turn it all back over tuh him. Our week is up anyway, an' you've had enough o' playin' Jessica Fletcher."

"Okay, you're right. Let's get these interviews done and go home."

Maybe our first knock would be the last.

"Hello! My name is Evangeline Delafose and this is my partner, Shorty Cormier. And..."

"Look, I'm not buying anything! I've got religion, cable TV, a weekly newspaper, and enough magazines to keep me occupied. So, you can be on your way."

Shorty took a turn.

"No ma'am. We're workin' with the sheriff's department on the murder o' Michael Cook. Yore neighbor, Edith Dixon, is an alibi for one o' the suspects. We're jus' tryin' *t'con-furm* that."

No woman was immune to Shorty's charms.

"Well, why didn't you say so! Come on in! I've just made a fresh batch of sweet tea, and I think I have some saltines in the pantry."

Lila needed to give this woman her helpful hints on what to serve during a murder investigation. Maybe Hugh could run an article in the *Gazette*? If only I had those Ooh La La sugar cookies!

"Why, thank ya' ma'am! Saltines an' some sweet tea shore would hit the spot!"

After digging around in her kitchen, Lurlene Foret produced three glasses with ice, a plastic pitcher of tea, and a box of saltine crackers. Maybe Hugh's article should include the proper serving dishes for murder investigation snacks.

"Oh, it was terrible, just terrible, what happened to that poor Cook boy! And dear Edith! She just made herself sick, worrying about her granddaughter being involved. Then when the deputies came out and questioned all of us, well, it was just awful."

Lurlene dabbed her eyes a bit, then turned her sights on me. Or so I thought.

"Tell me, Miss...Delafose, isn't it? Do you feel safe interviewing all those suspects and such?"

No need to answer—Lurlene hadn't wanted one, anyway.

"Well, of course you do! With a big, strong man escorting you everywhere, you must feel safe and protected."

Had I really believed Lurlene cared about my safety?

"Tell me, are you two an item? Or just colleagues, like Detectives Baez and Reagan on *Bluebloods*?"

At least she had good taste in television shows.

"Oh no, we ain't datin'! We're jus' *call-eegs*."

My question of the hour: would Shorty mention Annabelle?

"Now, y'said the deputies interviewed ya. Right, Miss Foret?"

Lurlene definitely felt there was hope. "Oh, please! Call me *Lurlene*. Yes, they wanted to know if I could verify that Faith's car had remained at her grandmother's house during the time of the murder. Unfortunately, I couldn't. I'd been watching the *Matlock* marathon, just like Edith and her granddaughter."

Not much help with Faith's alibi, but definitely great taste in television shows. Shorty and I exchanged a glance as we stood up.

"Thank ya' ma'am! We 'preciate yore time, but we still have a few more neighbors t'interview."

As we edged closer to the door, I could see our hostess panicking. Her potential boyfriend had one foot out the door without asking for a date. What was a girl to do?

"Uh, but my nephew could vouch for Faith! He knows her car was at her grandmother's all night."

What nephew? Nate's detailed notes included an interview with Lurlene, but not her nephew.

"What are you talking about? How could your nephew confirm Faith's alibi for that evening?"

Not even a blink. "Because he'd parked down the street from Edith's house and watched Faith's car all night. He knows she parked in the driveway at 4:32 p.m. and didn't leave until 9:07 p.m."

Should I ask? Did I want to know?

"Lurlene, why was your nephew watching Faith's car all evening?"

Our hostess began convulsing. Or was she batting her eyes at Shorty? It was hard to tell.

"Why, when you meet your soulmate but they don't realize it yet, you've got to stay close to them. You've got to be nearby. That way, when they finally come to their senses, you'll be right there." More batting. Or convulsing, I still wasn't sure.

Run, Shorty, run! Of course, Shorty had been around enough crazy to see it a mile away.

"Thank ya' for yore time, Miss Lurlene, but we'd best be goin'. My girlfriend'll be wonderin' where I am. Ya'll take care now!"

Thanks to a potential serial killer, we could cross Faith off our suspect list.

"Why didn't Lurlene or her nephew tell the sheriff what they knew? They could have cleared Faith over a year ago."

To his defense, Shorty had been trying harder to be patient with my lack of common sense. Sometimes he actually succeeded.

"Well, let's think 'bout this, Doc. Lurlene an' her nephew may have *jus-tee-fide* stalkin' people in their own crazy world. But they know the sheriff ain't gonna' be real pleased. Those two wanna' keep that off the radar, so t'speak. Don't forget, Miss Edith came forward an' gave Faith an alibi. In their minds, there's no need to *pub-lee-size* their looney toon *ten-dance-seez*."

He had some valid points. "Of course, if Faith had been arrested, I'm sure this stalking nephew would have come forward to clear her. All in the name of love, of course."

After our encounter with Lurlene Foret, we'd regrouped at home over supper. Cooking for someone had helped me enjoy eating again, although I'd have appreciated a more grateful dining partner.

"What're we havin' for supper, Doc? Personally, I was hopin' for some *ay-too-fay*."

"You know better than anyone that etouffee takes all day to prepare! We're having Cajun grilled cheese sandwiches."

Shorty dropped his voice to a stage whisper, just loud enough for me to hear.

"If someone would jus' plan a little, we could have had *ay-too-fay*. But nope! She can't do that."

Did he want me to hear his whining? No doubt.

"Listen, roomie! You are welcome to take over the cooking at any time. Just say the word!"

Not a peep from the food critic. As I pulled out the ingredients, Shorty stalked off to his bedroom. Zydeco remained at his station, between me and the entrance to the living room. Shorty had to hop over the dog, which made his exit less dramatic. And less dignified.

My Cajun grilled cheese sandwiches included Italian bread, pepper jelly, pepper jack and muenster cheese, and andouille sausage. A hole-in-the-wall market in Zachary sold the best sausage. But The Market Basket had a decent meat department, and their links would do in a pinch.

What was my PI hollering about? Was it the smell from the kitchen? My nose dipped closer to the skillet, taking a cautious whiff. Nope! Those sandwiches smelled some kind of good. So why was Shorty all worked up?

My roomie skidded into the kitchen, his socks sliding on the tile floor. What was that movie with Tom Cruise? Singing in his underwear and sunglasses? Tom slid into the camera shot thanks to his white socks, sporting sunglasses, while lip-synching into a candlestick microphone. Shorty's entrance reminded me of that scene, except he was completely dressed. Thank goodness!

"The water! The water's the key!"

Was he delirious from hunger? Maybe hallucinating? My arm reached for a glass in the cupboard.

"Don'tcha' get it, Doc? The water on the floor of the crime scene!"

Nope, still didn't make much sense.

"Take a breath, Shorty. Do you want some water?"

If looks could kill...well I'd have been dead long before that evening.

"No, listen tuh me. The report says the floor was damp, like someone cleaned up the blood. It says there was a jar o' marinara an' a package o' *spuh-getty* on the counter. Now, the stove was turned off, but mebbe the killer did that. What if..."

"Oh! Yeah, I see where you're going with that! Go on!"

Did Shorty's chest puff out just a little?

"What if Michael was boilin' water for the *spuh-getty*? The killer come in the kitchen with the gun, an' Michael threw a pot o' boilin' water at 'im. Or her. Then the murderer mops up the water an' the blood."

My mind whirled, processing the new theory.

"There was a pot on the counter by the stove—wasn't there? What did it look like? How big was it?"

Shorty opened the case file and grabbed the photo on top.

"Right here, Doc! It's about three quarts, same size as the one ya' use. It was empty. Mebbe cuz Michael had dumped it on his killer. Whatcha' think?"

Honestly, I thought my PI was pretty darn smart.

"Let's test your theory, Shorty, with room temperature water, of course."

My three-quart pot rested in the drainer by the sink, so I grabbed it and filled it halfway with water. Shorty reached for a wooden spoon out of the drawer and we began.

"Now Doc, you stand by the stove an' pretend yer stirrin' the water. Let me come atcha' with the spoon."

"Okay, so y'see the gun. Now grab the pot an' fling the water at me. Not the pot, though!"

Instinctively, I aimed the water towards the hand holding the weapon—Shorty's right hand.

No Academy Awards for us, but the theory worked. Shorty's right arm dripped water, and the right side of his shirt was pretty damp, too.

"This is fantastic, Shorty! Our murderer could have burn marks! The report mentions the killer fired the gun right-handed—correct? All our suspects are right-handed, so that doesn't narrow the field. Have we seen any of them wearing short sleeves?"

Who would have thought to note the clothing my suspects had worn? Next time, if there was a next time, I'd take better notes!

"When I met Faith at the coffee shop, she was wearing a short-sleeved Kane Brown t-shirt. No scars on either arm."

But what about the others?

"Well, in my interview with Rob, he had short sleeves too. Yeah, I remember, because he had a golfing type shirt. Like the ones I get Nate for Christmas."

"Okay, good—that's good! Now, let's think, Doc. Stella had on one o' those lacey flowy things. What are those goofy things called?"

Seriously? "They're called dusters. Stella's had long sleeves, which keeps Stella on our list, I suppose. Although from what we've heard, I don't think she's guilty."

"Yeah, probably so. What about our buddy, Josh? You've seen 'im twice—once at the grocery store an' once at Señor Sombrero's. He had on a jacket when he came tuh Señor's an' never took it off. Even at the table! What 'bout the grocery store?"

My mind creeped back to that day, but truthfully only his teeth and hair had caught my eye.

"He had a jacket on that day as well, I think. We need to get him to take off the jacket so we can prove he's our killer!"

During our conversation, Shorty had grabbed some paper towels and begun wiping up the water.

"No, Doc. 'Member today is our last day. Tomorrow, we turn everything over tuh yore brother an' walk away. In fact, I've already talked tuh him an' he's gonna' meet us at the coffee shop. 9 a.m. tomorrow t'do the handoff."

That was it? After all the weeks spent strategizing and interviewing? My eyes filled with tears, so I bent down to sop up the puddle. With my eyes on the floor, hopefully Shorty wouldn't notice a sniffle or three. But he knew me too well.

"Look Doc, don't cry! Hey, I'm jus' as disappointed as you. But we made some good progress, didn't we? Me n' you found out things the sheriff's department couldn't even figure out. We did good, Ev! An' who knows? Mebbe Nate will call on us again t'help out."

Maybe, but we hadn't actually solved the case. We weren't even sure if our boiling water theory held water. Ha! Good job, Ev—at least you still had your sense of humor.

Chapter 19

My heart needed a good cup of tea—lavender chamomile specifically. Prayer and lavender chamomile had brought me through disappointment and heartache. In the grand scheme of things, turning the case back over to Nate wasn't life-altering. On the surface anyway. So why did I feel like something had been yanked out of my body?

The case had given my life purpose, something to do after drinking a pot of tea and watching the local news. No matter. After Christmas, I'd start my adjunct job at LSU. Or, as Shorty called it, my junk job.

Shorty. We'd not kept in touch since high school, but the case had brought us closer than ever. Without an excuse to pick up the phone, our relationship would probably go back to how it was before. At least I'd gotten Zydeco out of this fiasco, and possibly a new friendship with Annabelle. Hopefully, Elizabeth would return home soon.

Shorty's phone buzzed. The guy always kept it on silent, so I'd never heard it ring. Wonder what his ringtone was? Probably whatever was programmed in it when he got the phone.

"Yes ma'am, I'll be right there. Thank ya'."

Before I could interrogate him, my PI gave me the news.

"Well dam the Cypress Bayou! Muh cows are runnin' aroun' on Highway 64, an' I gotta go get 'em! Son of a biscuit!"

Shorty's swearing had virtually disappeared. Hearing him suggest the state build a dam on Cypress Bayou and yell about the descendants of breakfast food made my heart happy.

"Doc, I really don't want t'leave ya'. Why don'tcha' come with me? Y'can sit in the car—I'll even fill yore favorite travel mug with more tea. Y'know, the one with the butterflies an' glitter."

Our friendship had progressed to gentle teasing and private jokes. Yes, I would definitely miss that. Maybe I could invite him over for supper once in a while?

"No, Shorty, I'll be fine. Besides, I've got the twenty-gauge by the couch and my primary detail by my feet."

As if on cue, Zy opened his eyes for a half-second. Shorty nodded at his security colleague.

"Yeah, okay, I guess it'll be fine. But don't open the door fer no one! I'm gonna' see if Mack Taylor an' Moe Gladstone can come help me out. Don't open the door!"

With that, my PI, partner, and dear friend slammed the front door.

"Well, Zy, what shall we do? Jessica Fletcher or DCI Barnaby? Oh, I know! Let's watch *Murder on the Orient Express*—the good one!"

My movie partner never moved a muscle, a sure sign he approved. Mmmm...my tea cart beside me with a fresh pot of tea and a light chenille throw tucked around my legs. Nothing else could improve my movie viewing. Thanks to movies on demand, a short time later I was deep into Agatha Christie and her characters.

Who would ring the doorbell this late at night? A glance at my phone told me it was only 8 p.m. Shorty left...what? Ten minutes ago?

My first instinct, to get up and answer the door, got shoved to the ground by Shorty's parting words: *Don't open the door.* Then my mother's voice sounded. *Ev, Southern hospitality dictates you must open the door.* What was a girl to do?

Maybe I could sneak a look and identify my evening visitor? Zydeco's growls at my movement told me, not a chance. My protector wouldn't let me get near the door.

"Miss Ev! It's Rob Dugas. Could you let me in? There's something really important I need to tell you."

At the sound of Rob's voice, Zydeco shifted into *you'd better get off my porch or I'll eat you alive* mode. Rob spoke a few more words, but I couldn't hear anything over Zy's barking and growling.

"Let me put up the dog. Give me a second."

Ev, was this the wisest move?

We'd cleared Rob, based on our theory. Our unproven theory. As I shoved Zy into his crate, my brain fought a civil war. Rob could have some important information, something that would solve the case. If I could hand over evidence that put the murderer in prison, I'd feel better about turning it all over to Nate in the morning. Except that Shorty said, *Don't open the door.* What if I talked to Rob through the door?

"You know, I don't feel safe letting you in. Could you just tell me through the door?"

"Not really, Miss Ev. My information is something I need to show you."

My desire to solve the case slammed my common sense to the ground. The Mossberg! If I unlocked the door, then stepped back while holding the shotgun, I'd be protected.

Shorty's voice echoed in my brain. *"Don't open the door!"*

My PI and my common sense won the war.

"I'm sorry, Rob. You need to leave. We're turning everything back over to the sheriff's department tomorrow. You can talk to them about any information you have."

Could he even hear me over my dog's commotion?

"It's okay Rob—you can leave now. I've got this under control."

The hairs on my neck stood at attention—a little late, guys! Should I turn around? Someone was behind me and probably had a gun. And how did they get in my house? No wonder Zy was going berserk. On another note, Shorty and I weren't as smart as we'd thought.

"Hands up, Miss Ev, and turn around, please."

Such a polite murderer—Stella's mother would be proud of her manners. The killing not so much, though.

As I faced Stella, my favorite sleuth popped in my mind. What did Jessica Fletcher do in these situations? Honestly, I was always so involved in the puzzle that I didn't pay attention. Didn't someone usually burst in and arrest the killer? Oh wait! Jessica always stalled for time.

"Okay, Stella, this is the part where you start at the beginning and confess the entire crime. Since you're going to kill me, anyway. Is that the murder weapon you're pointing at me?"

Smart, Ev. The story could take a good twenty minutes, maybe thirty. How long did it take to round up cattle on a highway? Hopefully less than twenty minutes, plus drive time.

"Let's start with how you got in here. Since I can barely hear myself think over my dog's barking, I'm guessing it wasn't too hard to slip in."

Ugh! Stella's cat eyes unsettled me once again, staring with unblinking coolness. That sealed the deal—I would never own a cat! Assuming I got out of this mess alive.

"Rob did a splendid job of distracting you at the front door and getting the dog all riled up so you wouldn't hear me come through the kitchen. The new owners will need to replace the pane of glass on your back door. You really should have had a double deadbolt on it, Miss Ev. All I had to do was break the pane and twist the lock."

To add insult to injury, the person set to kill me gave excellent advice on how to secure my home.

"So Rob had nothing to do with Michael's murder? Did he know about it?"

Stella's eyes remained cool, making her smile empty.

"Look, I don't have time to give a *Murder She Wrote* roundup. Thanks to my call, your friend ran out of here. But he will be back any moment. In summary, I killed Michael and River. They wanted to save me and got too nosey. Remember what I told you, Miss Ev. Some people don't want to be saved."

Shorty was right—Stella definitely knew who killed her brother. We hadn't suspected *her* guilt during the interview, not even a bit.

"Don't feel bad, Miss Ev. Ever since I was a little girl, I've been an excellent liar. It took my parents a long time to figure that out. Michael never trusted me, but he seriously underestimated me."

"What about Josh? Is he involved in all this?"

A little wave of her gun signaled the end of our conversation.

"Let's go to the living room. You'll be on the couch for your death. This time I'm using poison. It's so much quieter, and you've got a pot of tea ready to go. Oh, I'm definitely not using the gun—too loud! Small towns, what can you do?"

Should I test our hot water theory? My teapot sat innocently on my cart. Maybe offer Stella a cup of tea? No, too suspicious. Especially if she'd been burned by hot water in the past.

"Did Michael throw a pot of boiling water on you?"

Stella's cat eyes shifted just the tiniest bit.

"Mmmm...you figured that out? That's pretty good, because your brother glossed right over it."

Should I tell her that *Shorty* figured it out? He seemed to be off her radar, so probably best to keep it that way.

"Yeah, I've been seeing a dermatologist in Baton Rouge. Now that I've finally got access to Michael's money from our parents, I can get some skin grafts."

Zydeco had stopped barking, most likely so his vocal chords could have a break. *Crunch!*

Who stepped on the broken glass? Shorty?

As Stella swiveled at the waist, I grabbed my teapot.

"No!"

Why did I say *no*? Because it was the first word that popped into my head.

Stella swung back towards me, then shrieked as the steaming water hit her face. Or were those *my* screams of anguish? That was my favorite teapot, a gift from the kids and Doug one Christmas long ago.

"Stella Cook, you're under arrest." Nate Mirandized my house guest as he cuffed her. Zydeco had recovered, and his barking echoed through the house. "Ev, can you shut that dog up? He's giving me a headache!"

"Go take care of our buddy, Doc. Me n' Nate got this covered."

When did Shorty get back? My head throbbed as the adrenaline exited my nervous system. Where did I put Zy's leash? Why did my front yard look like a law enforcement convention? What did one serve to parish deputies as a late-night crime scene snack? Was it too late to call Lila?

Thanks to my bohemian border area rug, a gift from Nate and Bonnie, my teapot survived the fall. Only a small chip, which Shorty promised to fix.

Zydeco refused to leave my side, growling at anyone closer than two feet. Except Shorty, who sat by me on the couch. Was it the hot dogs and canned beans? Or did my dog finally accept my secondary security?

Thank You, Lord, for protecting me! Thank You for sending Nate to save me and thank You for keeping my precious teapot safe. Your blessings overflow!

The evening's excitement continued as Sheriff Dupre summoned Shorty and me to Baton Rouge. Although Nate would question the suspects, the sheriff thought we should see the evidence of our hard work. Rob and Josh had also been arrested, and Rob had been talking up a storm! With his previous drug convictions, he was eager to make a deal. Sheriff Dupre wanted Shorty and me behind the glass partition when Nate questioned Rob. My PI didn't bother to hide his excitement.

"Ain't this excitin', Doc? Just wait until I tell Annabelle all about our evenin', an' how I saved you an' everythin'. That woman'll be so impressed, I bet she'll bake me a Doberge cake. This evenin' couldn't get any better!"

Shorty saved me? Sure, why not? In a way, he did. Shorty's buddy, Monty the deputy, had been on duty. My friend knew that a call to Monty could confirm the exact location of the runaway cows. Except the deputy told Shorty there were no calls about any runaway animals, Shorty's or otherwise. My brilliant PI told Monty to hoof it over to my house, and bring backup. Then he called Nate, who was at home—two minutes away. My brother entered through the unlocked door in my kitchen and stepped on the glass. By the time Shorty arrived, Nate had Stella sitting on the floor in handcuffs. Monty and two other patrol cars screeched onto Pecan Street not too long after.

As we pulled into the parking lot of the sheriff's office, my stomach performed some acrobatic feats.

"Why do I feel nervous, Shorty? We've cracked the case! Yet, I feel a little unsettled."

My friend shifted his truck into park and turned off the engine.

"Who knows, Doc? Mebbe it's one o' those female thangs y'see on TV. Best not t'discuss it, okay?"

So much for a bonding moment at the end, like Jessica and Sheriff Amos Tupper. Maybe Nate could fill that spot for me? My mind replayed our last exchange, with my brother yelling about my best protector giving him a headache. Nope, I was on my own.

In exchange for his testimony and a guilty plea, Rob had been offered a lighter sentence. Shorty and I sat behind the one-way mirror and watched the jailbird sing.

"Rob, I'm Detective Nathan Bergeron. The district attorney's deal depends upon what you tell us. The first thing I want to know is, who broke into Dr. Delafose's house? What were they trying to achieve?"

"That was me, but I didn't want to do it. Stella told me to look around, see if I could find out how much she knew. Gosh, her handwriting was really neat—I could read every single word! But I told Stella she didn't have much in the file."

Despite my disgust, Rob had flattered me. All my teachers gave me high marks for penmanship. Should I let Lila know a felon agreed with her opinions on my handwriting?

"All right, moving on. Tell me about Stella."

"Yeah, so Michael figured out Stella was dealing drugs with Josh at his store. You know, Best Dry Cleaners? That's why those two were fighting the night before the murder. Michael thought it was all Josh's fault, and that he lured Stella back into the drug scene. Josh tried to tell him it was all Stella's idea, that she came to him wanting to earn some money. But Michael didn't believe him. He still thought his sister was just a recovering addict, weak and frail, needing his protection. Man, you don't want to cross Stella! That girl's scarier than Julia Brown!"

Rob grew up in Frenier, LA where the voodoo queen Julia Brown was a legend. She'd lived along the Manchac Swamp at the turn of the twentieth century, creeping out the whole town of Frenier. Parents told her story to scare their children, and Rob's family was no exception.

"Now, Michael promised Stella he wouldn't turn her in. He just wanted to sell the house and leave town. But Stella, she didn't believe him. Now, Josh tried to convince Stella that Michael wouldn't rat us out, and that he didn't have any real evidence, anyway. But Stella insisted her brother did have proof of our operation, because he'd been snooping around on her phone and her laptop. She claimed Michael was stalling until he could get enough information to turn us in."

Rob paused long enough to take a breath. "Hey, can I get another grape soda? How about a burger or something?"

Yeah, Rob definitely enjoyed all the attention. He leaned back in his chair like a rockstar, waiting for his wishes to be granted.

My brother didn't blink, obviously used to entitled criminals.

"Okay, I'll send someone out to find you some supper. In the meantime, we'll take a little break and get you another drink."

Ten minutes and a grape soda later, Rob continued his confession.

"A few days before Michael's death, Stella got suspicious and tailed him. She spied him in downtown Zachary, meeting with some lady. Man, she freaked! Said the woman was DEA, and Michael had enough evidence to testify against all of us. Josh already had the feds sniffing around—Stella said it was just a matter of time before they sifted through his evidence and prepared Michael to testify."

Did that mean the blonde woman having supper with Michael was a drug enforcement agent? Either way, Stella figured it all out and made sure her brother never had a chance.

Nate scribbled furiously, even though the camera was taping the entire interview. Taking his own notes made Nate a stellar detective. An irritating brother but a stellar detective.

"Stella and Josh have retained legal representation, so I can't question them at this time. Could you tell me about Michael Cook's murder? Did either of them speak with you about it?"

Rob's eyes glittered in the harsh fluorescent lighting. His fifteen minutes of fame had turned into forty-five. Why didn't anyone offer me a burger and grape soda? Why was it that only the criminals got to eat?

"Oh, Stella told me all about it! She called me from the library, asked me to pick her up. Said it was time to get rid of her brother, so she needed me to drive her to the bank. The plan was to catch Michael at work, and make up a story that she'd caught a ride to the bank but needed a ride home. She'd brought the gun, so she could force him to drive to Devil's Swamp. Then she'd kill him and dump the body."

Not a bad plan. Hiding a body there could guarantee getting away with murder. Between the alligators and the buzzards, there wouldn't be much to find. Rob continued.

"She didn't count on Michael leaving work early though, so I took her home. We saw Michael's car parked in the driveway, and Stella got out of my car. She tried the door, but it was locked. I guess she'd left her key at home by mistake, because she knocked on the door. Michael opened it and let her in, and I drove around the block. Stella called after she'd shot Michael, told me to swing back by and get her. So I did.

"Stella told me she'd killed Michael with their father's gun, because it was poetic justice. He thought he was so smart, making her believe he'd gotten rid of the gun. She said the look on Michael's face was priceless when she proved that she was smarter than he thought. More ruthless too."

My body shuddered. Shorty just shook his head.

Chapter 20

My body ached and my stomach craved food. Rob feasting on his hamburger only made me angry. Crime might not pay, but it sure ate better than the crime fighters. Shorty had disappeared but returned with two burgers, an orange soda, and a bottle of water. Perhaps he was my best friend after all, at least for that moment.

"Looks like when the deputy went fer Rob's burger, he brought a whole bag o' them! So I snatched a couple. An' I found some tea bags, but they weren't those fancy kind that ya like. I brought ya some water. Figured ya needed that more, anyway."

Who knew grease could taste so good? As we feasted on our burgers, Sheriff Dupre appeared.

"Hello, folks! I wanted to introduce myself—Sheriff Mitch Dupre. I'm the boss around here, although most days these people run circles around me."

The sheriff extended his hand, but both my PI and I preferred our burgers. My mouth was too full of greasy goodness to explain our dilemma.

"Yeah, if I was eating one of Dusty's burgers, I wouldn't shake hands, either." He chuckled and returned his hand to his pocket. "Say, Mrs. De-lafose, when you get a chance, both Stella and Josh would like a word with you. If you feel comfortable with that. Nate says it's your call, although he'd prefer you stayed away from those two."

The sheriff winked at me.

"Personally, I'd love to hear what they have to say! When we brought them in, they each said they wanted a lawyer. But when they heard you were here at the station, they said they'd talk, but only to you. Now, Nate or Shorty can be in there with you. Or both—whatever you feel comfortable with. It would really help our case, Mrs. Delafose, if you'd talk to them. I mean, the more they say without their lawyers, the better off we all are."

Who was he kidding? Heck, yeah I'd talk to them! Once I'd finished my burger of course. And the sweet potato fries that Shorty had found.

"Of course, Sheriff. Of course, I'll speak to them. Not a problem. Just let me take these last bites."

Shorty sat with me across from Stella. We'd started this journey together, and we would finish it that way too.

"Well done, Miss Ev. Well done. You've heard by now that I've refused to speak without my lawyer. But since you have been such a worthy opponent, I thought I'd answer any questions you have. Any questions except ones about my brother's death. Or River's."

Good grief! What other questions could I have? Where she purchased her V-neck, long-sleeved, floral print midi dress? Actually...

"Doc! Ask her why she went into bizness with Josh, when she twisted on the Inner Net that she's afraid o' him!"

Twisted on the Inner Net? "Shorty, do you mean when she tweeted on the internet that she's afraid of Josh?"

"That's what I said, Doc! Ask her!"

Note to self—find someone to give Shorty lessons on social media.

"Okay, Stella. A couple of years ago, you had a different Twitter account. You tweeted that Josh was trying to replace your father and kept telling you what to do. That he pretended to care about you and Michael, but it was all an act. You said Michael was afraid of Josh, and you probably should be too. Why did you do that?"

Funny, she didn't look like a serial killer. In another life, we might have met at Maggie's Coffee Shop for a drink and a chat.

"Maybe I was afraid of Josh. Maybe I still am."

The woman was playing us for sure, like a Cajun squeezebox. Stella saw the irritation in my eyes and threw me a bone.

"Or maybe it was a smokescreen, to make Josh look dangerous. Maybe I was planting the seeds of a good story, where Josh was capable of killing. But then Josh saw my tweets and made me delete the account. You still found them though—didn't you? And they made you think he killed Michael."

Shorty's nod confirmed his satisfaction with Stella's answer. As for me, I wanted to get as far away from her as possible. We made a hasty exit.

My visit with Josh was even faster. With my partner close beside me, I simply listened.

"Ev, I just wanted to tell you that I'm *so* sorry about all this! I told Stella to leave you alone. You thought I killed Michael, so she had nothing to fear. That was true, wasn't it? You *did* think I killed him, didn't you? And you were going to convince your brother to arrest me. Ahh...but that's Stella—always too impatient."

Josh's smile lit up the room, and I hoped it served him well in prison.

"Uh, the other thing I wanted to say was that I really like you. There's this vibe between us, you know? A connection. And I think we could be really good together. Have you ever seen the TV show *Love After Lockup*?

It's on the TLC channel, and it's about finding love off the beaten path. You see, one person is in prison and the other is on the outside, and..."

Shorty grabbed my arm. "Yeah, we're done here. Guard!"

The wrap up with Nate and Sheriff Dupre was all a blur. My brain shut down right after Josh's...suggestion? Proposal?

Sheriff Dupre's sandy blond hair and moss green eyes complemented his tan. Did he play golf? Hiking maybe? The man clearly spent time outdoors. No wedding ring probably meant he was single.

"We couldn't say much until now, but our parish drug enforcement team has been working closely with the Federal Bureau of Investigation and the Drug Enforcement Administration. Our task for the last two years has been to bring down Josh's drug operation. Thanks to Michael, they learned that Stella is more involved in the activities than originally believed. Michael had approached the DEA about testifying, but it was in the early stages. He'd provided no real evidence at the time of his death, which is why our homicide division was investigating his murder. We suspected his death could be related to drugs, but we didn't know for sure. Until you two stepped in and solved the case."

Nate, always the protective brother, called for my taxi.

"Shorty, why don't you get my sister home? It's been a long night and she looks exhausted. She's got circles under her eyes and she probably needs a shower." My brother, always the caretaker. Thanks to the people who loved me, I might never have a love life again. Thank goodness for Zydeco.

"Of course, Detective! Let's get our crime fighters home for some well-deserved sleep. Thank you, again, for helping out with the investigation." Sheriff Dupre's eyes widened as he opened his mouth just slightly. Did he want to say something else? Maybe chime in that indeed I could use a shower? "Mrs. Delafose, if we have any other questions—regarding the investigation, of course—would it be all right to call you?"

"Yeah, yeah Sheriff, whatever y'need. Me an' Miz Delafose are at yore *diss-poze-zull*. But you'll wanna' call *me*. Miz Delafose dudn't git up 'til almost seven ev'ry mornin'. An' she's in her *puh-jaw-muz* by seven ev'ry night. That's a mighty short winduh t'talk tuh her, so you'd best call me."

My brain conjured up a talk show set, with me seated in a plush red velvet chair facing my host. Kelly Clarkson perhaps? Maybe even Rachael Ray—I could cook my Cajun grilled cheese sandwiches.

"Tell me, Ev, did you ever date again after your husband's death?"

"Well, no, I didn't, Kelly. It wasn't for lack of trying, believe me! Unfortunately, my first opportunity turned out to be a charming but dangerous drug kingpin. We toyed with the idea of dating while he served his prison term, but in the end I walked away."

"Oh, Ev! That is so unfair! We can't choose who we love, can we, audience?"

Cheering and encouraging clapping from said audience echoed in my head.

"What about now? Is there anyone on Ev Delafose's radar?"

My face turned up the heat a little, as I flipped the grilled cheese. No, this story worked better with Rachael Ray. The two of us behind a stove with pepper jelly and andouille sausage.

"Not especially, Rachael. Thanks to well-meaning friends and family, I just never had the chance."

Cries of outrage and empathy poured from my adoring fans, seated in tiered plastic seats before me. Rachael placed an encouraging hand on my shoulder.

"You hang in there, Ev! Love comes along when you least expect it. Now let's sample these Cajun grilled cheese sandwiches!"

Rachael was right. In the meantime, God had blessed me with a home I loved, friends I adored, and a dog who thought I hung the moon. Life was good.

"Y'know, Doc. That sheriff was eyein' ya' real good. He's gonna' throw some more cases our way fer sure!"

"Let's hope they don't involve crazy serial killers intent on making me the next victim."

"Whatcha' talkin' about Doc? Those cases are the best kind."

Shorty summed up our suspects in just a few iconic words. "That Josh Hamilton is the sorriest man that ever wore a shirt."

"Agreed. What's your opinion on Stella? During our interview, she convinced you she didn't do it."

"Well, Doc. Here in the South, we don't hide crazy. We put it on the front porch and give it a drink."

Well said, my friend.

As for Shorty's relationship with Annabelle, it was rock solid.

"Guess what Annabelle told me, Doc! *You're a hero*, she said. *No ma'am*, I told her. *I'm just a man with heroic tendencies.*"

That was my best friend, humble to the core.

"By the way, Doc. Couldja change my ringtone? Anythin' but Garth Brooks' "I've Got Friends in Low Places" please?"

Yikes! That was meant for my ears only. "Shorty, how did you know your ringtone?"

"Cuz your daddy told me—teases me about it every chance he gets. So, can ya change it?"

How could I say no? "Okay, which ringtone would you like?"

Cue the now endearing horse snort. "C'mon, Doc, which song do ya think fits me the best?"

Which song do I think...of course! "Would that be the theme from *The Rockford Files*?"

My PI flashed a bigger grin than an alligator feasting on a mess of catfish.

LAGNIAPPE

Here in Louisiana, a lagniappe is a little something extra, a bonus. An additional donut in your order at the donut shop, an extra play for a season ticket holder, a little something special tucked into your order at the boutique. My lagniappe to you, my dear reader, is this short piece about one of my characters. It has nothing to do with the story you just read. Instead, it gives more insight into the character.

"Women who wear glasses are incredibly sexy. At least, in my opinion."

Seriously? It was my junior year, the week of spring finals! What was this guy doing? Didn't I have enough going on? My lips pressed into a thin line, complimenting my furrowed eyebrows. Squaring my shoulders toward the voice, I prepared to unleash the full effect of my irritation.

Those eyes!

My face disobeyed the order to flash annoyance. How could I blame my body for ignoring my brain? It wasn't anyone's fault, really. Was this incredibly handsome guy actually flirting with me? My heart skipped a beat, and my eyebrows and mouth scurried to regroup. Unfortunately, my face rarely changed looks so quickly. My eyebrows arched as my jaw dropped slightly. Nope, not the sweet and sexy look my brain had ordered up. My face resembled those teenage girls in slasher movies just before they're ...well...slashed.

"Oh, I'm sorry! I didn't mean to scare you! Hey, I'll just leave you alone."

The only man who'd ever told me glasses were sexy prepared for a hasty retreat. His eyes widened considerably, then softened. The color of my Darjeeling tea—charcoal made lighter with two teaspoons of milk.

Take a breath, Ev, and calm yourself. I studied the guy standing before me, pushing up my glasses for a clearer perspective.

My would-be suitor towered over me. The look on his face reminded me of my dog Beau, friendly but hopeful for a kind word. The guy ran his hand through the most beautiful curly waves, the color of my Darjeeling without milk. His nervousness relaxed me, and I felt a smile sneak onto my face. My new admirer calmed me somehow. My breath slowed and my smile fit my face naturally. Normally, new people made me nervous. I wasn't shy, but I could count on one hand the number of people I called, friend.

Twenty-nine years and two kids later, I still counted Douglas Charles Delafose as a friend. We'd survived college, grad school (me), the police academy (Doug), a doctorate degree (me again). We were navigating the teenage years, or what we liked to call The Black Hole. No GPS and no exit ramps, but definitely a lot of twists and turns. Every morning, I thanked God for giving me Doug as my traveling companion.

"Evangeline, are you ready? The car's packed."

The man still didn't need glasses. Except for the gray woven through his curls, my husband had not aged.

Glancing in the mirror, my lips automatically pushed downward. Did I actually get both my own and Doug's crows' feet? My face looked tired—I hadn't slept well.

"I'll be right there!"

Enough with the mirror! The day was not for focusing on my shortcomings.

"Mom! I don't want to be late! Let's go!"

Oh great! Matty was irritated with me. Ellie would be next, so best to hustle. Maybe tomorrow I'd do something right. Running a brush through my hair, I snatched my purse and fled out the door.

Sitting in the back with Ellie, I closed my eyes to keep from crying. Was that an elbow in my ribs? Would someone please remind me...why did I have children?

"Geez, Mom! Are you going to act like this when I go off to college? Matty's just going down the road, not even to another state. And he said you can visit him whenever you want. Which is ridiculous because who wants their parents hanging out with them at college? And...he already said he's coming home in a couple of weeks. Why are you being so dramatic?"

I didn't have to open my eyes to know Doug was studying me in the rearview mirror. Deep breaths, Ev. You still have Ellie at home, for what that was worth.

Eyes tightly shut, I took another breath. "No, Ellie, rest assured I won't act like this when you leave for college. In fact, your father and I will be on a month-long cruise through Europe. You will be the last thing on our minds."

Ev's Next Adventure

Evangeline Delafose is settling back into Graisseville, Louisiana—but she'd really like to solve another case! The sheriff has offered her a missing person investigation, only because he doesn't think Remy Robichaux is actually missing.

Follow Ev as she works to find Remy, all with her frustrating but loveable private investigator by her side. And of course a bit of help from the quirky residents of her small town.

This book is the second of the Small-Town Girl Mystery Series.

Boudin and Bloodshed

"Ya' need a new washin' machine, Doc! This one ain't gonna patch together much longer. Yeah, that's what you need, a new washer! Hey, now that yore teachin' at LSU, those high falutin' pro-fessers over there gotta be payin' ya' enough money t'get a new washin' machine!"

"For the fifteenth time, Shorty, I'm only teaching two classes at LSU right now. That's an extra $2,000 for the semester. With gas and taxes, I'm bringing home about $300 a month. And that's been covering repairs to my car."

My mechanic and I had been nursing my seventeen-year-old Volvo for the last six months. We both knew I needed to pull the plug, but I couldn't afford any car payments. My plan was to coax my car to the end of the semester, and convince the LSU powers that be to let me teach four classes during the summer session. My mechanic had been on the lookout for a decent used car, something reliable and relatively cheap.

"No need to be testy! All I'm sayin' is that your washer ain't gonna make it to Mardi Gras. So, you'd better save your quarters for the Fluff n' Fold in Zachary, or start plannin' to do yore laundry at someone else's house. And before ya' ask, ya' can't use mine. I can't have ya' bringing over yore unmentionables t'wash at my place. Neither of us need any tongue waggin' from the village gossips."

Should I argue that doing my laundry at Shorty's place probably wasn't even a blip on the gossip radar? No, I didn't want to do laundry over there, anyway. Between my father and my best friend Elizabeth Trahan, I should have plenty of laundry access. And no tongues would be wagging if I brought my unmentionables to their homes, either. What was an unmentionable anyway? In the world we lived in, I didn't realize those still existed.

"Don't worry, I'll figure out something. And if you hear of any inexpensive, reliable cars, please let me know. My vintage Volvo is on its last legs."

A familiar horse's snort from my handyman. "Vintage? Doc, that car's just old! Callin' it vintage or retro or antique don't make it worth any more money. But I do have a buddy who takes cars like that for parts. Want me t'see how much he'd give ya' for it? And I can ask him if he's got any leads on a car t'replace it. Do ya' have any pref-uh-rinses?"

"Preferences? Just that it runs and won't cost me more money once I pay for it. Poor people can't afford to be choosey, that's for sure."

Doug and I had always pinched our pennies, but without my full-time salary I had been struggling. Not to mention, my husband's pension was 80% of his salary. The additional money for losing his life while on duty helped, but I needed to teach more classes. Or win the Louisiana Powerball.

"Hey, has Nate said anythin' about givin' us another case? It's been a few months, and I figured we'd have one by now."

Although the sheriff had generously thanked us, he hadn't handed out any more cases. My dad said it was because we'd made the sheriff look bad.

"Now don't get me wrong, Evangeline. Sheriff Mitch Dupre is a good guy. Best sheriff we've had in a long time, in fact. But you made him look bad. That Michael Cook case stumped the entire department—including your brother—for eighteen months. Then you and Shorty come along and solve it within a week. How does that make those highly trained and experienced law enforcement people look? Not good, I'll tell you."

Nate had thanked me for solving the case, but he had paid for it with some serious digs at his detective skills. Hugh Cormier wanted to publish the headline *Detective's Big Sister Solves His Case*, but I begged him to go with something else.

"Hugh, you can't publish that! That isn't even the truth, and you know it. Nate did a lot of legwork on that case before I even saw it. Not to mention, the only reason I cracked the case is because the murderer showed up at my house, and confessed before trying to kill me. Otherwise, I don't know if I would have solved the case either. We had no real evidence. And let's not forget Nate walked in my back door and arrested the murderer. Just as she was about to shoot me, I might add. He absolutely saved my life. So you'd better come up with a more accurate headline!"

Hugh went back to the drawing board and a few days letter produced a paper proclaiming *Detective Nathan Bergeron Solves Murder with Help from Big Sister*. Personally, I could have done without the big part, but it was better than older sister. And it gave credit to my brother, which was what I'd wanted. Of course, Shorty complained his name wasn't in the headline.

"And the next case we help the sheriff with, I want credit in the paper!" My friend couldn't let that one go.

"Look Shorty, we've been over this. You got credit in the article itself. Headlines are limited in the number of words. Hugh probably thought the brother and sister angle worked better."

My handyman's eyes grew dark, like the sky just before a thunderstorm. "I put in just as much work as you did, Doc. Mebbe even more, truth be told. But where's my name in that rag of a paper? In the third para-graph—the third! Annabelle's still proud of me, of course, but my buddies can't stop teasin' me that I didn't even make the headline. Next time my cuzzin Hugh wants some work done on his house, he can kiss my assets!"

Between me and Annabelle Brochet, Shorty's librarian girlfriend, we'd put a stop to the cursing. His substitutions made us both chuckle, but he got an A for effort.

"Let's cross that bridge when we come to it. For now, we don't have any cases. How's it going down at the Gas n' More? Have you gotten any new clients?"

The thunderstorm disappeared in Shorty's eyes, replaced with muddy pools. Like mud puddles after a rainstorm. "Well, I found Annie Landry's dog. And Lila Trahan paid me to follow her husband for a few days. Turned out the guy was goin' to Moe Gladstone's to play dominoes. But nothin' else. Say, could ya' call the sheriff yore self? He seemed kinda sweet on ya', mebbe you could flirt a little and get us a case. You still remember how to do that, right?"

Should I express outrage Shorty wanted me to use my charms to secure a case? Truthfully, I was flattered he thought I had charms.

"Well, I don't know about flirting to get a case. But Sheriff Dupre sent Nate home with his Detective Lou Bergeron books for me to sign. How about I call him and offer to swing by his office to return them? Then I could ask him about giving us another case."

The mud puddles changed to sparkling pools of...well, still mud. Shorty's eyes definitely were dark brown no matter his mood.

"Doc, I could just about kiss you! And Annabelle wouldn't mind neither, cuz you cheered me up! But in the interest of our friendship and my relationship with my girl, I'm not gonna do that."

Oh, thank goodness! If Shorty kissed me, my heart would probably stop from shock.

"Yes, let's definitely not have any kissing. I'll give Sheriff Dupre a call tomorrow morning and set up a meeting. Don't worry, I'll let you know when the meeting is, and I'll call you as soon as I leave said meeting."

Shorty had many qualities, but patience had not made the list. And it never would.

"Fantastic! But why don't you call him right now? No time like the present, I always say."

Did he? For the life of me, I couldn't remember those words ever coming out of his mouth.

"Okay, I'll call him right now. See, I'm picking up my phone. I'm looking up the phone number of the station. Here is my finger clicking the number. Oh! It's ringing on the other end. Shhh! Let's be quiet so I can talk."

Interrupting was a personality trait that followed impatience like a shadow. Reminding Shorty to be quiet might or might not work. I had a 50% chance of success.

"Hello, this is Evangeline Delafose. I'd like to speak with Sheriff Dupre. Yes, I'll hold."

"Shorty, I'm on hold right now while the receptionist checks to see if the sheriff is free. So, I don't know anything yet."

Sometimes if I relayed my information to my friend, he wouldn't ask irritating questions such as *what's going on*? Or *have you talked to the sheriff yet*? Again, a 50% chance of success. Raising two children had prepared me well for my friendship with Shorty.

"Hello, Sheriff! Thank you for taking my call. Listen, I've got your books all signed and ready to go. I'm teaching a couple of classes at LSU, so I'll be in Baton Rouge tomorrow. Could I swing by the station and drop off the books? And maybe we could catch up."

As Sheriff Dupre relayed his schedule, I nodded to Shorty. Hopefully, my smiling and nodding would keep him quiet.

"Uh, lunch? Well, I guess so. My first class is over at 11:30 a.m. and my next one is at 2 p.m. Lunch would work. Okay, I'll meet you at the station right after my class. Goodbye."

Was this a date? How did that happen? No, it couldn't be. The sheriff and I hadn't spoken in three months, after Shorty's revelations about my personal life.

"Sheriff, Miz Delafose dudn't git up 'til almost seven every mornin'. An' she's in her *puh-jaw-muz* by seven ev'ry night. That's such a short winduh t'talk tuh her, you'd best call me if ya' have questions."

After my so-called best friend broadcast my hermit tendencies to the sheriff, I'd avoided all situations involving law enforcement. No, lunch was just a friendly, casual time between two professionals. At least it would give me a chance to hit up the sheriff for a case. Shorty had the same idea.

"Lunch with the sheriff? Doc, that's perfect! You'll have him cornered at a table, with no escape. He'll have t'give us a case. Good thinkin'!"

Did he hear the conversation? Lunch definitely wasn't my idea. No matter—he was off and running.

"Okay, so when you have the sheriff cornered at the table, be sure and remind him what a great job we did on the Michael Cook case. Both of us—don't forget to mention me too. Why, we risked our lives to catch that crazy Stella Cook."

Our lives? Hmmm...the way I remembered it, Stella pointed the gun at me. Shorty didn't show up until Nate had the woman in handcuffs. It didn't really matter. Without my PI's help, we'd have never solved the crime. Writing crime fiction is not the same as solving a crime. If Shorty wanted to entertain people with his version of the truth, it was fine by me. He enjoyed the spotlight much more than I did, anyway.

"Don't ask for a case, Doc. Demand one! After our great detective work, he should be beggin' us to take a case. We even did it for free, to show him how valuable our services are. Which reminds me—for this next case, we need t'be chargin' the sheriff a consultin' fee. Be sure and bring that up. I'm thinkin' $200 a day plus expenses."

Shorty was an avid fan of *The Rockford Files*, a television show that ran for six years. It featured James Garner as Jim Rockford, a private investigator. Jim charged $200 a day plus expenses, mentioning his fees in practically every episode. Shorty and I both watched *The Rockford Files* with our dads, and my friend used the television show as his business model.

"Let me just get through the lunch and see how it goes, okay? We don't want to make the sheriff angry by demanding cases and charging fees. Believe me, I understand what you're saying, and I will make every effort to get us a case. But let's hold off on the fees, okay? Because I'd rather take a case for free than lose out on one just because I demanded to be paid."

Shorty shrugged his shoulders, but the thunderstorm had rolled back into his eyes. Silence was worse, because it signaled the calm before the storm. If I didn't return with a case and the promise of being paid, I'd definitely be caught in a monsoon. What would be worse: trying to flirt with the sheriff, or suffering through Shorty's anger? Yeah, it was time to dust off my feminine wiles.

"Thanks for bringing my books, Mrs. Delafose. I still can't believe I'm meeting the author of my favorite book series in person."

Maybe this would be easier than I'd hoped. "Not a problem, and please call me Ev. Shall we head out to lunch? Where are we going?"

Sheriff Dupre ran his fingertips across the book on the top, *Guns and Girlfriends*. "Huh? Oh, how about Louie's Café on State Street?"

Louie's had been an LSU tradition since 1941. Many hours during my post graduate work were spent at one of the 1950's style tables, munching on French fries drenched in Swiss and Colby cheese. Upon my graduation for my masters, Doug had bought me a Louie's Café t-shirt. And for my doctorate, a $100 gift card, which we spent upon my celebratory lunch.

"Perfect! Should I meet you there?" Please don't let the sheriff see my aging Volvo.

"Why don't we take my car? The parking's usually scarce anyway, so we'll just have t'scare up one space."

As we stepped into the parking lot, my eyes locked in the opposite direction of my sun faded blue car.

"Here we are...let me open your door for you."

Time to break out the feminine wiles, Ev. "Why thank you so much! What a gentleman."

Too drippy with feminine wiles? Did it even sound sincere? How long had it been since I'd flirted? Doug passed three years before, plus almost twenty years of marriage...as my father would say, it had been a coon's age. Although I was pretty sure raccoons didn't live twenty-three years.

"Now please call me Mitch, and I just have to ask this question. Do you think you'll ever write another Detective Lou Bergeron mystery? My brother turned me on to your novels, and when he finds out my copies have been signed by the author...why, he'll be fit to be tied."

Not the first time I'd been asked that question, and my answer remained the same. "My husband was the inspiration for my novels. Without Doug, I just don't feel right about continuing the books. But who knows? Maybe

I'll create a new series with a different detective. Nate has already volunteered to be my protagonist. Honestly, though, I'm enjoying teaching crime fiction at my old stomping grounds for now."

Mitch nodded as he watched the road, but his chin barely dipped towards his chest. Another fan disappointed in my answer.

"Say, if I managed to steal my brother's books, would you sign them too? His wife could help me sneak them out, and that would be the best birthday present I could ever give him. If that's too much to ask, I understand."

A way back into the sheriff's good graces! "Oh, not too much trouble at all. I'd be happy to do that for you...Mitch."

Okay, let's just forget about flirting and focus on making the sheriff happy. From the chuckle at my response, I was succeeding at that.

"Fantastic! Mike's birthday is next month. I'll talk to his wife and get his books. Thanks so much Ev! Oh, look—a spot right up front. You must be my lucky charm."

Was that flirting? Ugh, even in my twenties I stunk at reading men. If Doug hadn't walked up to me in the library and told me women wearing glasses were sexy, I'd probably still be single.

Focus on getting a case, Ev. Enduring Shorty's irritation was literally like being in a thunderstorm without rain gear.

"I'll have the sauteed seafood salad and water with lemon, please."

"Forgive me, Ev, but I didn't eat breakfast." Mitch eyed the menu. "Give me a sauteed crawfish po' boy and a glass of sweet tea, please."

During the three years after Doug's death, I'd lost forty pounds, which needed to be lost and never found again. During the Michael Cook case, though, I'd found my appetite. Over the last few months, I'd become reacquainted with thirty of my missing pounds. My stomach protested the salad over the po' boy, but I drank a glass of water to keep it quiet. Gaining weight had been a lot more fun.

"Ev, thank you again for helping with the Michael Cook case. And please let me apologize for putting you in danger. After all that, Nate insisted that I keep you off any future cases."

Ah hah! Mystery solved. "You are very welcome—it was a lot of fun! And while I appreciate Nate's concerns, Shorty and I would like you to give us another case. Could you do that, and we just won't tell Nate?"

My brother was eight years younger than me, but after Doug's death he'd made it his mission in life to protect me. He felt a duty to Doug, since they'd been the best of friends. Doug had mentored Nate, and written him a letter of recommendation when he applied to the sheriff's department. As I tried to push back my annoyance, I focused on Nate's good intentions.

Mitch sipped his tea—was he searching for a case to hand me, or a way to refuse my request?

"Honestly, Ev I promised Nate not to give you any more cases. But I do have a situation that's not an official case. Have you heard of Remy Robichaux?"

"No, I haven't. But I bet Shorty has. That guy knows everyone. Is he from Graisseville?"

Mitch leaned back and slid his tea glass towards the middle of the table. Our server brought his crawfish po' boy on a large platter, overflowing with French fries. My stomach muttered a protest and I shushed it with more water. My sauteed seafood salad slid comfortably right in front of me, and my stomach gurgled with happiness. Eating healthy could also taste good. Not as good as a po' boy and fries, but still pretty good.

Mitch clasped his hands together on the table. "I always say a prayer before eating. Would you like to join me?"

"Oh absolutely!" Such a nice change from Shorty, who scarfed up four bites before I could bow my head.

"God don't mind, Doc. As long as we get the prayer in before we finish dessert, it still counts." With three brothers and two sisters, Shorty had learned to eat quickly before someone else ate it for him.

As we dug into our meal, Mitch filled me in on the case that wasn't a case. "Remy's been missing since Saturday night. His girlfriend is hysterical, keeps calling the station asking for updates. The problem is that Remy's an adult—age thirty-three to be exact. He's been missing four days, so technically we've classified him as a missing person. But his boss says it's not unusual for Remy to drive to Bossier and hit the boats. Sometimes the guy's gone for more than a week. His girlfriend Amy Whitehall says Remy always calls her when he heads to Bossier. But he's not answering his phone and she's convinced he's in trouble. Amy's got Remy's folks all up in arms too, and they're offering a $1,000 reward for any information. If you want it, then it's yours. And you might get some money out of it too."

"Thanks Mitch—it sounds right up our alley. And it should make Nate happy too, because it sounds pretty tame. But if you could avoid telling him, that would be ideal."

The sheriff grinned, a walking billboard for his dentist. "That works for me. All I promised was to not put you on a case. And this most definitely is not a case. I'll have my assistant scan and email you what we've got on Remy. Just keep me posted, okay?"

As we moved the conversation to small talk, my shoulders dropped a few inches and so did my ribcage. With my mission accomplished, the rest of the lunch became pleasant. And too short.

"Thank you for lunch, Mitch. That was nice of you to pay." My debit card appreciated it for sure.

"My pleasure. We should do it again, if you're okay with that. In fact, when you have some updates on the Remy Robichaux situation, you could give me a call. We could discuss it over lunch."

Okay, that was definitely not a date. No offer to take me to supper, or a movie, or anything. Just two colleagues having lunch. What was that bitter taste in my mouth? Oh yeah, it was the taste of disappointment.

Also By Jann Franklin

Sometimes life throws you curveballs.

Jen Guidry thrives in the big city, but her husband Mike finds the bright lights blinding. He moves their family back to the tiny town in Louisiana where he grew up, a place that doesn't even have a coffee shop! How will Jen cope with being a fish out of water?

That doesn't mean you lose hope.

God puts us all where we're needed, and it isn't long before Jen is living a life she never knew she wanted. Can she give up the bright lights of the big city and truly appreciate her yard full of lightning bugs? Join Jen and her family in the first book of this delightful small-town series, as she finds new friends and new adventures (and misadventures) while navigating small-town life.

Find this and other books at

jannfranklin.com

www.ingramcontent.com/pod-product-compliance
Lightning Source LLC
Chambersburg PA
CBHW060135130626
46556CB00006B/2354